STAR TREK ®

VOLUME 7

THE KHITOMER CONFLICT

STAR TREK ®

VOLUME 7

THE KHITOMER CONFLICT

Collection Cover by **Erfan Fajar**, Colors by **Ifansyah Noor**

Collection Edits by **Justin Eisinger** and **Alonzo Simon**

Collection Design by **Chris Mowry**

Star Trek created by Gene Roddenberry.
Special thanks to Risa Kessler and John Van Citters of CBS Consumer Products for their invaluable assistance.

ISBN: 978-1-61377-882-1

17 16 15 14   1 2 3 4

IDW
www.IDWPUBLISHING.com
IDW founded by Ted Adams, Alex Garner, Kris Oprisko, and Robbie Robbins

Ted Adams, CEO & Publisher
Greg Goldstein, President & COO
Robbie Robbins, EVP/Sr. Graphic Artist
Chris Ryall, Chief Creative Officer/Editor-in-Chief
Matthew Ruzicka, CPA, Chief Financial Officer
Alan Payne, VP of Sales
Dirk Wood, VP of Marketing
Lorelei Bunjes, VP of Digital Services
Jeff Webber, VP of Digital Publishing & Business Development

Facebook: facebook.com/idwpublishing
Twitter: @idwpublishing
YouTube: youtube.com/idwpublishing
Instagram: instagram.com/idwpublishing
deviantART: idwpublishing.deviantart.com
Pinterest: pinterest.com/idwpublishing/idw-staff-faves

Written by

MIKE JOHNSON

Story Consultant

ROBERTO ORCI

Art by

ERFAN FAJAR

Colors by

SAKTI YUWONO, IFANSYAH NOOR,
and **BENY MAULANA** of Stellar Labs

Letters by

TOM B. LONG, CHRIS MOWRY, and **GILBERTO LAZCANO**

Series Edits by

SARAH GAYDOS

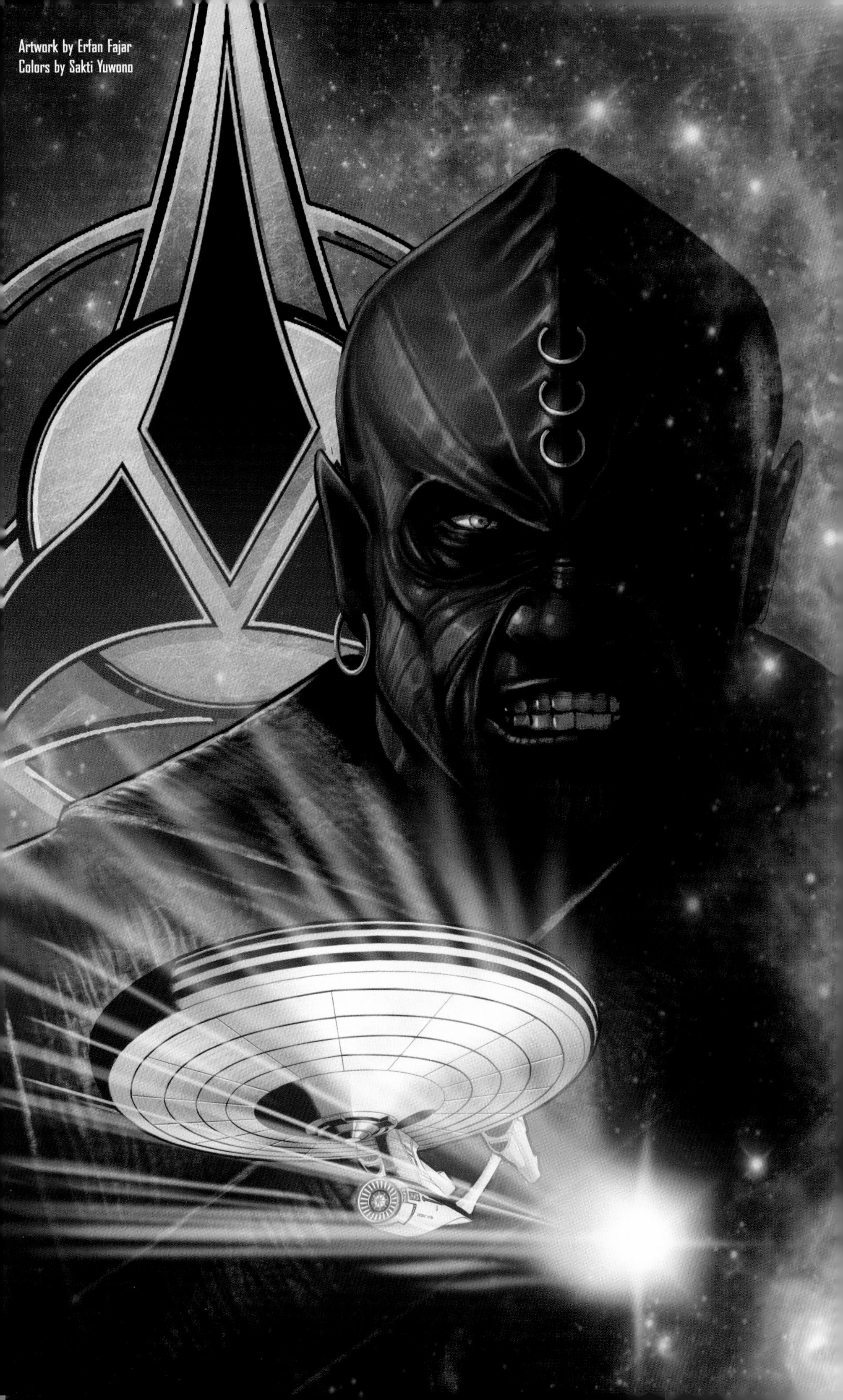

Artwork by Erfan Fajar
Colors by Sakti Yuwono

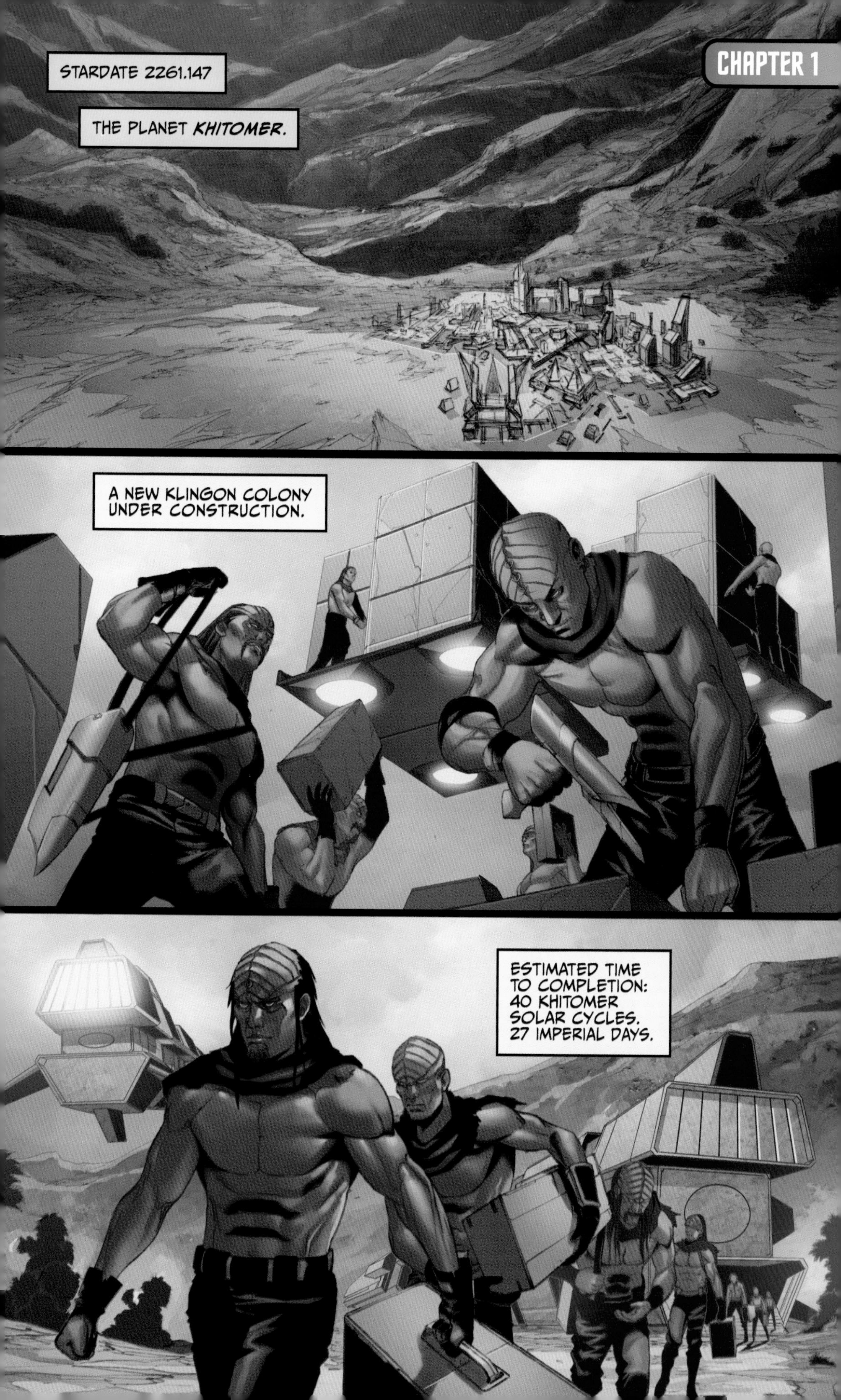
CHAPTER 1
STARDATE 2261.147
THE PLANET KHITOMER.
A NEW KLINGON COLONY UNDER CONSTRUCTION.
ESTIMATED TIME TO COMPLETION: 40 KHITOMER SOLAR CYCLES. 27 IMPERIAL DAYS.

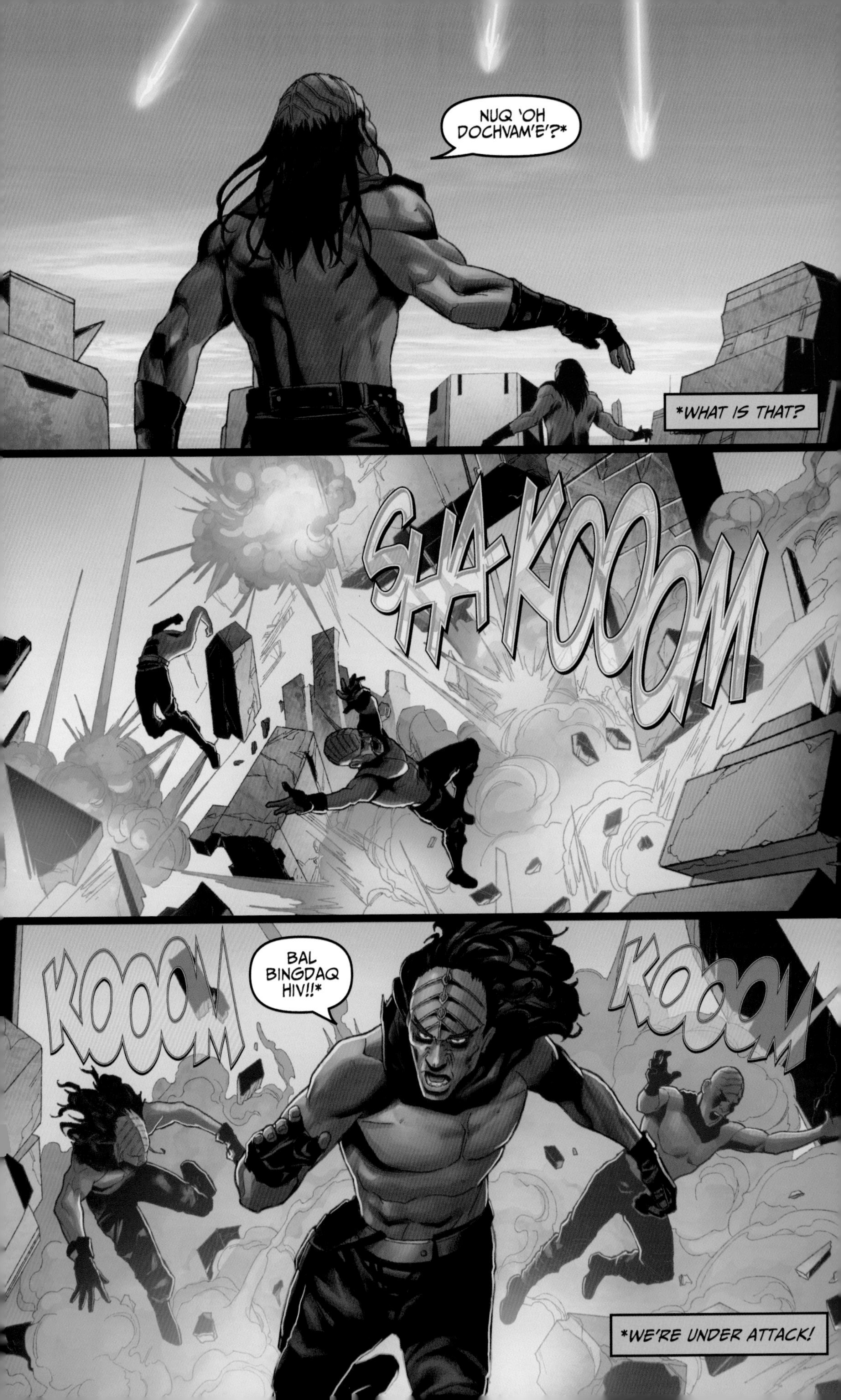
NUQ 'OH DOCHVAM'E'?*
*WHAT IS THAT?
SHAKOOOM
KOOOM
BAL BINGDAQ HIV!!*
KOOOM
*WE'RE UNDER ATTACK!

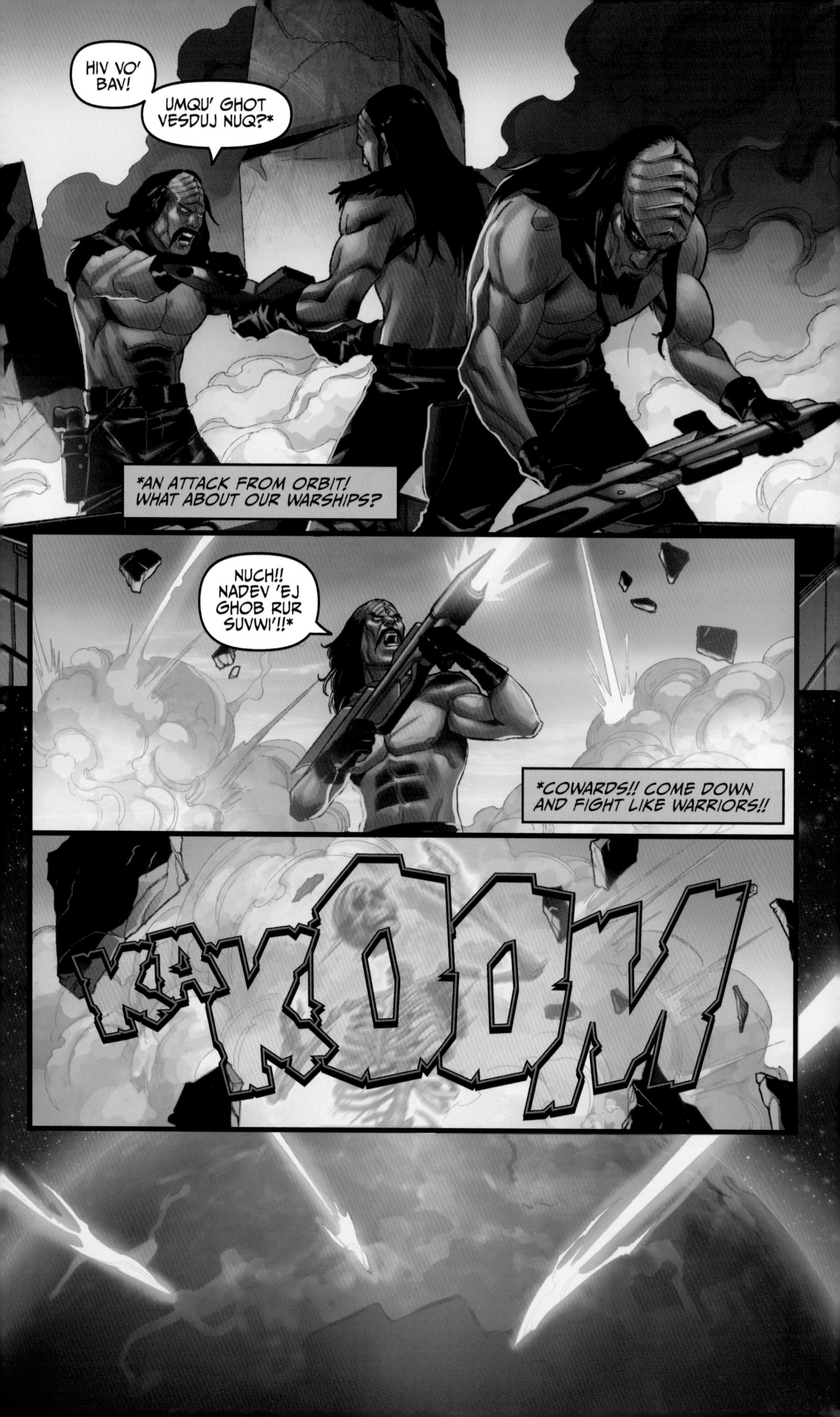
HIV VO' BAV!
UMQU' GHOT VESDUJ NUQ?*
*AN ATTACK FROM ORBIT! WHAT ABOUT OUR WARSHIPS?
NUCH!! NADEV 'EJ GHOB RUR SUVWI'!!*
*COWARDS!! COME DOWN AND FIGHT LIKE WARRIORS!!
KAKOOM

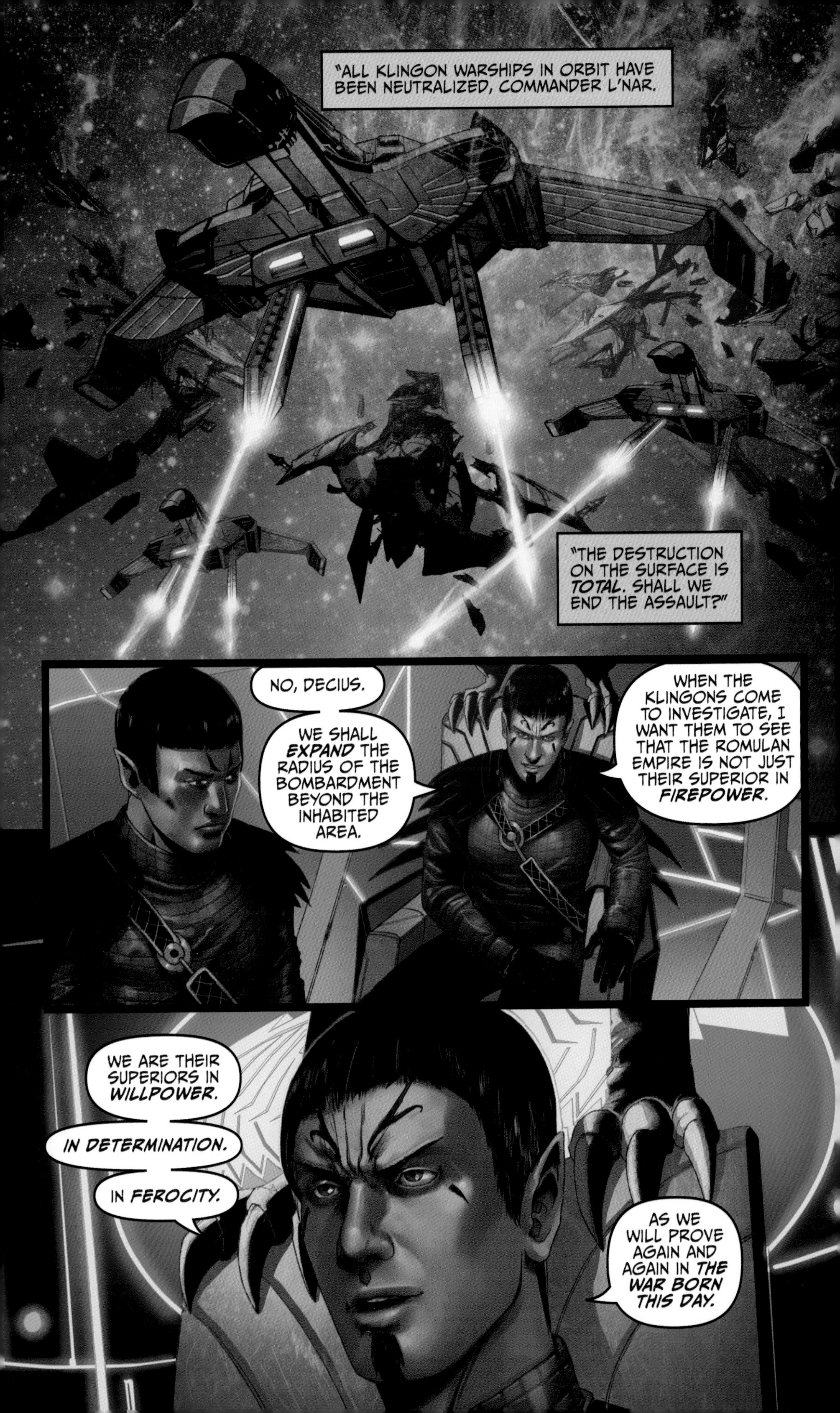
"ALL KLINGON WARSHIPS IN ORBIT HAVE BEEN NEUTRALIZED, COMMANDER L'NAR.
"THE DESTRUCTION ON THE SURFACE IS TOTAL. SHALL WE END THE ASSAULT?"
NO, DECIUS.
WE SHALL EXPAND THE RADIUS OF THE BOMBARDMENT BEYOND THE INHABITED AREA.
WHEN THE KLINGONS COME TO INVESTIGATE, I WANT THEM TO SEE THAT THE ROMULAN EMPIRE IS NOT JUST THEIR SUPERIOR IN FIREPOWER.
WE ARE THEIR SUPERIORS IN WILLPOWER.
IN DETERMINATION.
IN FEROCITY.
AS WE WILL PROVE AGAIN AND AGAIN IN THE WAR BORN THIS DAY.

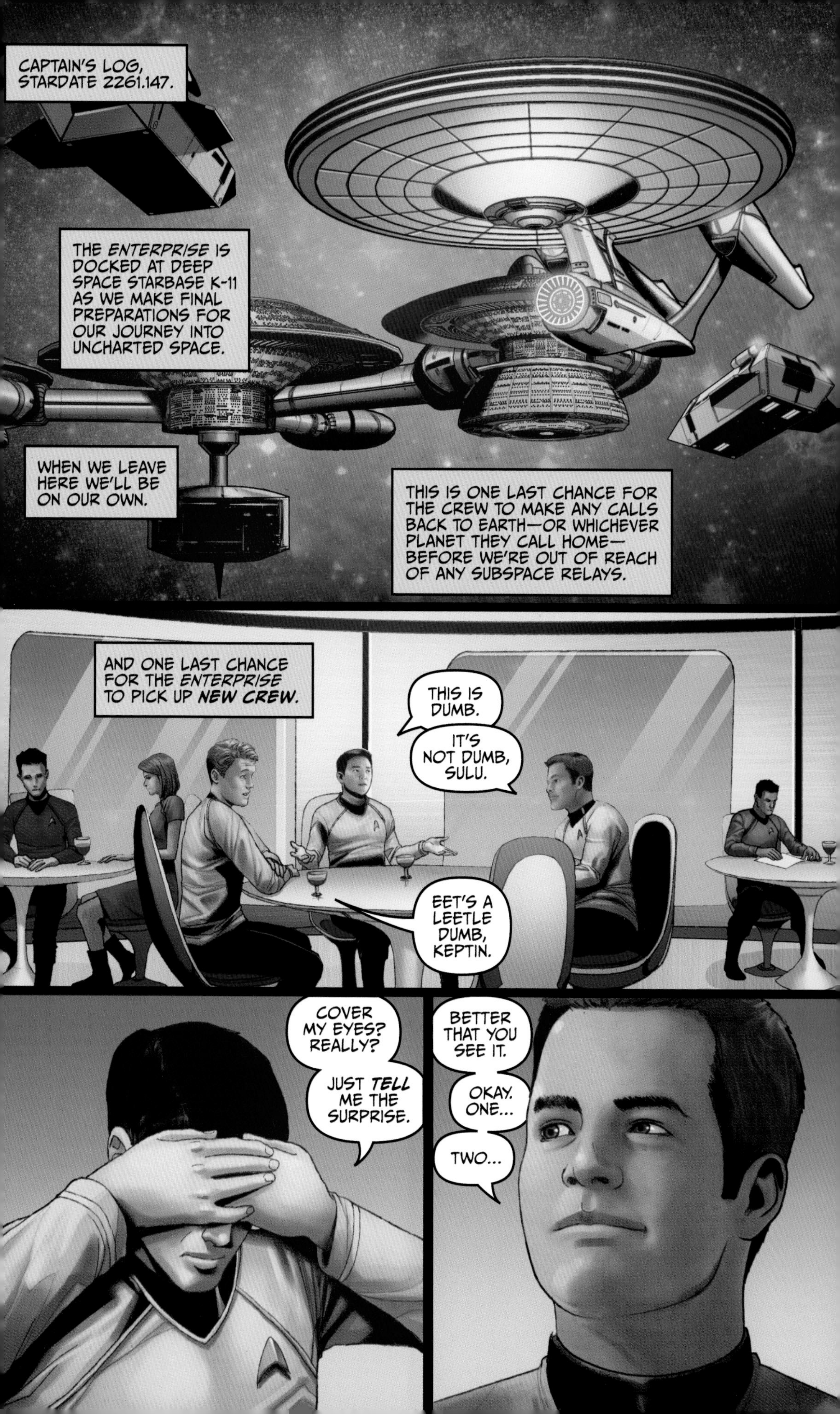
CAPTAIN'S LOG, STARDATE 2261.147.
THE *ENTERPRISE* IS DOCKED AT DEEP SPACE STARBASE K-11 AS WE MAKE FINAL PREPARATIONS FOR OUR JOURNEY INTO UNCHARTED SPACE.
WHEN WE LEAVE HERE WE'LL BE ON OUR OWN.
THIS IS ONE LAST CHANCE FOR THE CREW TO MAKE ANY CALLS BACK TO EARTH—OR WHICHEVER PLANET THEY CALL HOME—BEFORE WE'RE OUT OF REACH OF ANY SUBSPACE RELAYS.
AND ONE LAST CHANCE FOR THE *ENTERPRISE* TO PICK UP ***NEW CREW.***
THIS IS DUMB.
IT'S NOT DUMB, SULU.
EET'S A LEETLE DUMB, KEPTIN.
COVER MY EYES? REALLY?
JUST ***TELL*** ME THE SURPRISE.
BETTER THAT YOU SEE IT.
OKAY. ONE...
TWO...

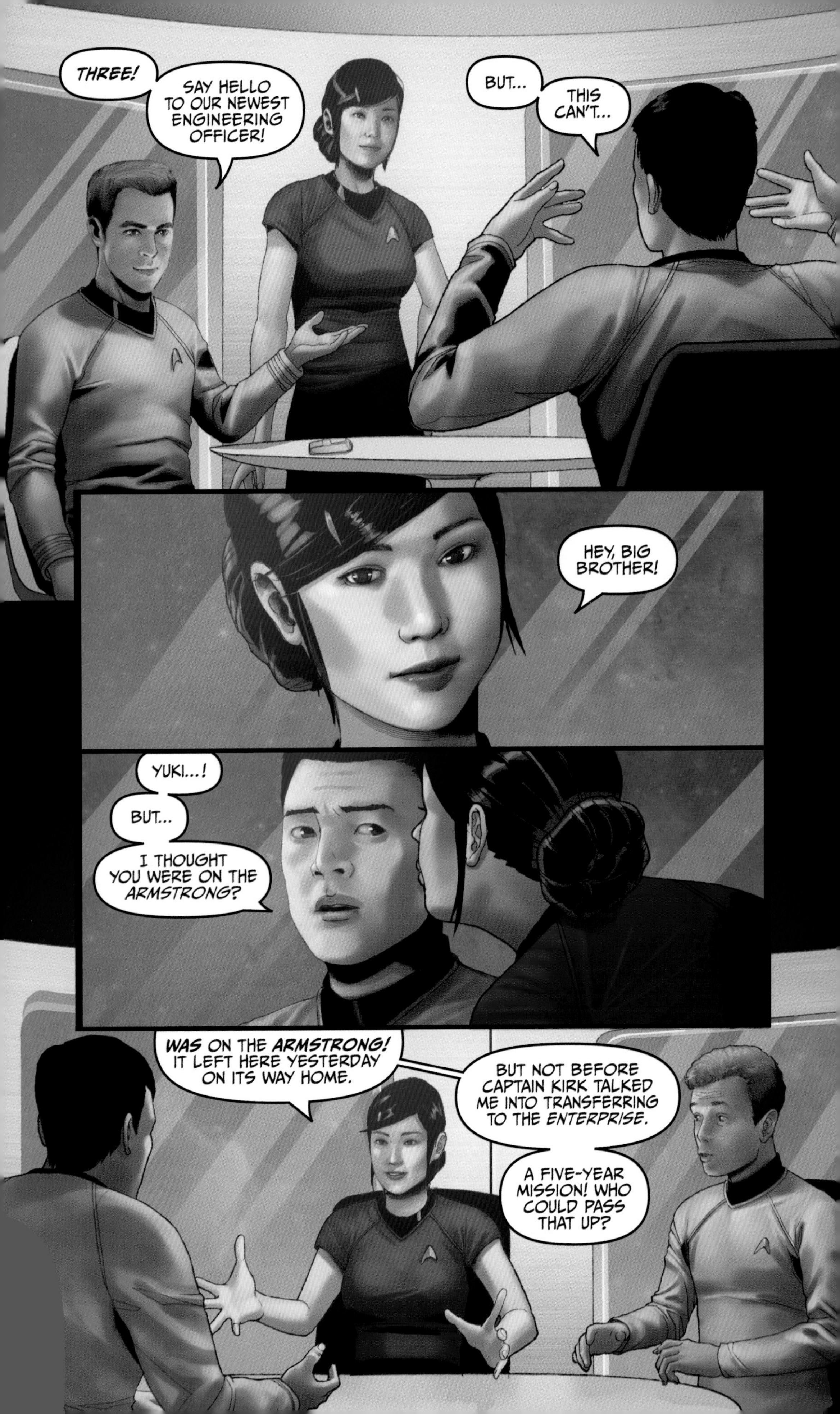
THREE!
SAY HELLO TO OUR NEWEST ENGINEERING OFFICER!
BUT...
THIS CAN'T...
HEY, BIG BROTHER!
YUKI...!
BUT...
I THOUGHT YOU WERE ON THE *ARMSTRONG*?
WAS ON THE *ARMSTRONG!* IT LEFT HERE YESTERDAY ON ITS WAY HOME.
BUT NOT BEFORE CAPTAIN KIRK TALKED ME INTO TRANSFERRING TO THE *ENTERPRISE*.
A FIVE-YEAR MISSION! WHO COULD PASS THAT UP?

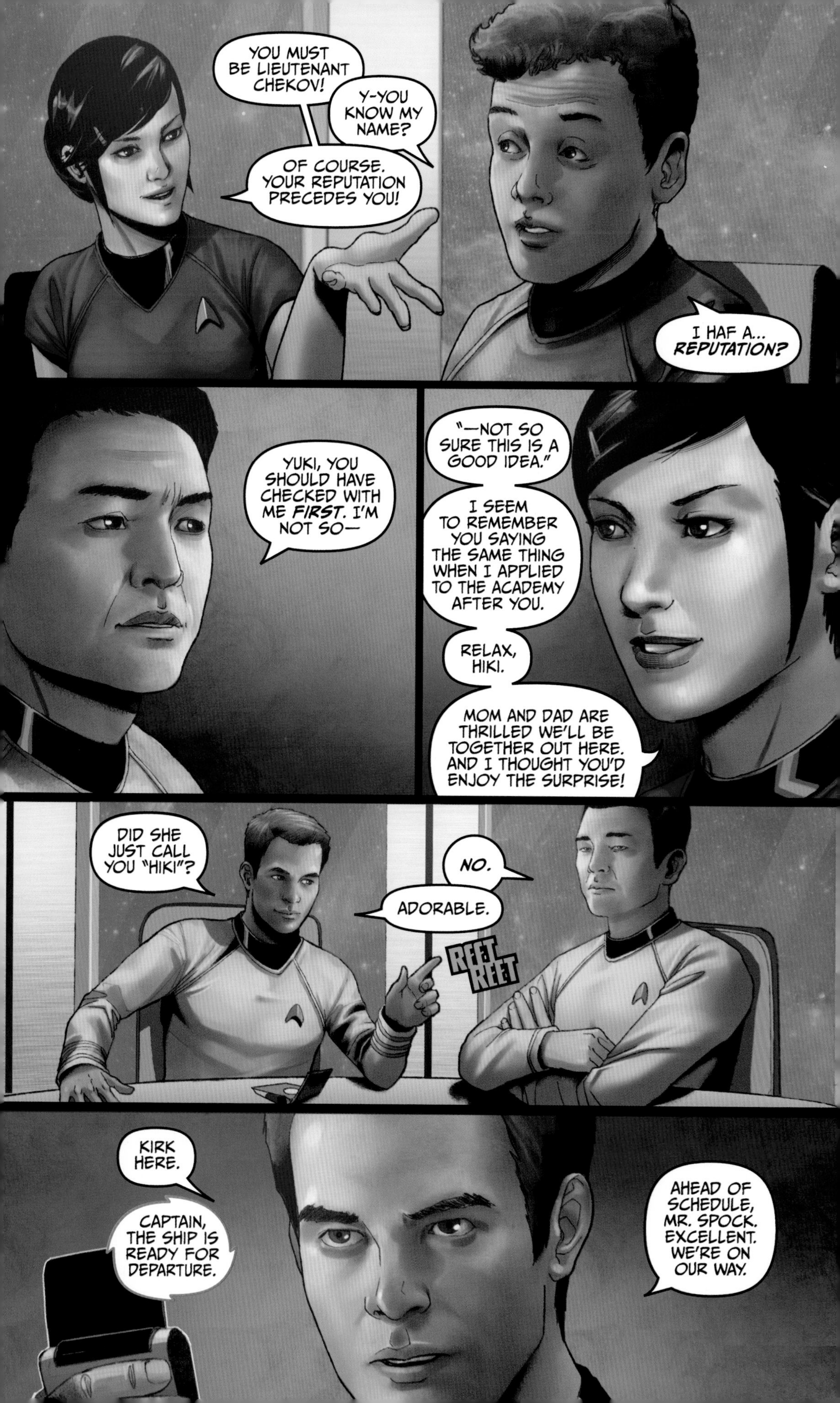

YOU MUST BE LIEUTENANT CHEKOV!
Y-YOU KNOW MY NAME?
OF COURSE. YOUR REPUTATION PRECEDES YOU!
I HAF A... *REPUTATION?*
YUKI, YOU SHOULD HAVE CHECKED WITH ME *FIRST*. I'M NOT SO—
"—NOT SO SURE THIS IS A GOOD IDEA."
I SEEM TO REMEMBER YOU SAYING THE SAME THING WHEN I APPLIED TO THE ACADEMY AFTER YOU.
RELAX, HIKI.
MOM AND DAD ARE THRILLED WE'LL BE TOGETHER OUT HERE. AND I THOUGHT YOU'D ENJOY THE SURPRISE!
DID SHE JUST CALL YOU "HIKI"?
NO.
ADORABLE.
REET REET
KIRK HERE.
CAPTAIN, THE SHIP IS READY FOR DEPARTURE.
AHEAD OF SCHEDULE, MR. SPOCK. EXCELLENT. WE'RE ON OUR WAY.

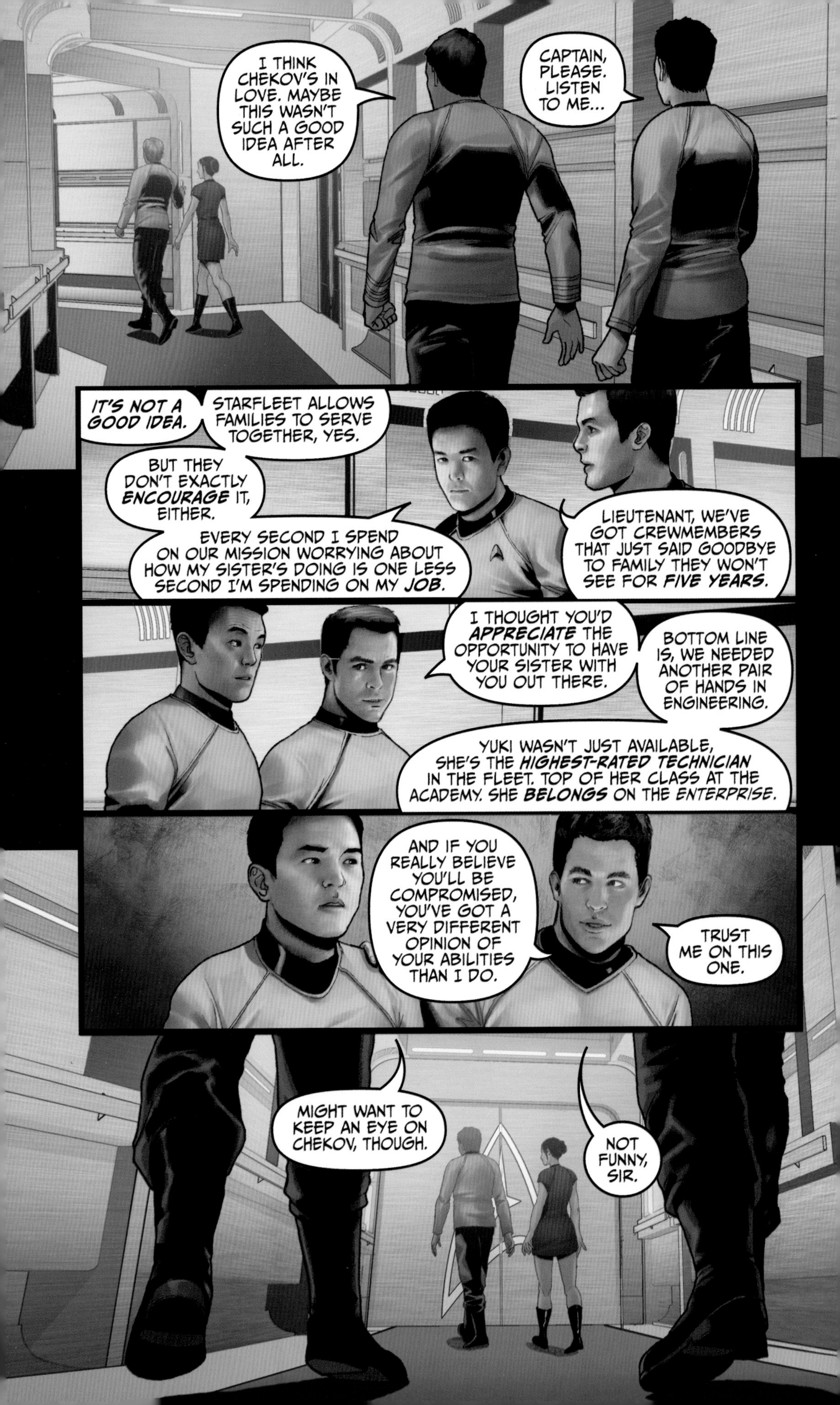
I THINK CHEKOV'S IN LOVE. MAYBE THIS WASN'T SUCH A GOOD IDEA AFTER ALL.
CAPTAIN, PLEASE. LISTEN TO ME...
IT'S NOT A GOOD IDEA.
STARFLEET ALLOWS FAMILIES TO SERVE TOGETHER, YES.
BUT THEY DON'T EXACTLY ENCOURAGE IT, EITHER.
EVERY SECOND I SPEND ON OUR MISSION WORRYING ABOUT HOW MY SISTER'S DOING IS ONE LESS SECOND I'M SPENDING ON MY JOB.
LIEUTENANT, WE'VE GOT CREWMEMBERS THAT JUST SAID GOODBYE TO FAMILY THEY WON'T SEE FOR FIVE YEARS.
I THOUGHT YOU'D APPRECIATE THE OPPORTUNITY TO HAVE YOUR SISTER WITH YOU OUT THERE.
BOTTOM LINE IS, WE NEEDED ANOTHER PAIR OF HANDS IN ENGINEERING.
YUKI WASN'T JUST AVAILABLE, SHE'S THE HIGHEST-RATED TECHNICIAN IN THE FLEET. TOP OF HER CLASS AT THE ACADEMY. SHE BELONGS ON THE ENTERPRISE.
AND IF YOU REALLY BELIEVE YOU'LL BE COMPROMISED, YOU'VE GOT A VERY DIFFERENT OPINION OF YOUR ABILITIES THAN I DO.
TRUST ME ON THIS ONE.
MIGHT WANT TO KEEP AN EYE ON CHEKOV, THOUGH.
NOT FUNNY, SIR.

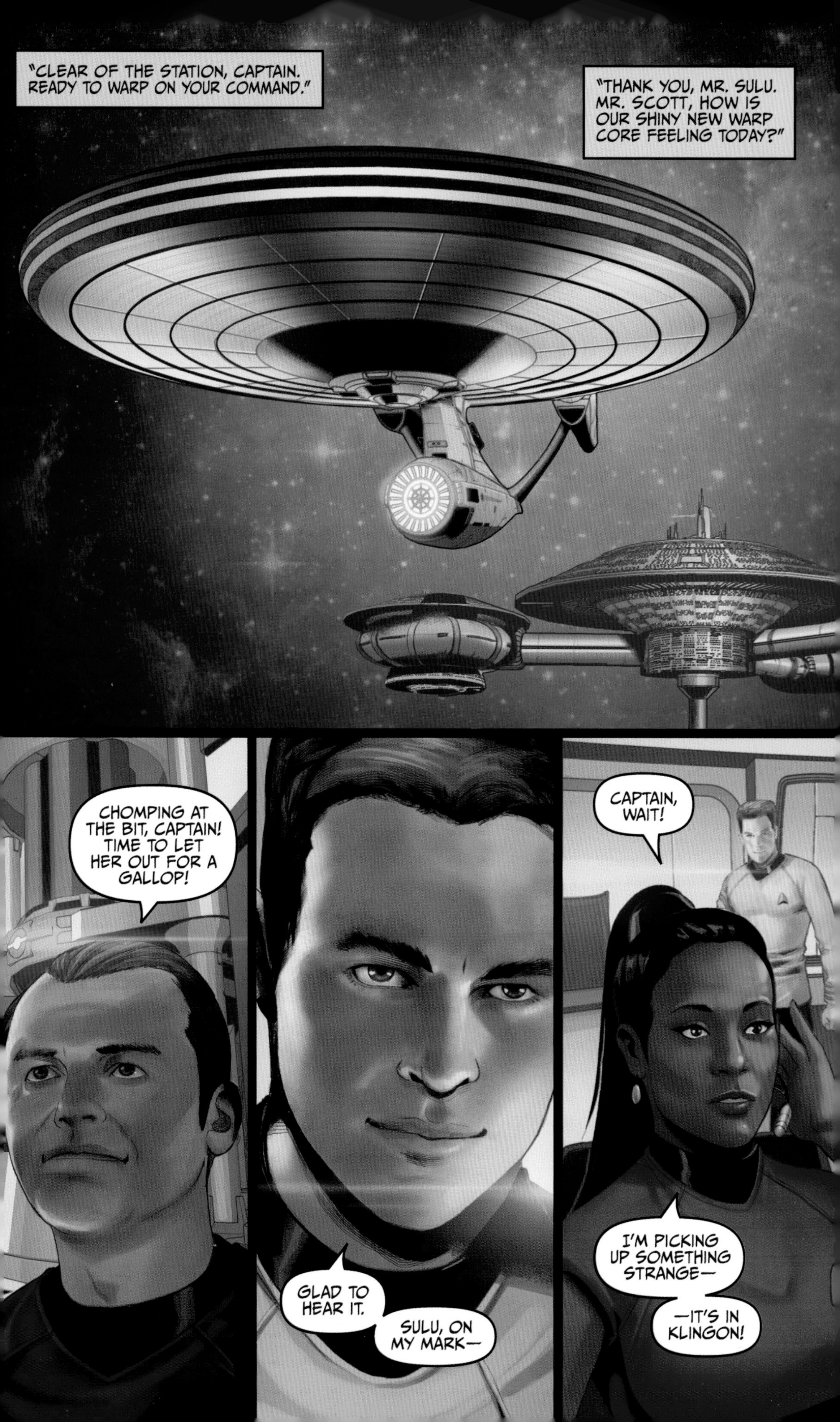
"CLEAR OF THE STATION, CAPTAIN. READY TO WARP ON YOUR COMMAND."
"THANK YOU, MR. SULU. MR. SCOTT, HOW IS OUR SHINY NEW WARP CORE FEELING TODAY?"
CHOMPING AT THE BIT, CAPTAIN! TIME TO LET HER OUT FOR A GALLOP!
GLAD TO HEAR IT.
SULU, ON MY MARK—
CAPTAIN, WAIT!
I'M PICKING UP SOMETHING STRANGE—
—IT'S IN KLINGON!

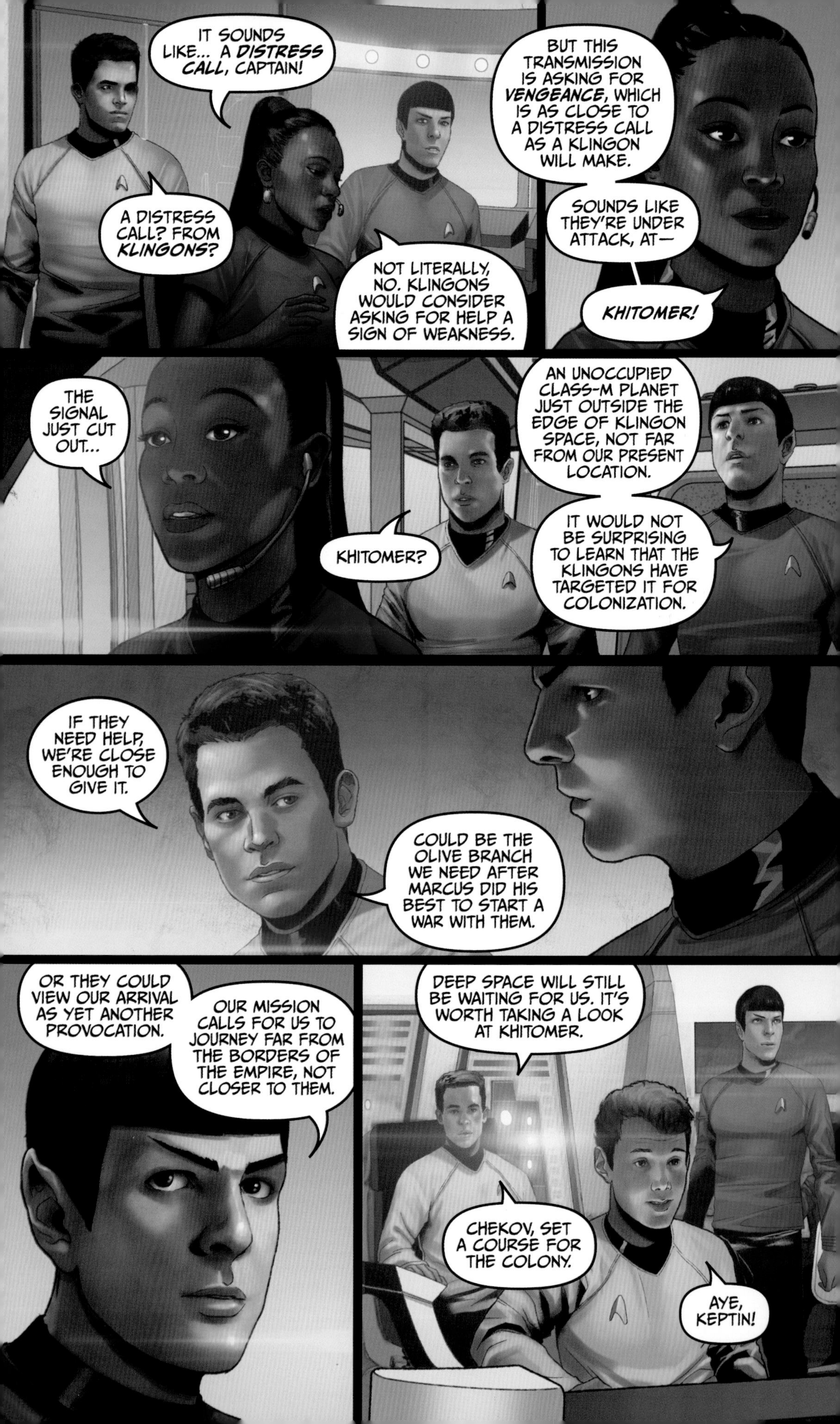
IT SOUNDS LIKE... A DISTRESS CALL, CAPTAIN!
A DISTRESS CALL? FROM KLINGONS?
NOT LITERALLY, NO. KLINGONS WOULD CONSIDER ASKING FOR HELP A SIGN OF WEAKNESS.
BUT THIS TRANSMISSION IS ASKING FOR VENGEANCE, WHICH IS AS CLOSE TO A DISTRESS CALL AS A KLINGON WILL MAKE.
SOUNDS LIKE THEY'RE UNDER ATTACK, AT—
KHITOMER!
THE SIGNAL JUST CUT OUT...
KHITOMER?
AN UNOCCUPIED CLASS-M PLANET JUST OUTSIDE THE EDGE OF KLINGON SPACE, NOT FAR FROM OUR PRESENT LOCATION.
IT WOULD NOT BE SURPRISING TO LEARN THAT THE KLINGONS HAVE TARGETED IT FOR COLONIZATION.
IF THEY NEED HELP, WE'RE CLOSE ENOUGH TO GIVE IT.
COULD BE THE OLIVE BRANCH WE NEED AFTER MARCUS DID HIS BEST TO START A WAR WITH THEM.
OR THEY COULD VIEW OUR ARRIVAL AS YET ANOTHER PROVOCATION.
OUR MISSION CALLS FOR US TO JOURNEY FAR FROM THE BORDERS OF THE EMPIRE, NOT CLOSER TO THEM.
DEEP SPACE WILL STILL BE WAITING FOR US. IT'S WORTH TAKING A LOOK AT KHITOMER.
CHEKOV, SET A COURSE FOR THE COLONY.
AYE, KEPTIN!

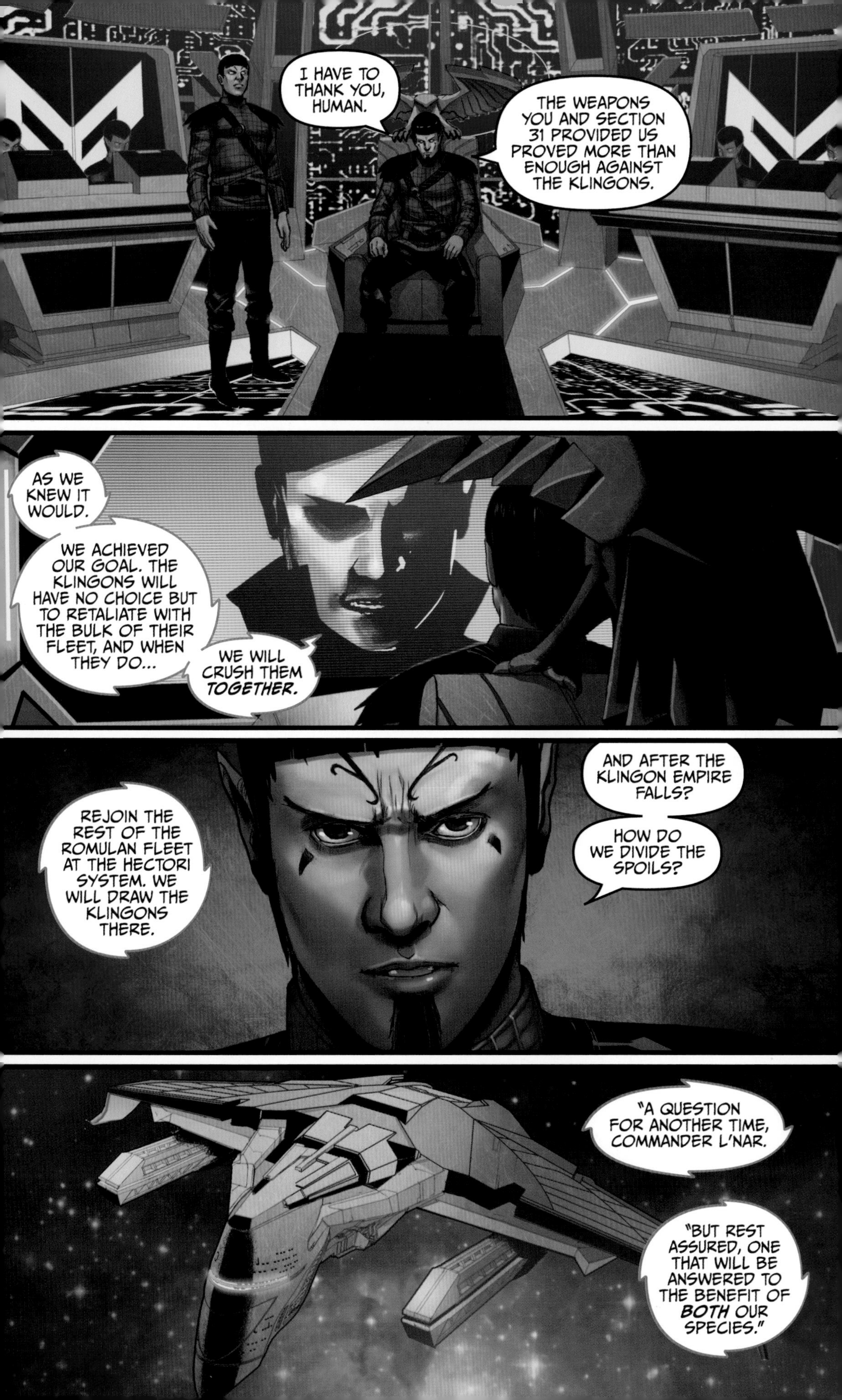

I HAVE TO THANK YOU, HUMAN.
THE WEAPONS YOU AND SECTION 31 PROVIDED US PROVED MORE THAN ENOUGH AGAINST THE KLINGONS.
AS WE KNEW IT WOULD.
WE ACHIEVED OUR GOAL. THE KLINGONS WILL HAVE NO CHOICE BUT TO RETALIATE WITH THE BULK OF THEIR FLEET, AND WHEN THEY DO...
WE WILL CRUSH THEM *TOGETHER.*
REJOIN THE REST OF THE ROMULAN FLEET AT THE HECTORI SYSTEM. WE WILL DRAW THE KLINGONS THERE.
AND AFTER THE KLINGON EMPIRE FALLS?
HOW DO WE DIVIDE THE SPOILS?
"A QUESTION FOR ANOTHER TIME, COMMANDER L'NAR.
"BUT REST ASSURED, ONE THAT WILL BE ANSWERED TO THE BENEFIT OF *BOTH* OUR SPECIES."

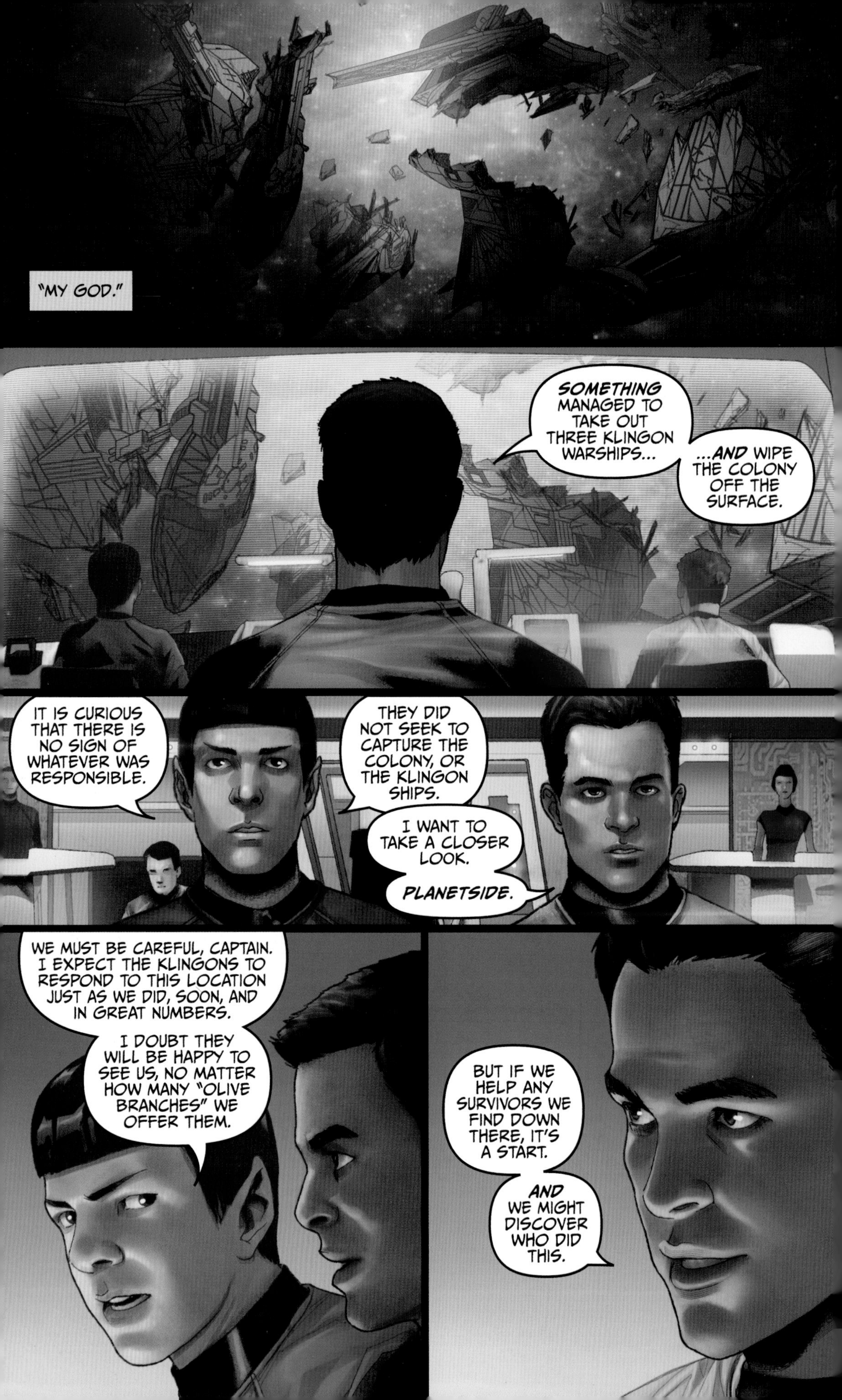
"MY GOD."
SOMETHING MANAGED TO TAKE OUT THREE KLINGON WARSHIPS...
...AND WIPE THE COLONY OFF THE SURFACE.
IT IS CURIOUS THAT THERE IS NO SIGN OF WHATEVER WAS RESPONSIBLE.
THEY DID NOT SEEK TO CAPTURE THE COLONY, OR THE KLINGON SHIPS.
I WANT TO TAKE A CLOSER LOOK.
PLANETSIDE.
WE MUST BE CAREFUL, CAPTAIN. I EXPECT THE KLINGONS TO RESPOND TO THIS LOCATION JUST AS WE DID, SOON, AND IN GREAT NUMBERS.
I DOUBT THEY WILL BE HAPPY TO SEE US, NO MATTER HOW MANY "OLIVE BRANCHES" WE OFFER THEM.
BUT IF WE HELP ANY SURVIVORS WE FIND DOWN THERE, IT'S A START.
AND WE MIGHT DISCOVER WHO DID THIS.

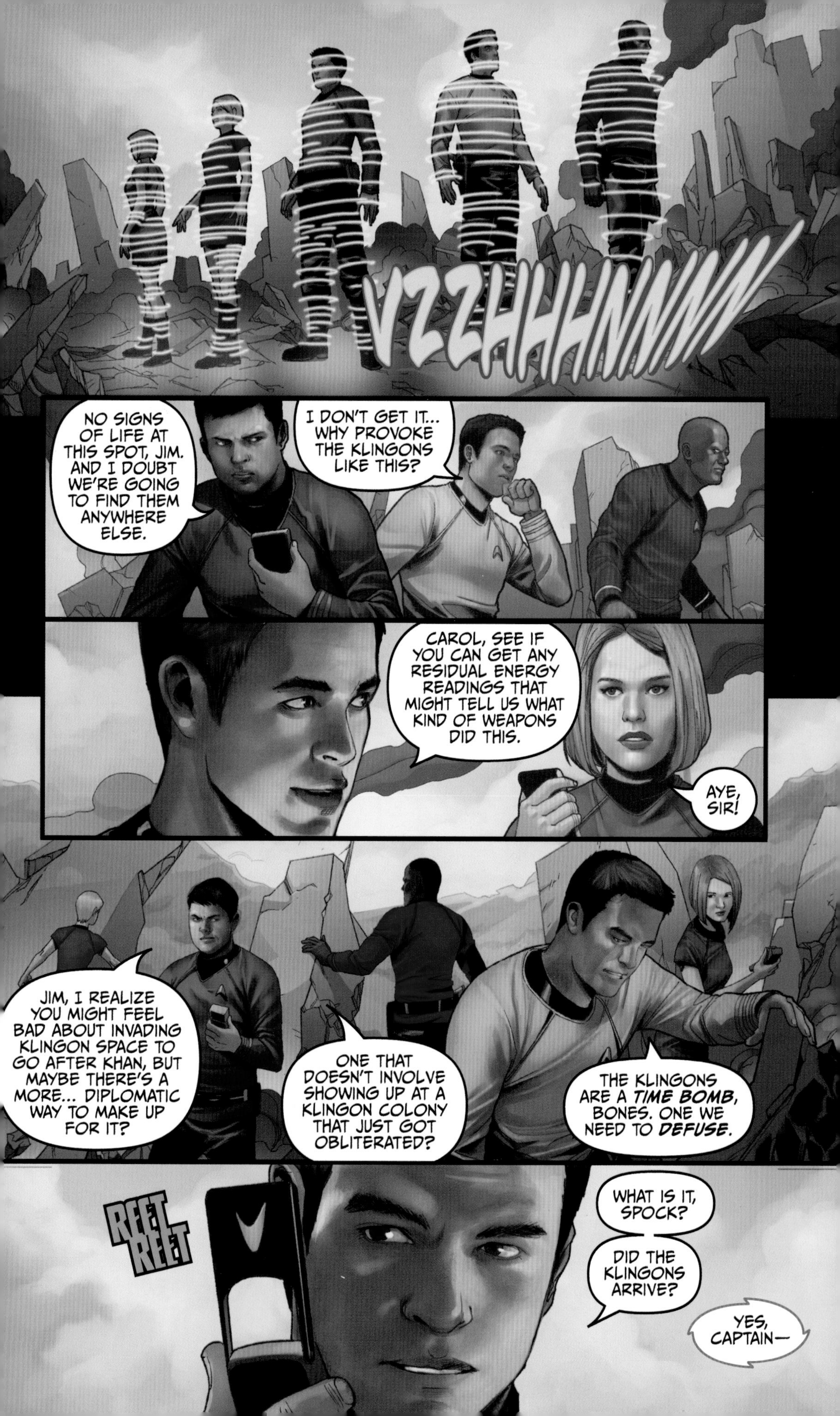
VZZHHHNNNN
NO SIGNS OF LIFE AT THIS SPOT, JIM. AND I DOUBT WE'RE GOING TO FIND THEM ANYWHERE ELSE.
I DON'T GET IT... WHY PROVOKE THE KLINGONS LIKE THIS?
CAROL, SEE IF YOU CAN GET ANY RESIDUAL ENERGY READINGS THAT MIGHT TELL US WHAT KIND OF WEAPONS DID THIS.
AYE, SIR!
JIM, I REALIZE YOU MIGHT FEEL BAD ABOUT INVADING KLINGON SPACE TO GO AFTER KHAN, BUT MAYBE THERE'S A MORE... DIPLOMATIC WAY TO MAKE UP FOR IT?
ONE THAT DOESN'T INVOLVE SHOWING UP AT A KLINGON COLONY THAT JUST GOT OBLITERATED?
THE KLINGONS ARE A *TIME BOMB*, BONES. ONE WE NEED TO ***DEFUSE***.
REET REET
WHAT IS IT, SPOCK?
DID THE KLINGONS ARRIVE?
YES, CAPTAIN—

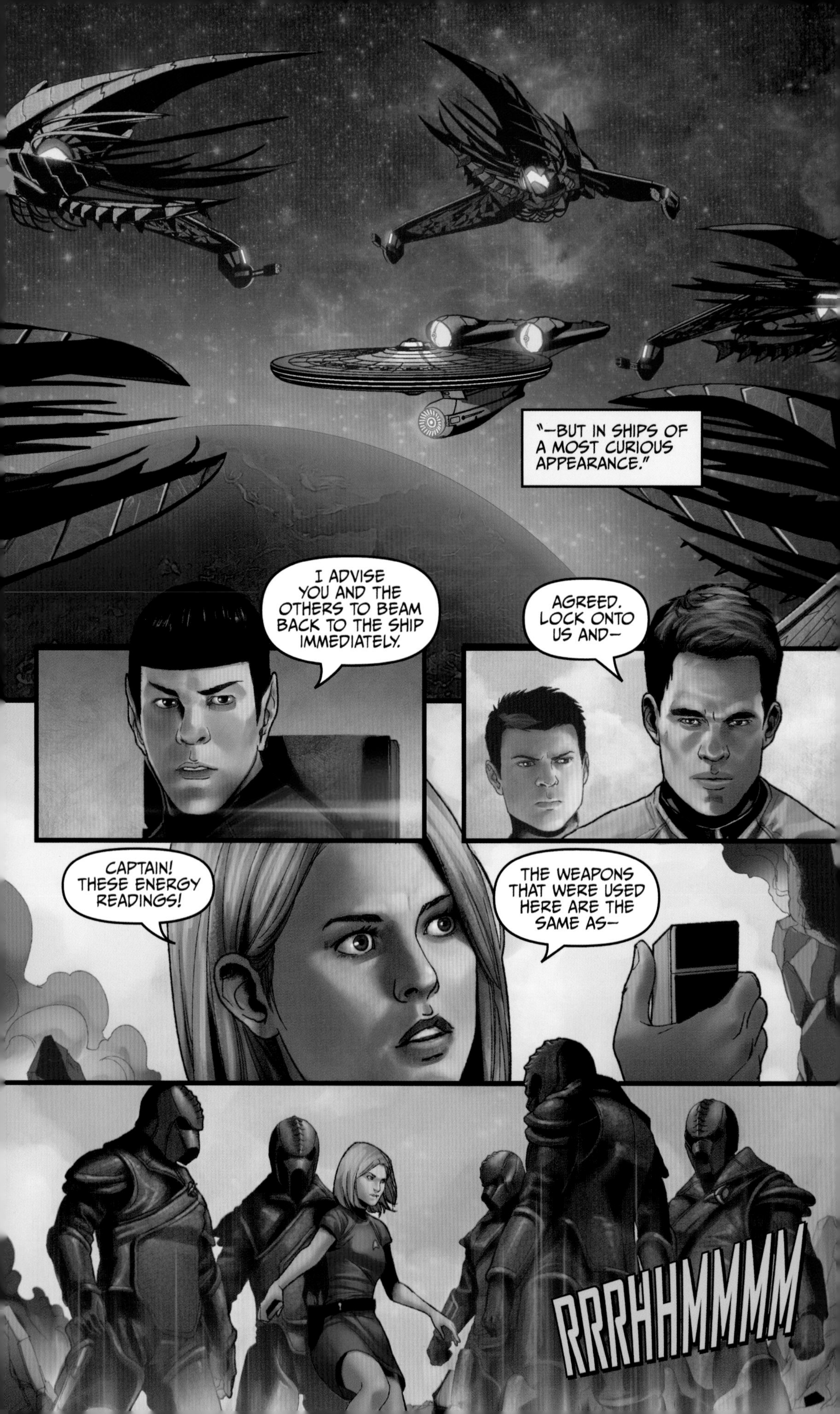
"—BUT IN SHIPS OF A MOST CURIOUS APPEARANCE."
I ADVISE YOU AND THE OTHERS TO BEAM BACK TO THE SHIP IMMEDIATELY.
AGREED. LOCK ONTO US AND—
CAPTAIN! THESE ENERGY READINGS!
THE WEAPONS THAT WERE USED HERE ARE THE SAME AS—
RRRHMMMM

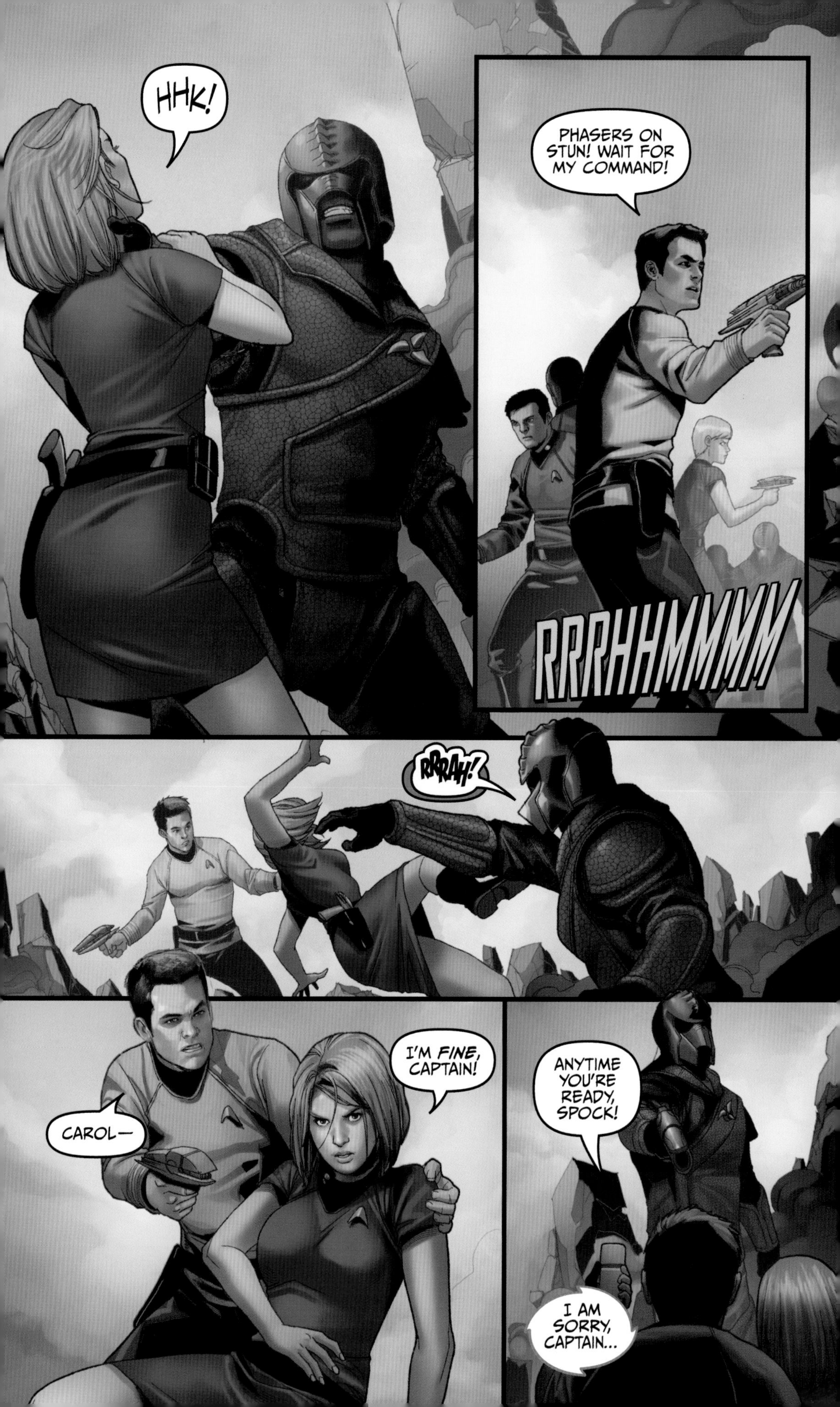
HHK!
PHASERS ON STUN! WAIT FOR MY COMMAND!
RRRHMMMMM
RRRAH!
CAROL—
I'M *FINE*, CAPTAIN!
ANYTIME YOU'RE READY, SPOCK!
I AM SORRY, CAPTAIN...

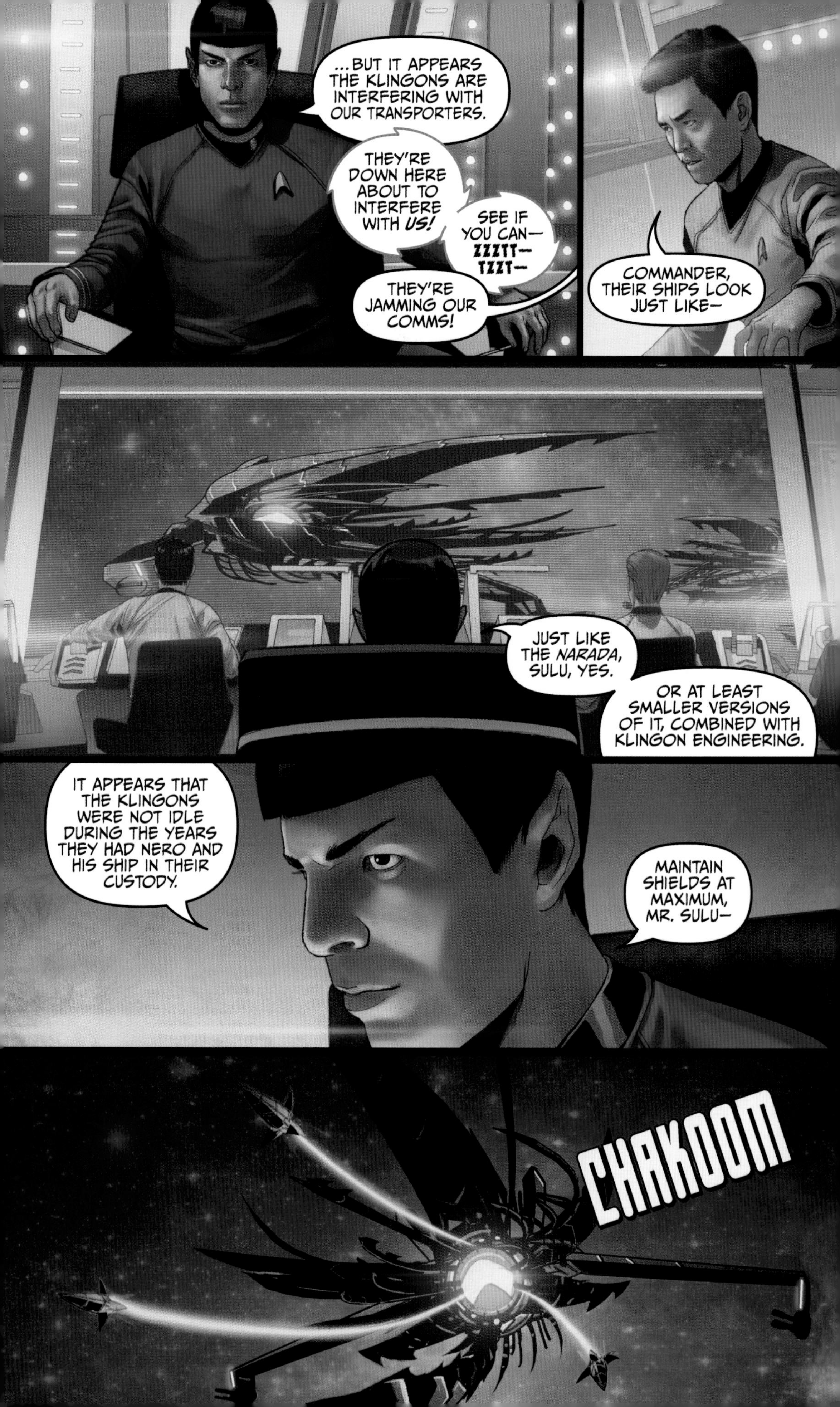
...BUT IT APPEARS THE KLINGONS ARE INTERFERING WITH OUR TRANSPORTERS.
THEY'RE DOWN HERE ABOUT TO INTERFERE WITH *US!*
SEE IF YOU CAN— ZZZTT— TZZT—
THEY'RE JAMMING OUR COMMS!
COMMANDER, THEIR SHIPS LOOK JUST LIKE—
JUST LIKE THE *NARADA,* SULU, YES.
OR AT LEAST SMALLER VERSIONS OF IT, COMBINED WITH KLINGON ENGINEERING.
IT APPEARS THAT THE KLINGONS WERE NOT IDLE DURING THE YEARS THEY HAD NERO AND HIS SHIP IN THEIR CUSTODY.
MAINTAIN SHIELDS AT MAXIMUM, MR. SULU—
CHAKOOM

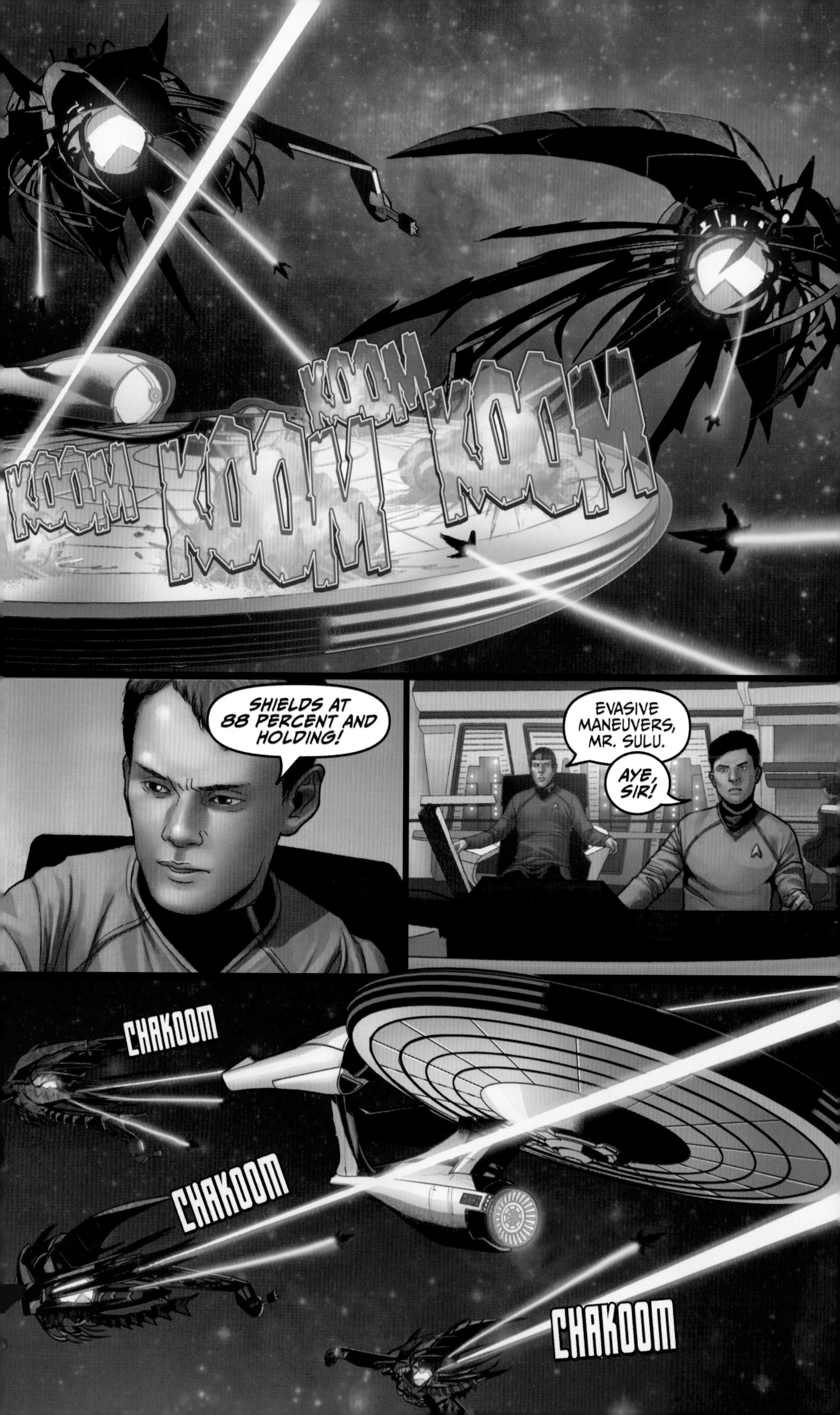
KOOM
KOOM
KOOM
KOOM
SHIELDS AT 88 PERCENT AND HOLDING!
EVASIVE MANEUVERS, MR. SULU.
AYE, SIR!
CHAKOOM
CHAKOOM
CHAKOOM

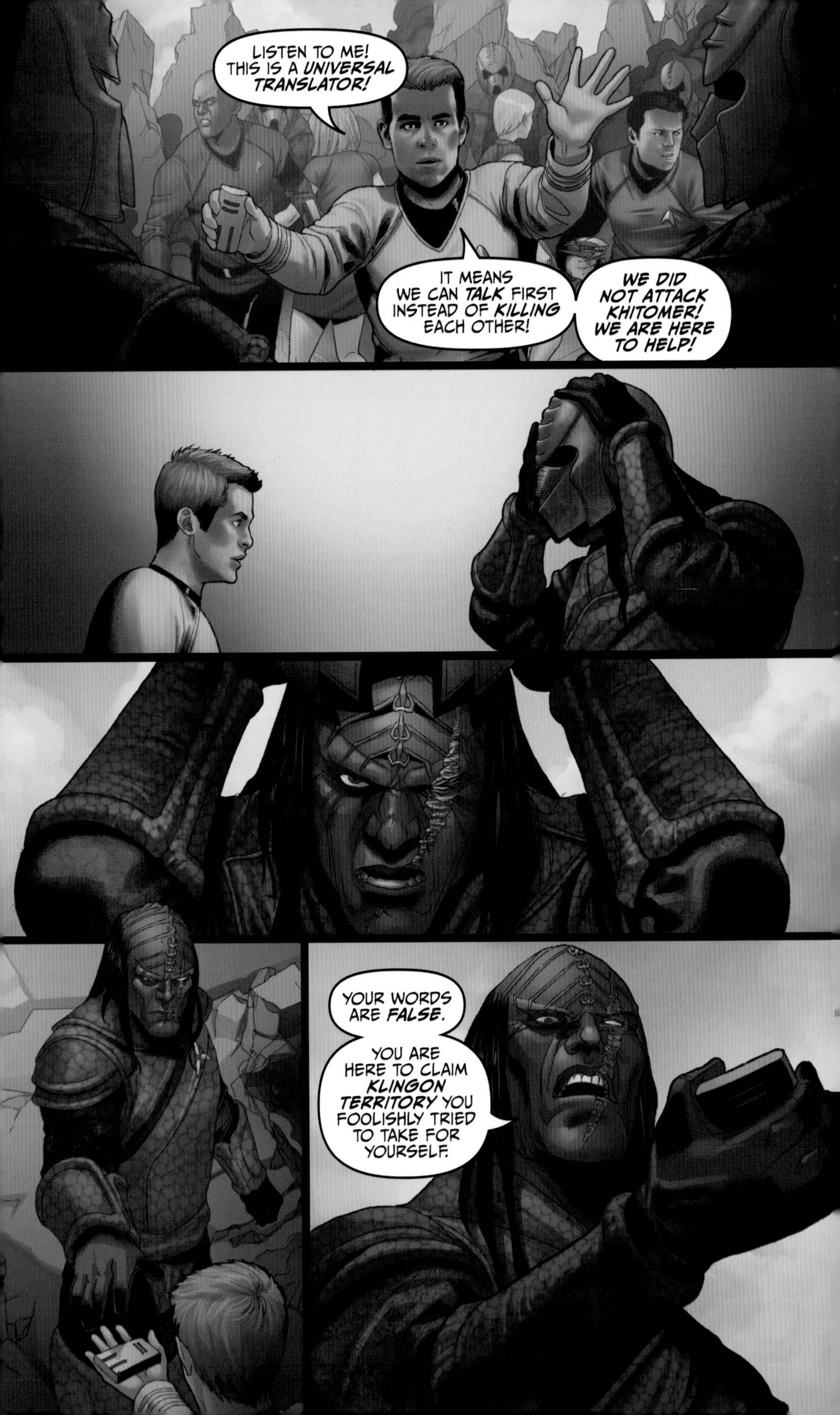
LISTEN TO ME! THIS IS A UNIVERSAL TRANSLATOR!
IT MEANS WE CAN TALK FIRST INSTEAD OF KILLING EACH OTHER!
WE DID NOT ATTACK KHITOMER! WE ARE HERE TO HELP!
YOUR WORDS ARE FALSE.
YOU ARE HERE TO CLAIM KLINGON TERRITORY YOU FOOLISHLY TRIED TO TAKE FOR YOURSELF.

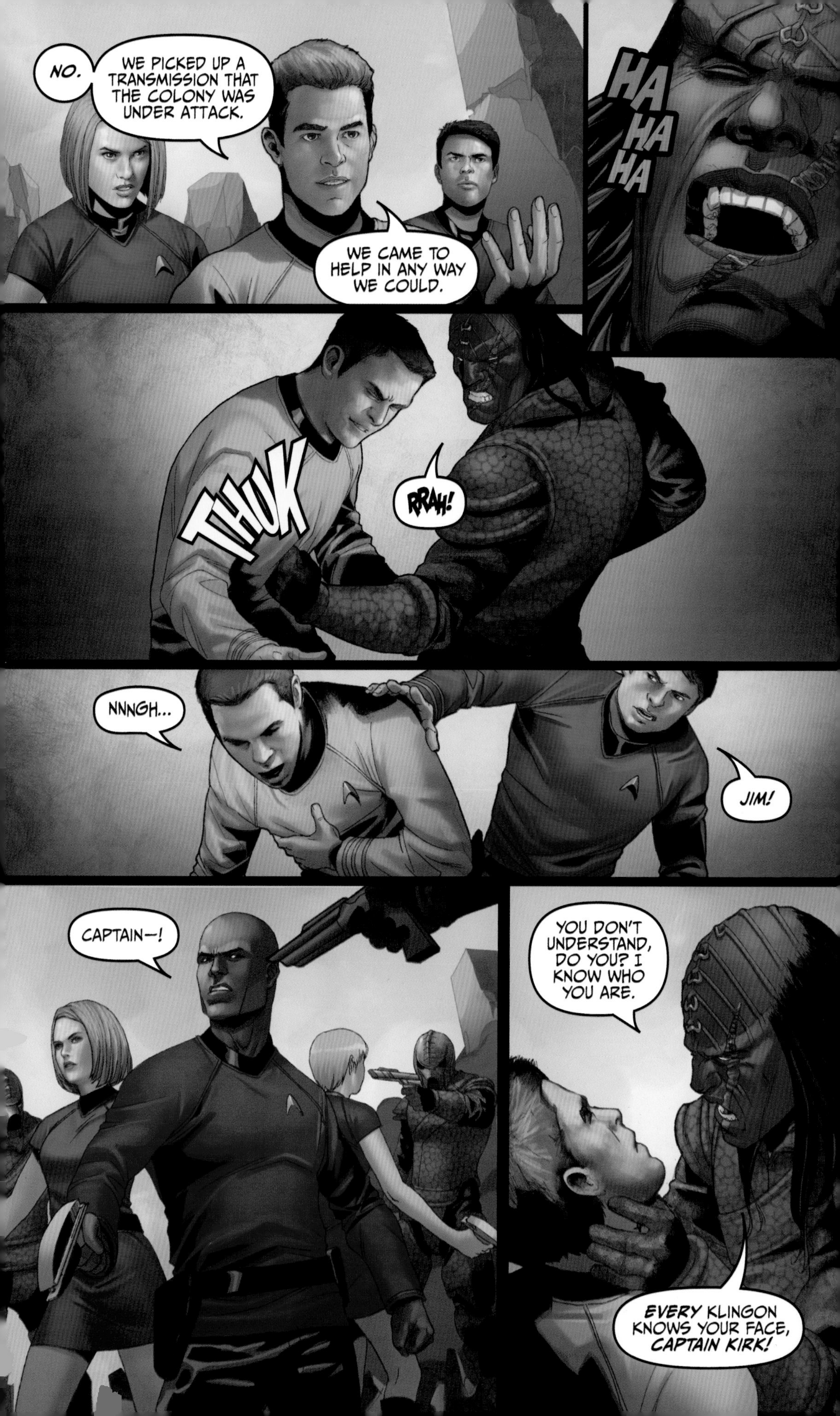
NO.
WE PICKED UP A TRANSMISSION THAT THE COLONY WAS UNDER ATTACK.
WE CAME TO HELP IN ANY WAY WE COULD.
HA HA HA
THUK
RRAH!
NNNGH...
JIM!
CAPTAIN—!
YOU DON'T UNDERSTAND, DO YOU? I KNOW WHO YOU ARE.
EVERY KLINGON KNOWS YOUR FACE, CAPTAIN KIRK!

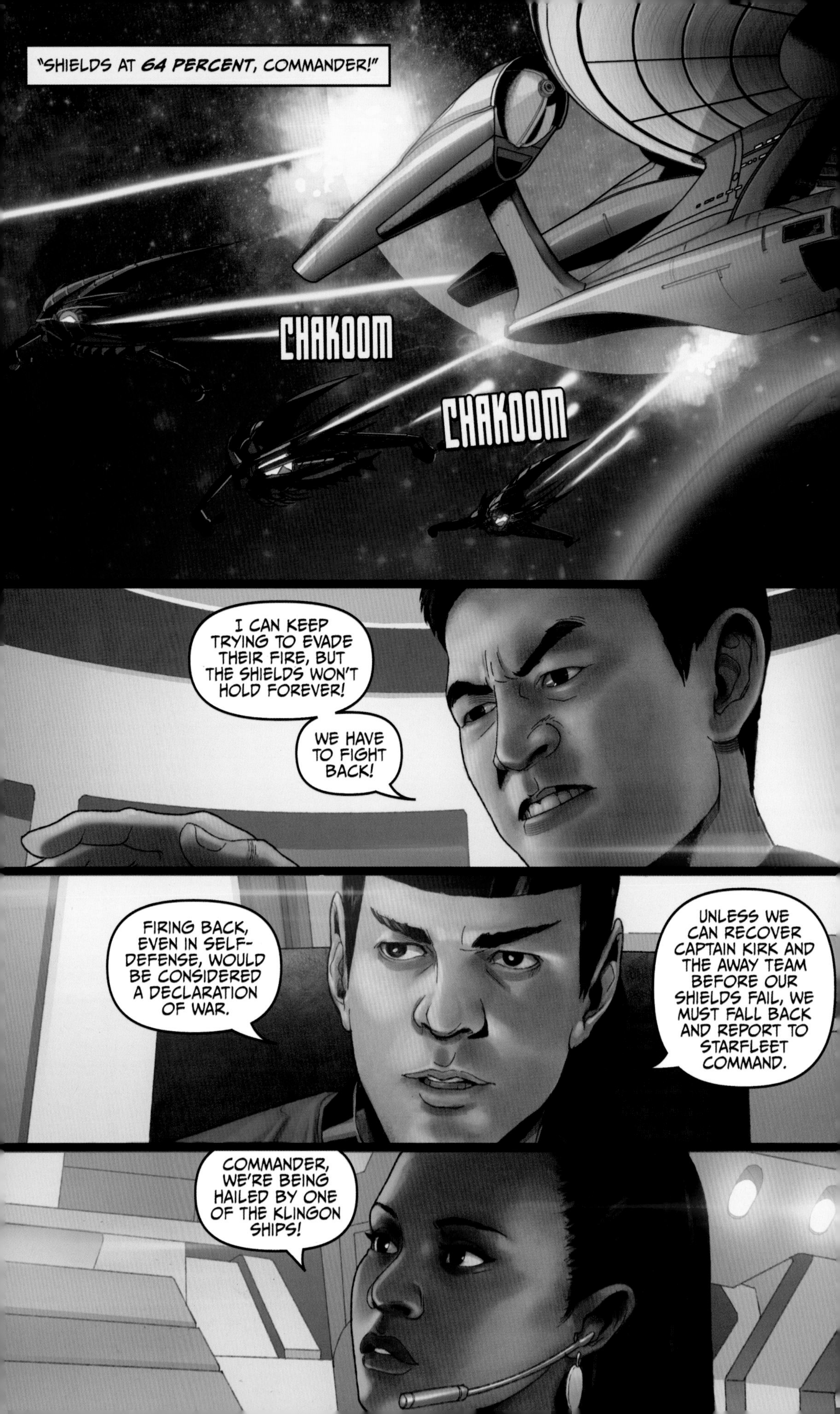
"SHIELDS AT 64 PERCENT, COMMANDER!"
CHAKOOM
CHAKOOM
I CAN KEEP TRYING TO EVADE THEIR FIRE, BUT THE SHIELDS WON'T HOLD FOREVER!
WE HAVE TO FIGHT BACK!
FIRING BACK, EVEN IN SELF-DEFENSE, WOULD BE CONSIDERED A DECLARATION OF WAR.
UNLESS WE CAN RECOVER CAPTAIN KIRK AND THE AWAY TEAM BEFORE OUR SHIELDS FAIL, WE MUST FALL BACK AND REPORT TO STARFLEET COMMAND.
COMMANDER, WE'RE BEING HAILED BY ONE OF THE KLINGON SHIPS!

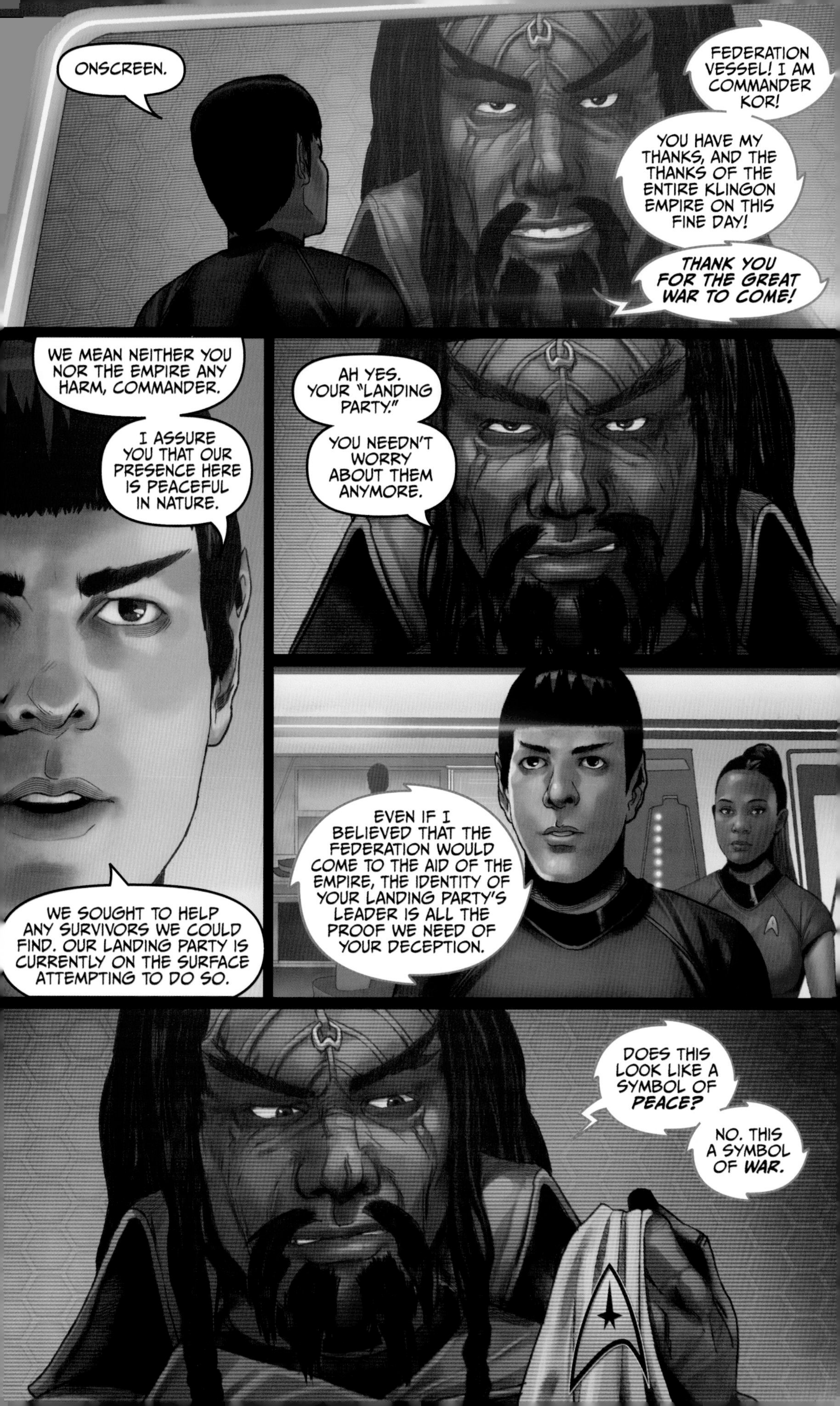
ONSCREEN.
FEDERATION VESSEL! I AM COMMANDER KOR!
YOU HAVE MY THANKS, AND THE THANKS OF THE ENTIRE KLINGON EMPIRE ON THIS FINE DAY!
THANK YOU FOR THE GREAT WAR TO COME!
WE MEAN NEITHER YOU NOR THE EMPIRE ANY HARM, COMMANDER.
I ASSURE YOU THAT OUR PRESENCE HERE IS PEACEFUL IN NATURE.
WE SOUGHT TO HELP ANY SURVIVORS WE COULD FIND. OUR LANDING PARTY IS CURRENTLY ON THE SURFACE ATTEMPTING TO DO SO.
AH YES. YOUR "LANDING PARTY."
YOU NEEDN'T WORRY ABOUT THEM ANYMORE.
EVEN IF I BELIEVED THAT THE FEDERATION WOULD COME TO THE AID OF THE EMPIRE, THE IDENTITY OF YOUR LANDING PARTY'S LEADER IS ALL THE PROOF WE NEED OF YOUR DECEPTION.
DOES THIS LOOK LIKE A SYMBOL OF *PEACE?*
NO. THIS A SYMBOL OF *WAR.*

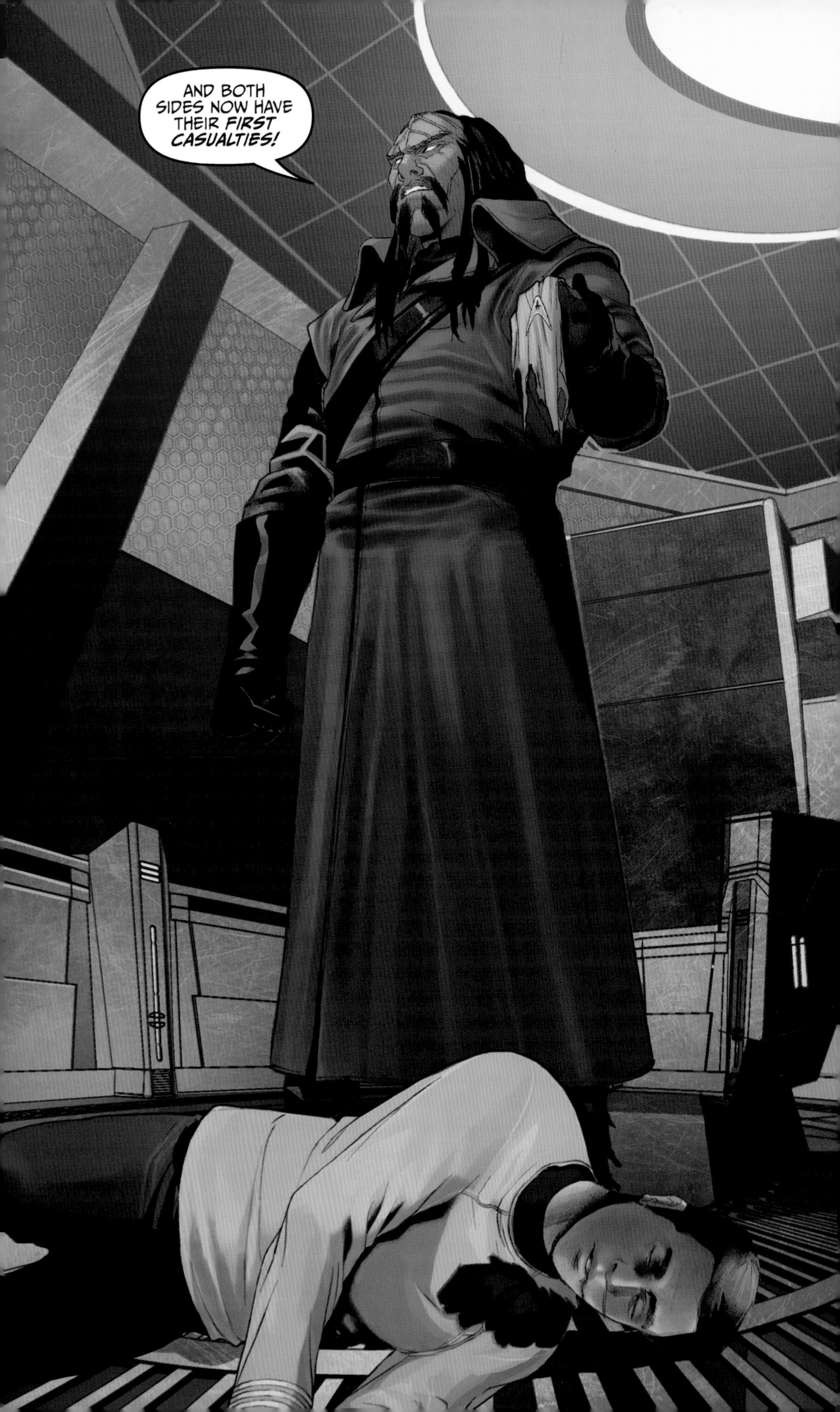
AND BOTH SIDES NOW HAVE THEIR *FIRST CASUALTIES!*

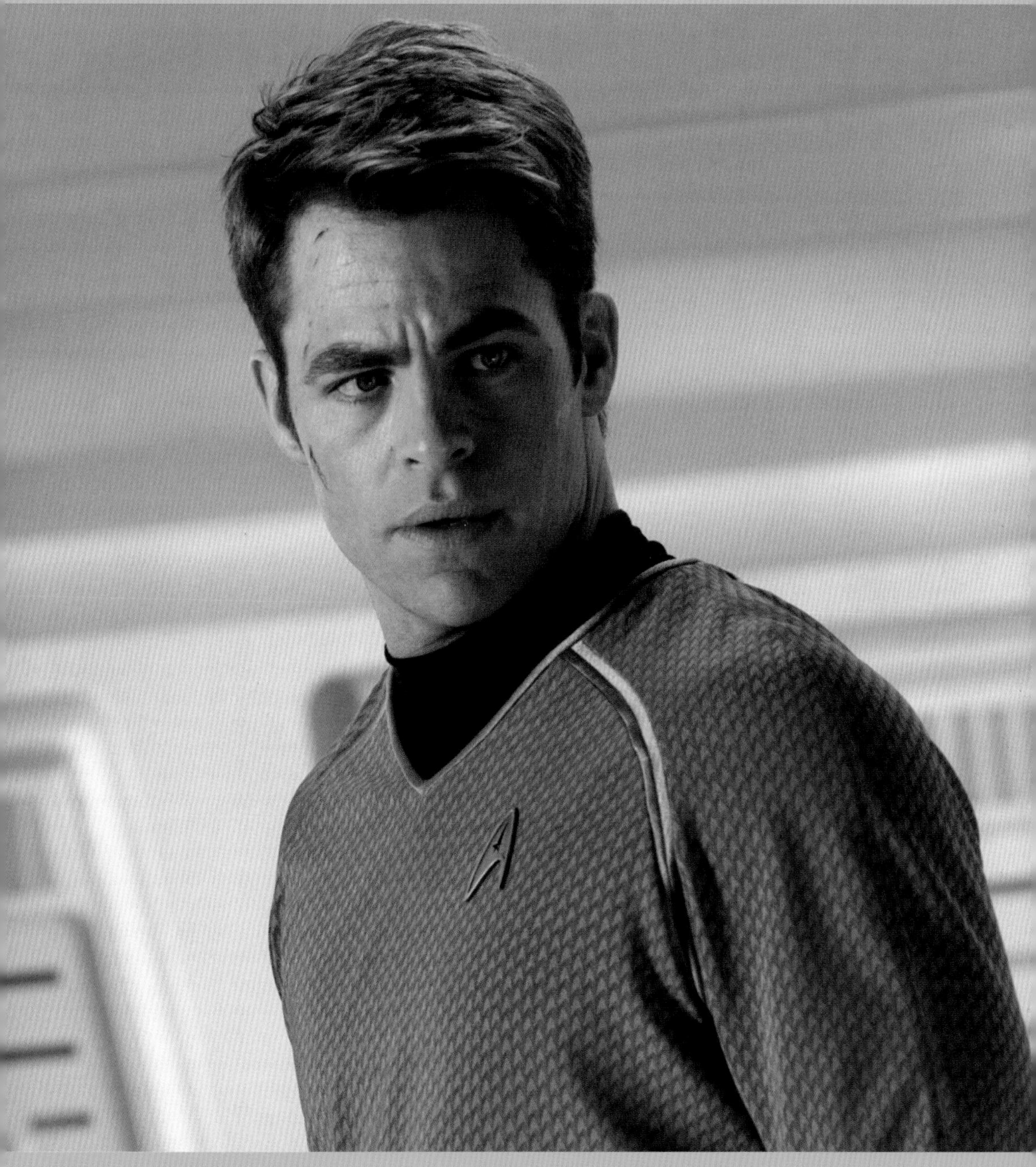

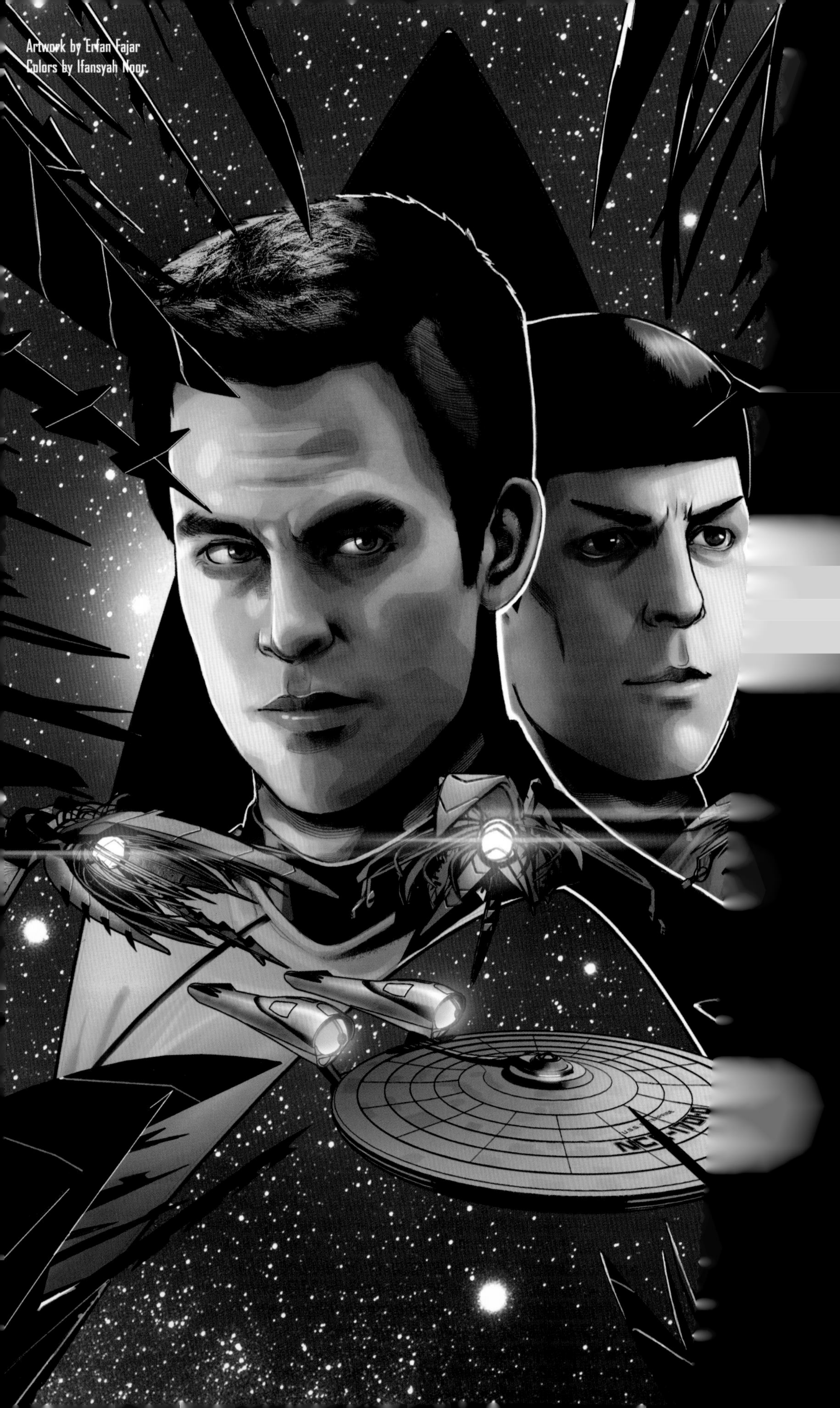
Artwork by Erfan Fajar
Colors by Ifansyah Noor.

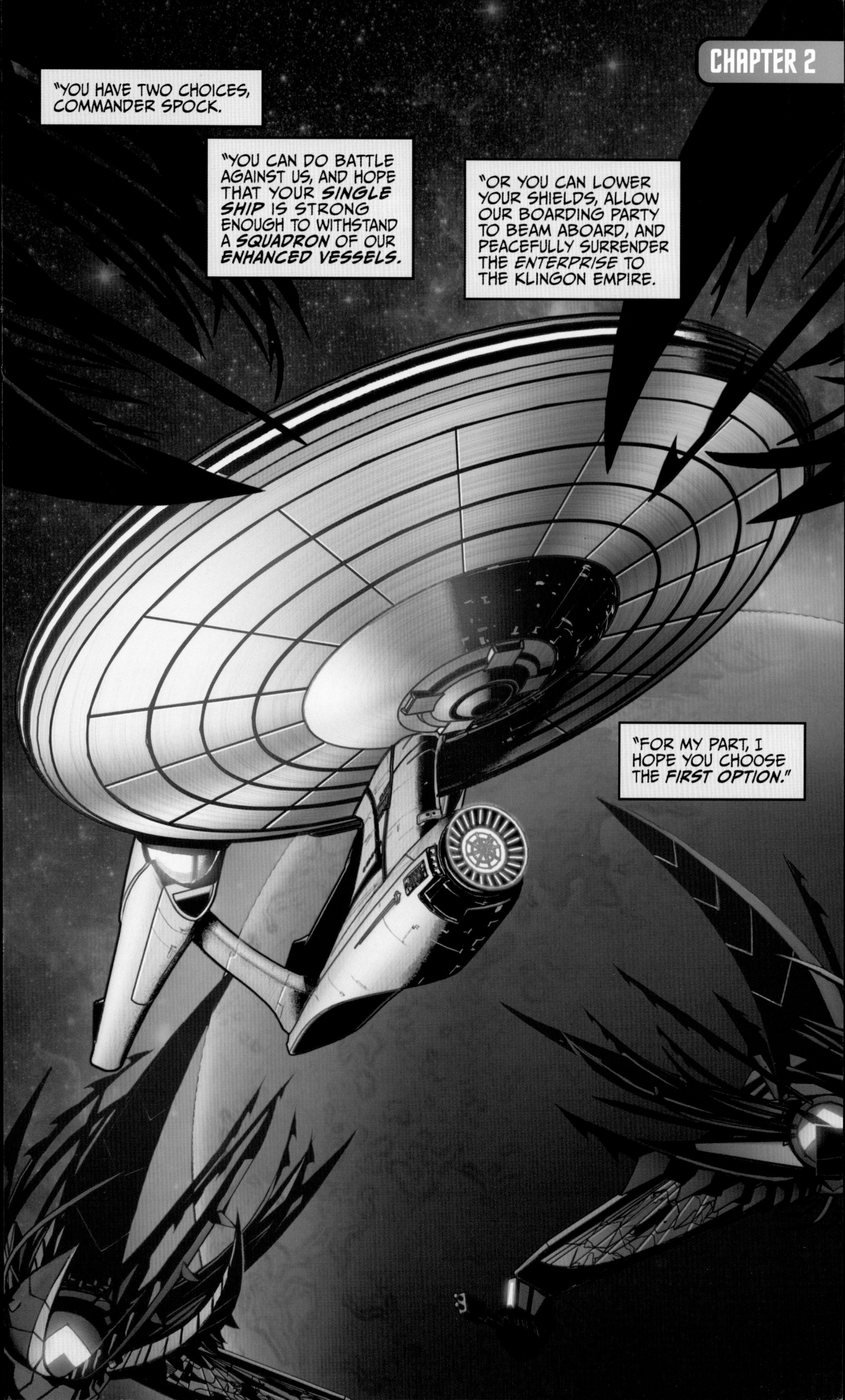
CHAPTER 2
"YOU HAVE TWO CHOICES, COMMANDER SPOCK.
"YOU CAN DO BATTLE AGAINST US, AND HOPE THAT YOUR *SINGLE SHIP* IS STRONG ENOUGH TO WITHSTAND A *SQUADRON* OF OUR *ENHANCED VESSELS.*
"OR YOU CAN LOWER YOUR SHIELDS, ALLOW OUR BOARDING PARTY TO BEAM ABOARD, AND PEACEFULLY SURRENDER THE *ENTERPRISE* TO THE KLINGON EMPIRE.
"FOR MY PART, I HOPE YOU CHOOSE THE *FIRST OPTION.*"

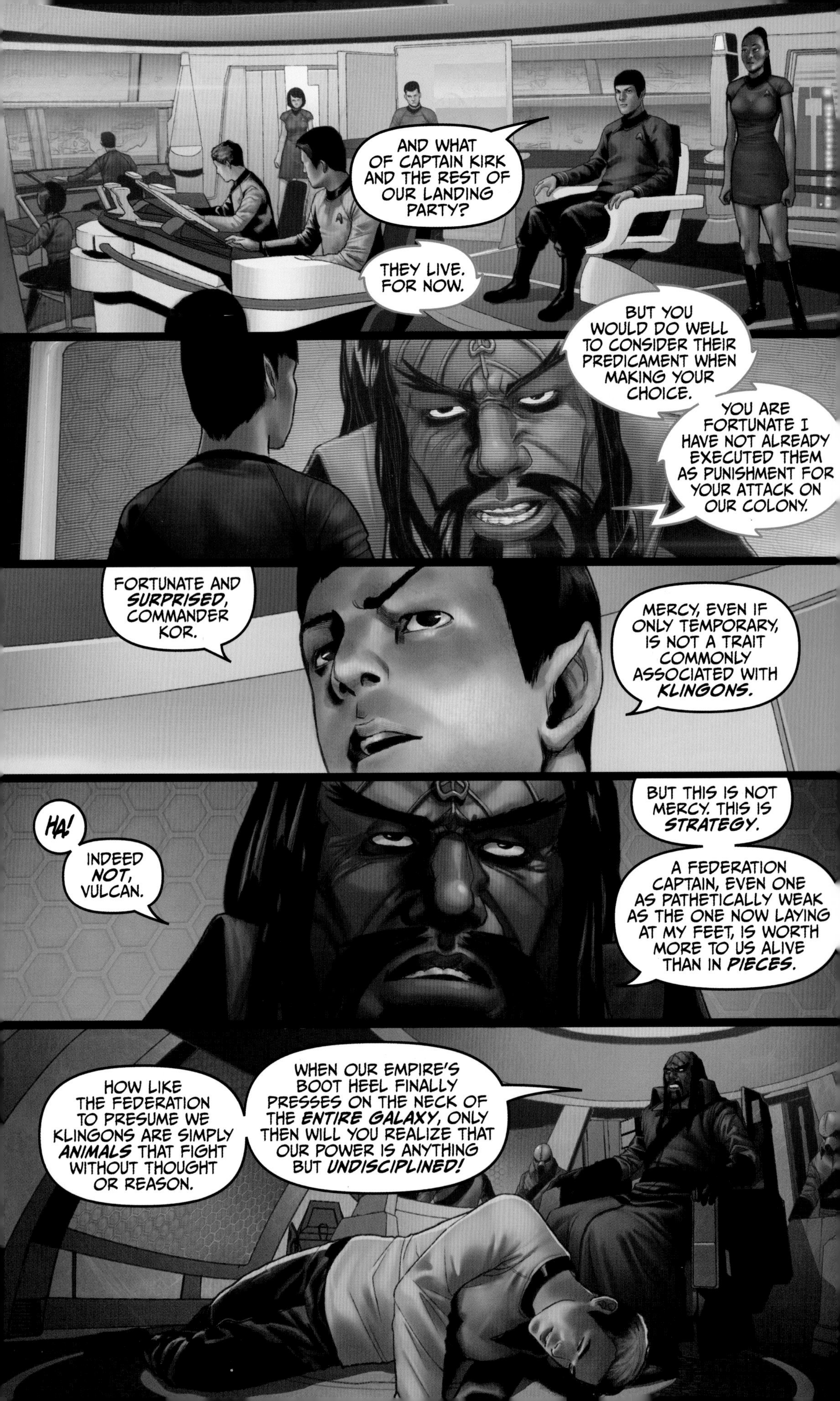
AND WHAT OF CAPTAIN KIRK AND THE REST OF OUR LANDING PARTY?
THEY LIVE. FOR NOW.
BUT YOU WOULD DO WELL TO CONSIDER THEIR PREDICAMENT WHEN MAKING YOUR CHOICE.
YOU ARE FORTUNATE I HAVE NOT ALREADY EXECUTED THEM AS PUNISHMENT FOR YOUR ATTACK ON OUR COLONY.
FORTUNATE AND *SURPRISED*, COMMANDER KOR.
MERCY, EVEN IF ONLY TEMPORARY, IS NOT A TRAIT COMMONLY ASSOCIATED WITH *KLINGONS*.
HA!
INDEED *NOT*, VULCAN.
BUT THIS IS NOT MERCY. THIS IS *STRATEGY*.
A FEDERATION CAPTAIN, EVEN ONE AS PATHETICALLY WEAK AS THE ONE NOW LAYING AT MY FEET, IS WORTH MORE TO US ALIVE THAN IN *PIECES*.
HOW LIKE THE FEDERATION TO PRESUME WE KLINGONS ARE SIMPLY *ANIMALS* THAT FIGHT WITHOUT THOUGHT OR REASON.
WHEN OUR EMPIRE'S BOOT HEEL FINALLY PRESSES ON THE NECK OF THE *ENTIRE GALAXY*, ONLY THEN WILL YOU REALIZE THAT OUR POWER IS ANYTHING BUT *UNDISCIPLINED!*

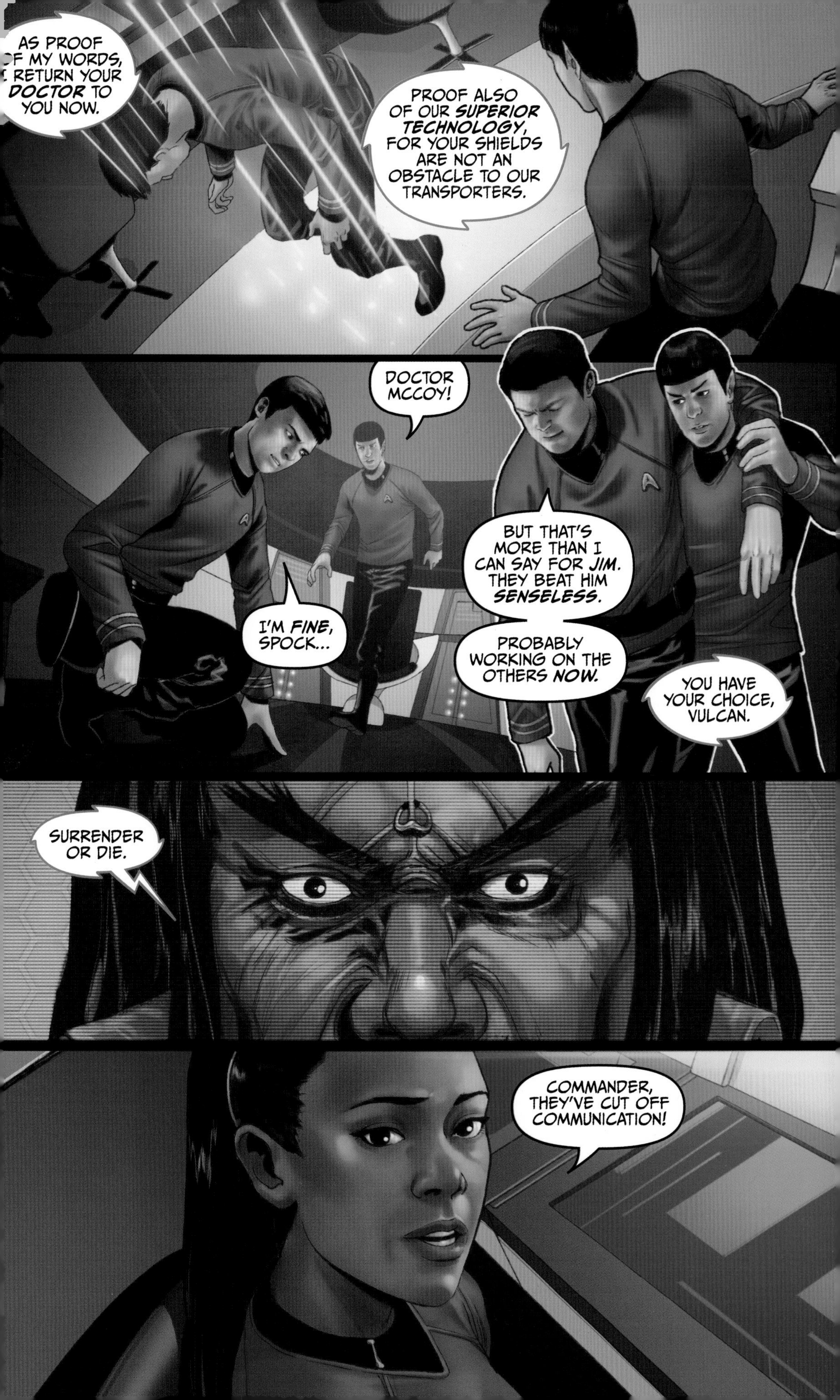
AS PROOF OF MY WORDS, I RETURN YOUR DOCTOR TO YOU NOW.
PROOF ALSO OF OUR SUPERIOR TECHNOLOGY, FOR YOUR SHIELDS ARE NOT AN OBSTACLE TO OUR TRANSPORTERS.
DOCTOR MCCOY!
I'M FINE, SPOCK...
BUT THAT'S MORE THAN I CAN SAY FOR JIM. THEY BEAT HIM SENSELESS.
PROBABLY WORKING ON THE OTHERS NOW.
YOU HAVE YOUR CHOICE, VULCAN.
SURRENDER OR DIE.
COMMANDER, THEY'VE CUT OFF COMMUNICATION!

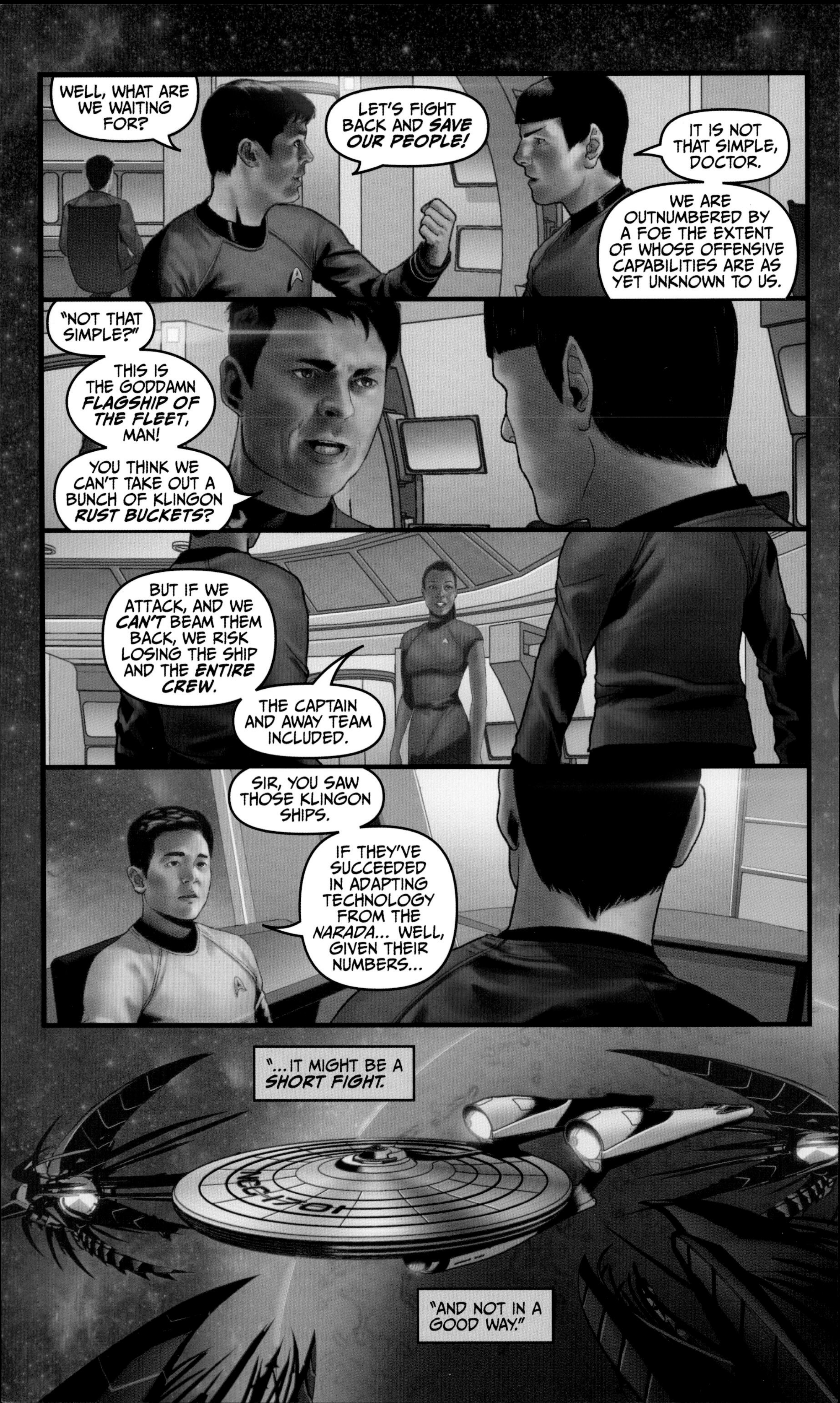
WELL, WHAT ARE WE WAITING FOR?
LET'S FIGHT BACK AND SAVE OUR PEOPLE!
IT IS NOT THAT SIMPLE, DOCTOR.
WE ARE OUTNUMBERED BY A FOE THE EXTENT OF WHOSE OFFENSIVE CAPABILITIES ARE AS YET UNKNOWN TO US.
"NOT THAT SIMPLE?"
THIS IS THE GODDAMN FLAGSHIP OF THE FLEET, MAN!
YOU THINK WE CAN'T TAKE OUT A BUNCH OF KLINGON RUST BUCKETS?
BUT IF WE ATTACK, AND WE CAN'T BEAM THEM BACK, WE RISK LOSING THE SHIP AND THE ENTIRE CREW.
THE CAPTAIN AND AWAY TEAM INCLUDED.
SIR, YOU SAW THOSE KLINGON SHIPS.
IF THEY'VE SUCCEEDED IN ADAPTING TECHNOLOGY FROM THE NARADA... WELL, GIVEN THEIR NUMBERS...
"...IT MIGHT BE A SHORT FIGHT.
NCC-1701
"AND NOT IN A GOOD WAY."

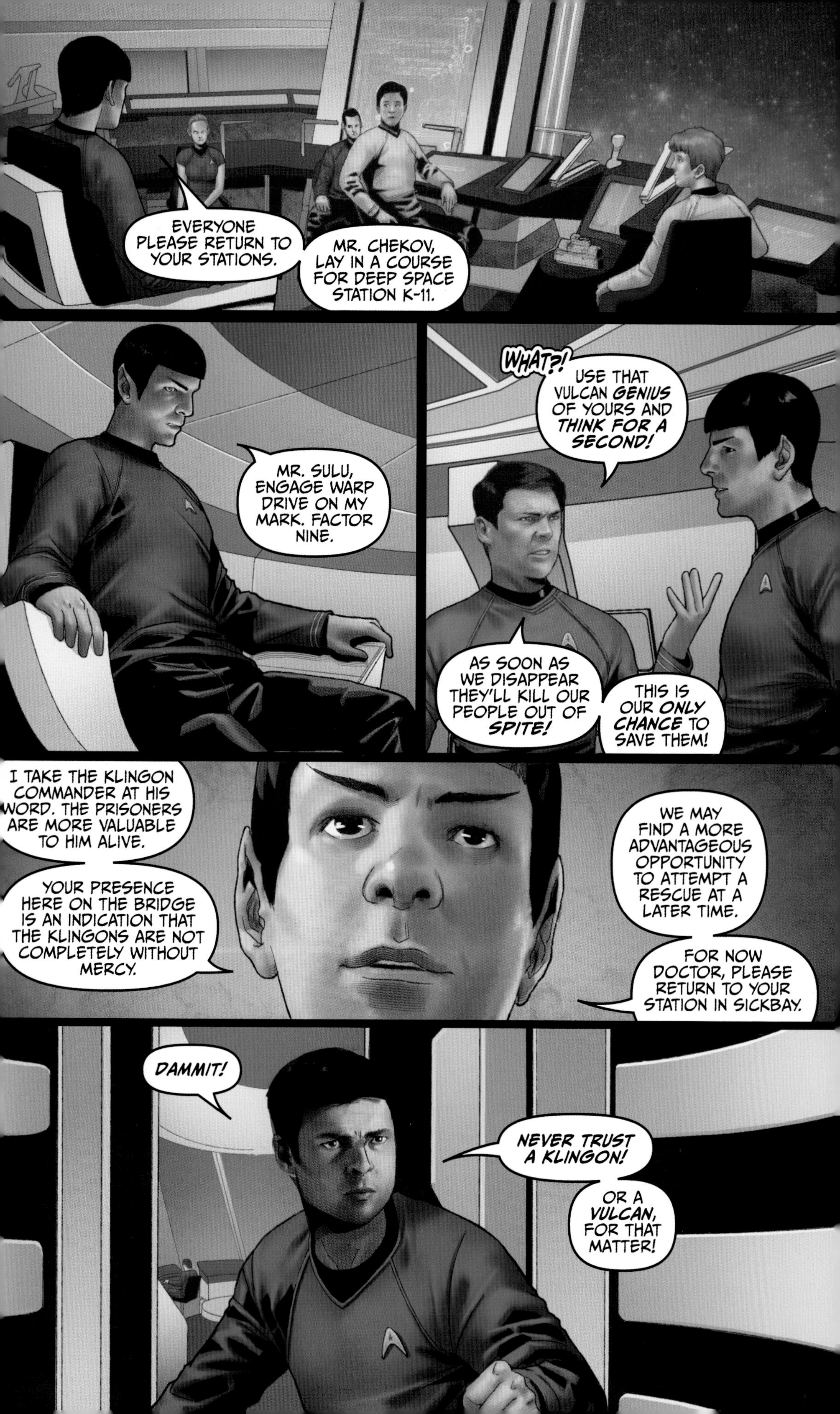
EVERYONE PLEASE RETURN TO YOUR STATIONS.
MR. CHEKOV, LAY IN A COURSE FOR DEEP SPACE STATION K-11.
MR. SULU, ENGAGE WARP DRIVE ON MY MARK. FACTOR NINE.
WHAT?!
USE THAT VULCAN GENIUS OF YOURS AND THINK FOR A SECOND!
AS SOON AS WE DISAPPEAR THEY'LL KILL OUR PEOPLE OUT OF SPITE!
THIS IS OUR ONLY CHANCE TO SAVE THEM!
I TAKE THE KLINGON COMMANDER AT HIS WORD. THE PRISONERS ARE MORE VALUABLE TO HIM ALIVE.
YOUR PRESENCE HERE ON THE BRIDGE IS AN INDICATION THAT THE KLINGONS ARE NOT COMPLETELY WITHOUT MERCY.
WE MAY FIND A MORE ADVANTAGEOUS OPPORTUNITY TO ATTEMPT A RESCUE AT A LATER TIME.
FOR NOW DOCTOR, PLEASE RETURN TO YOUR STATION IN SICKBAY.
DAMMIT!
NEVER TRUST A KLINGON!
OR A VULCAN, FOR THAT MATTER!

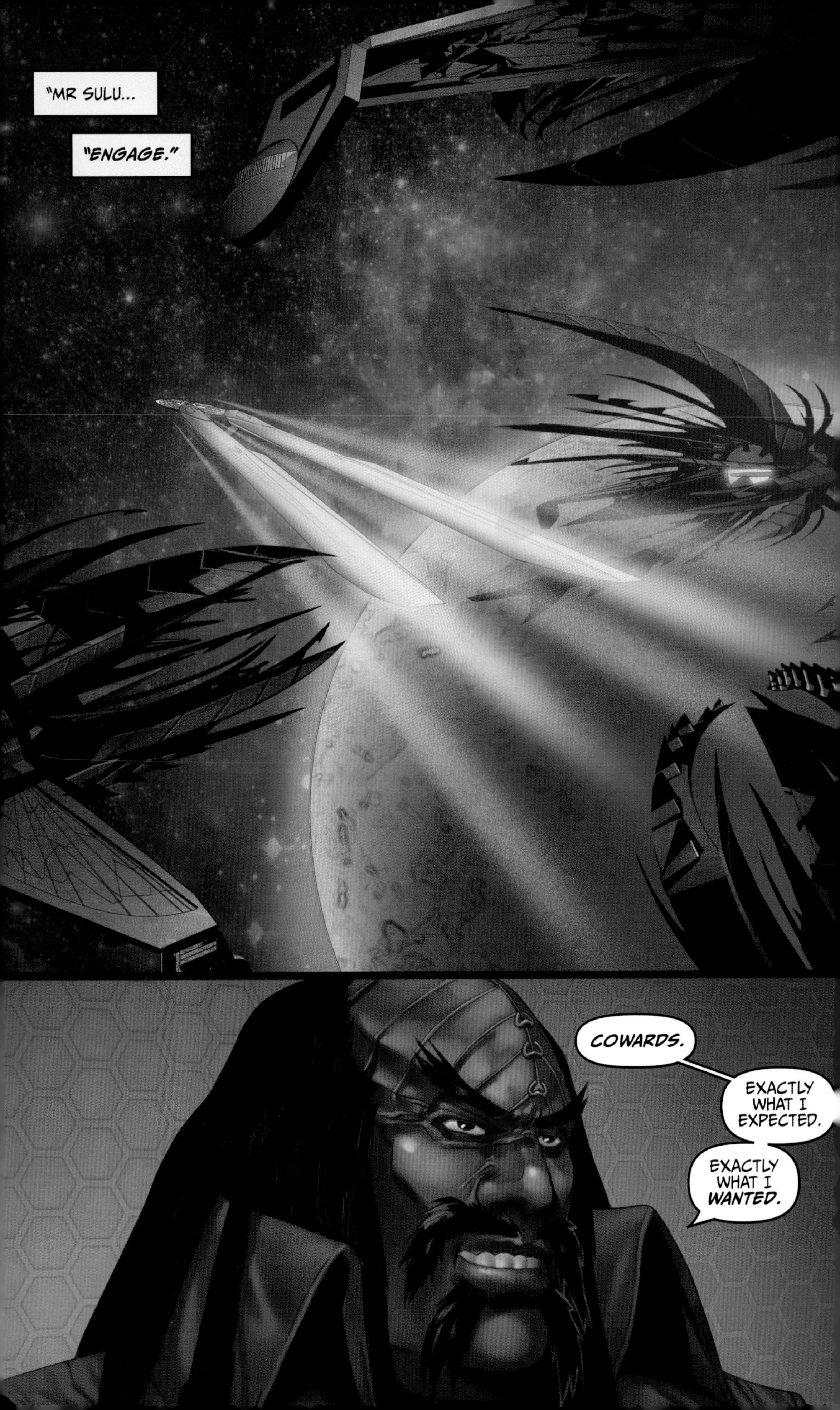
"MR SULU...
"ENGAGE."
COWARDS.
EXACTLY WHAT I EXPECTED.
EXACTLY WHAT I WANTED.

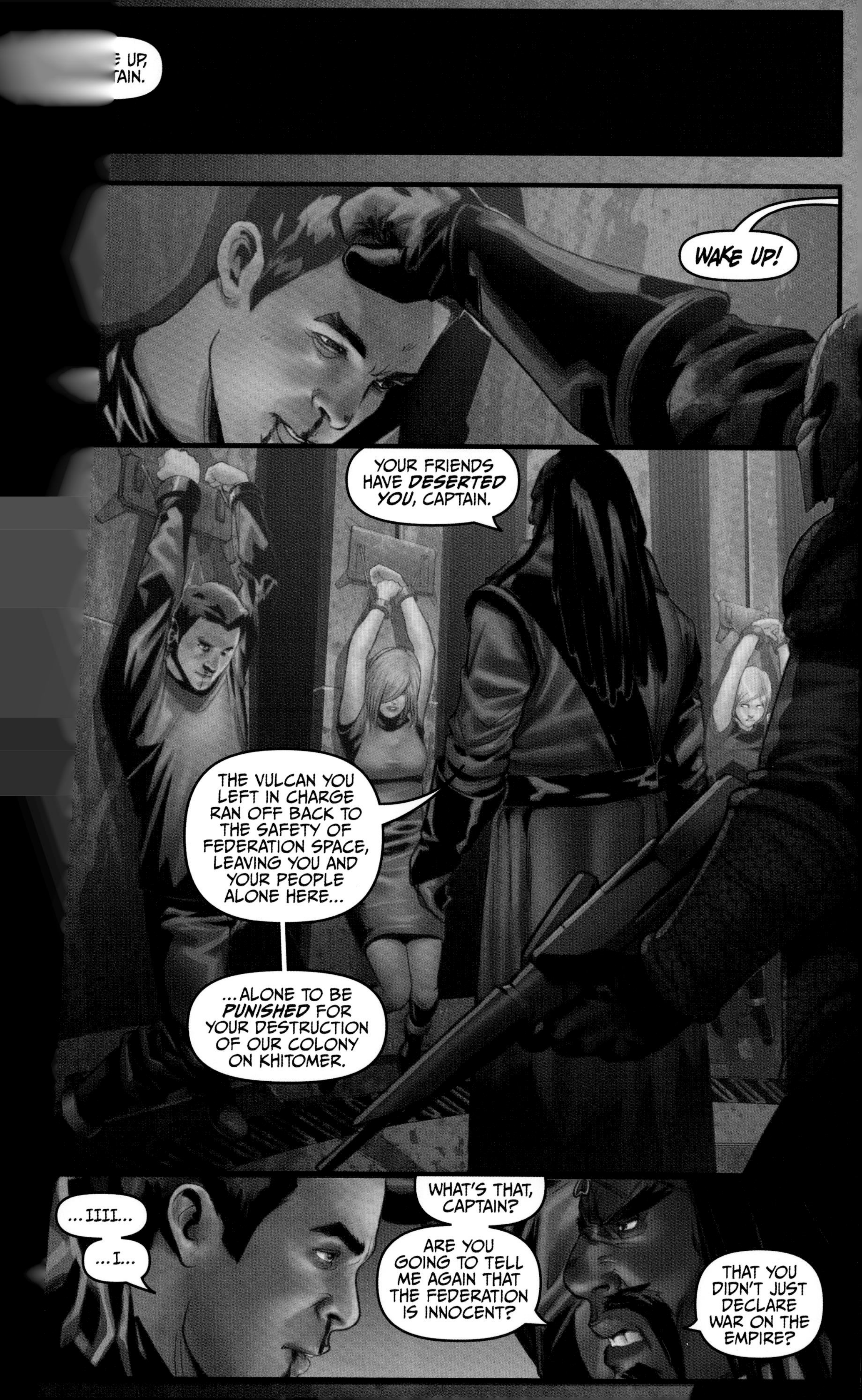
E UP,
TAIN.
WAKE UP!
YOUR FRIENDS HAVE DESERTED YOU, CAPTAIN.
THE VULCAN YOU LEFT IN CHARGE RAN OFF BACK TO THE SAFETY OF FEDERATION SPACE, LEAVING YOU AND YOUR PEOPLE ALONE HERE...
...ALONE TO BE PUNISHED FOR YOUR DESTRUCTION OF OUR COLONY ON KHITOMER.
...IIII...
...I...
WHAT'S THAT, CAPTAIN?
ARE YOU GOING TO TELL ME AGAIN THAT THE FEDERATION IS INNOCENT?
THAT YOU DIDN'T JUST DECLARE WAR ON THE EMPIRE?

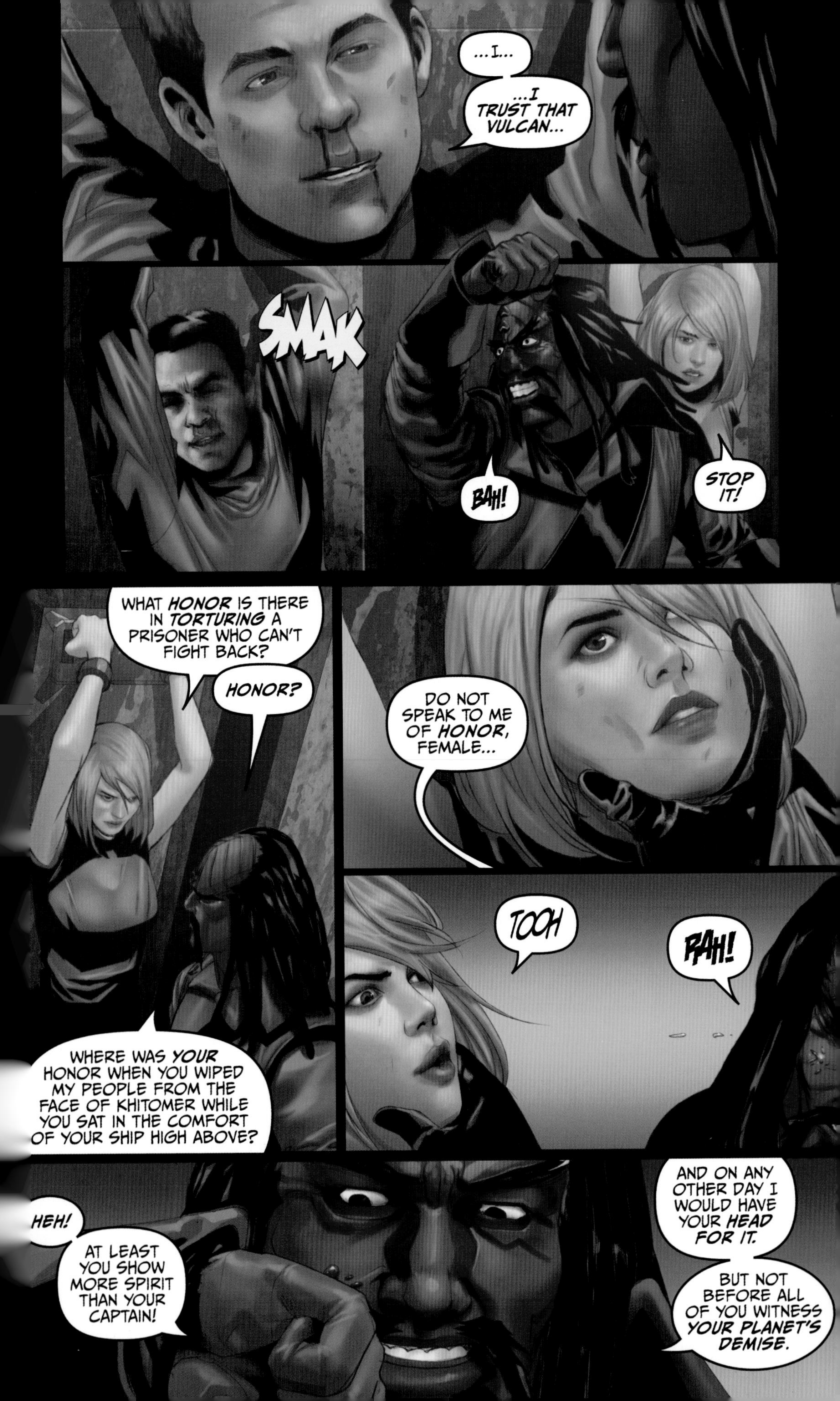

...I...
...I TRUST THAT VULCAN...
SMAK
BAH!
STOP IT!
WHAT HONOR IS THERE IN TORTURING A PRISONER WHO CAN'T FIGHT BACK?
HONOR?
WHERE WAS YOUR HONOR WHEN YOU WIPED MY PEOPLE FROM THE FACE OF KHITOMER WHILE YOU SAT IN THE COMFORT OF YOUR SHIP HIGH ABOVE?
DO NOT SPEAK TO ME OF HONOR, FEMALE...
TOOH
RAH!
HEH!
AT LEAST YOU SHOW MORE SPIRIT THAN YOUR CAPTAIN!
AND ON ANY OTHER DAY I WOULD HAVE YOUR HEAD FOR IT.
BUT NOT BEFORE ALL OF YOU WITNESS YOUR PLANET'S DEMISE.

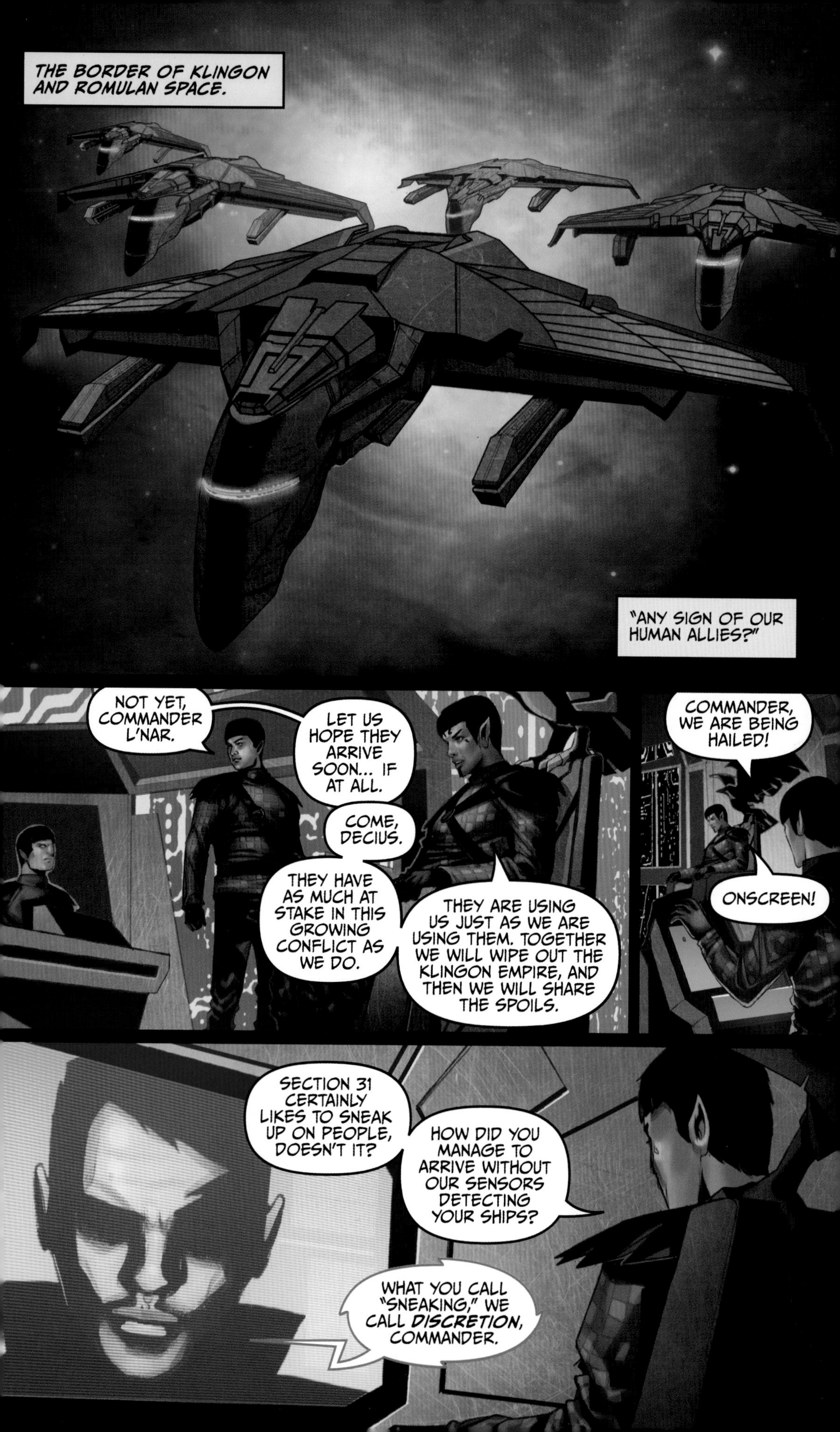
THE BORDER OF KLINGON AND ROMULAN SPACE.
"ANY SIGN OF OUR HUMAN ALLIES?"
NOT YET, COMMANDER L'NAR.
LET US HOPE THEY ARRIVE SOON... IF AT ALL.
COME, DECIUS.
THEY HAVE AS MUCH AT STAKE IN THIS GROWING CONFLICT AS WE DO.
THEY ARE USING US JUST AS WE ARE USING THEM. TOGETHER WE WILL WIPE OUT THE KLINGON EMPIRE, AND THEN WE WILL SHARE THE SPOILS.
COMMANDER, WE ARE BEING HAILED!
ONSCREEN!
SECTION 31 CERTAINLY LIKES TO SNEAK UP ON PEOPLE, DOESN'T IT?
HOW DID YOU MANAGE TO ARRIVE WITHOUT OUR SENSORS DETECTING YOUR SHIPS?
WHAT YOU CALL "SNEAKING," WE CALL *DISCRETION*, COMMANDER.

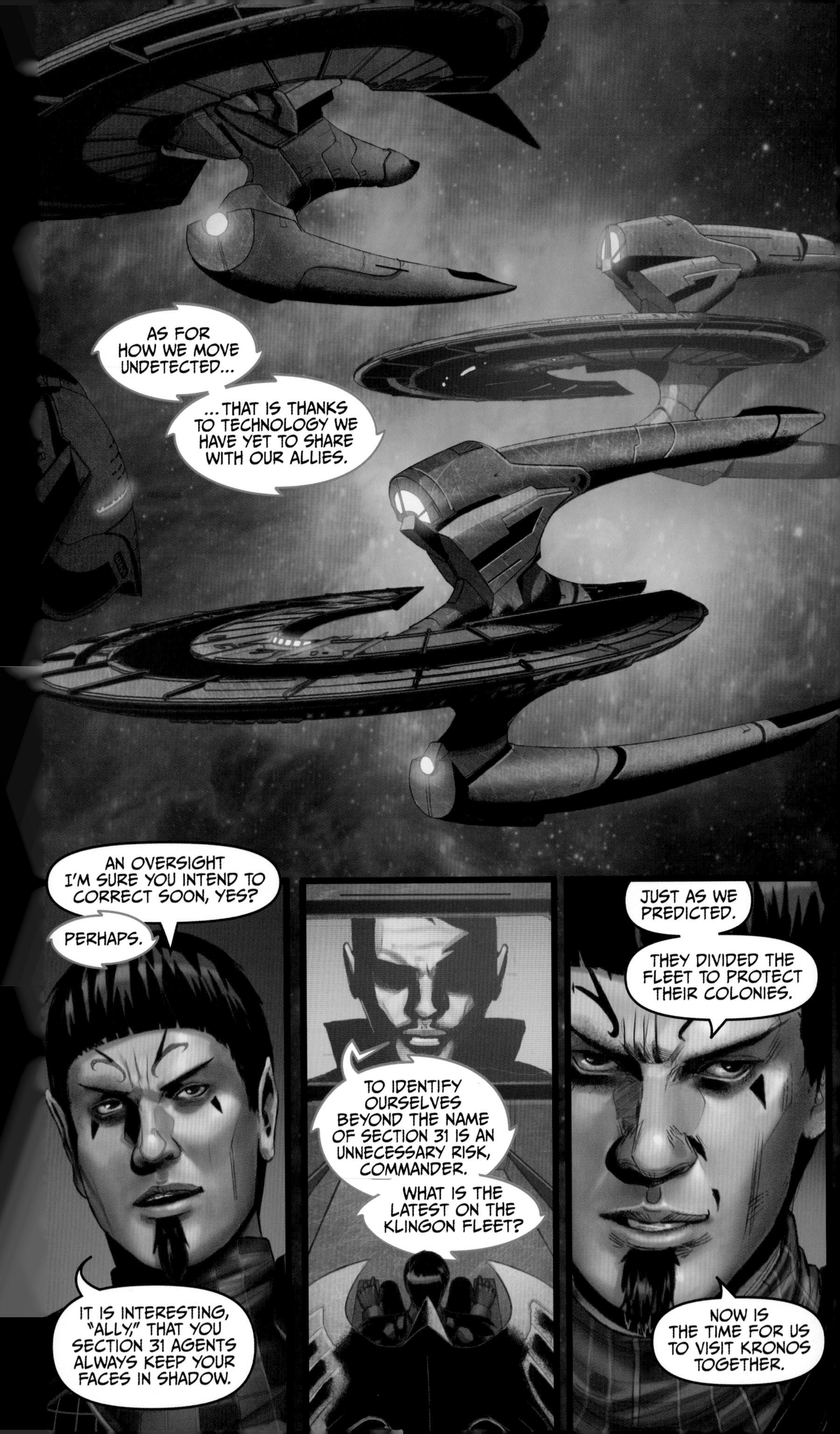
AS FOR HOW WE MOVE UNDETECTED...
...THAT IS THANKS TO TECHNOLOGY WE HAVE YET TO SHARE WITH OUR ALLIES.
AN OVERSIGHT I'M SURE YOU INTEND TO CORRECT SOON, YES?
PERHAPS.
IT IS INTERESTING, "ALLY," THAT YOU SECTION 31 AGENTS ALWAYS KEEP YOUR FACES IN SHADOW.
TO IDENTIFY OURSELVES BEYOND THE NAME OF SECTION 31 IS AN UNNECESSARY RISK, COMMANDER.
WHAT IS THE LATEST ON THE KLINGON FLEET?
JUST AS WE PREDICTED.
THEY DIVIDED THE FLEET TO PROTECT THEIR COLONIES.
NOW IS THE TIME FOR US TO VISIT KRONOS TOGETHER.

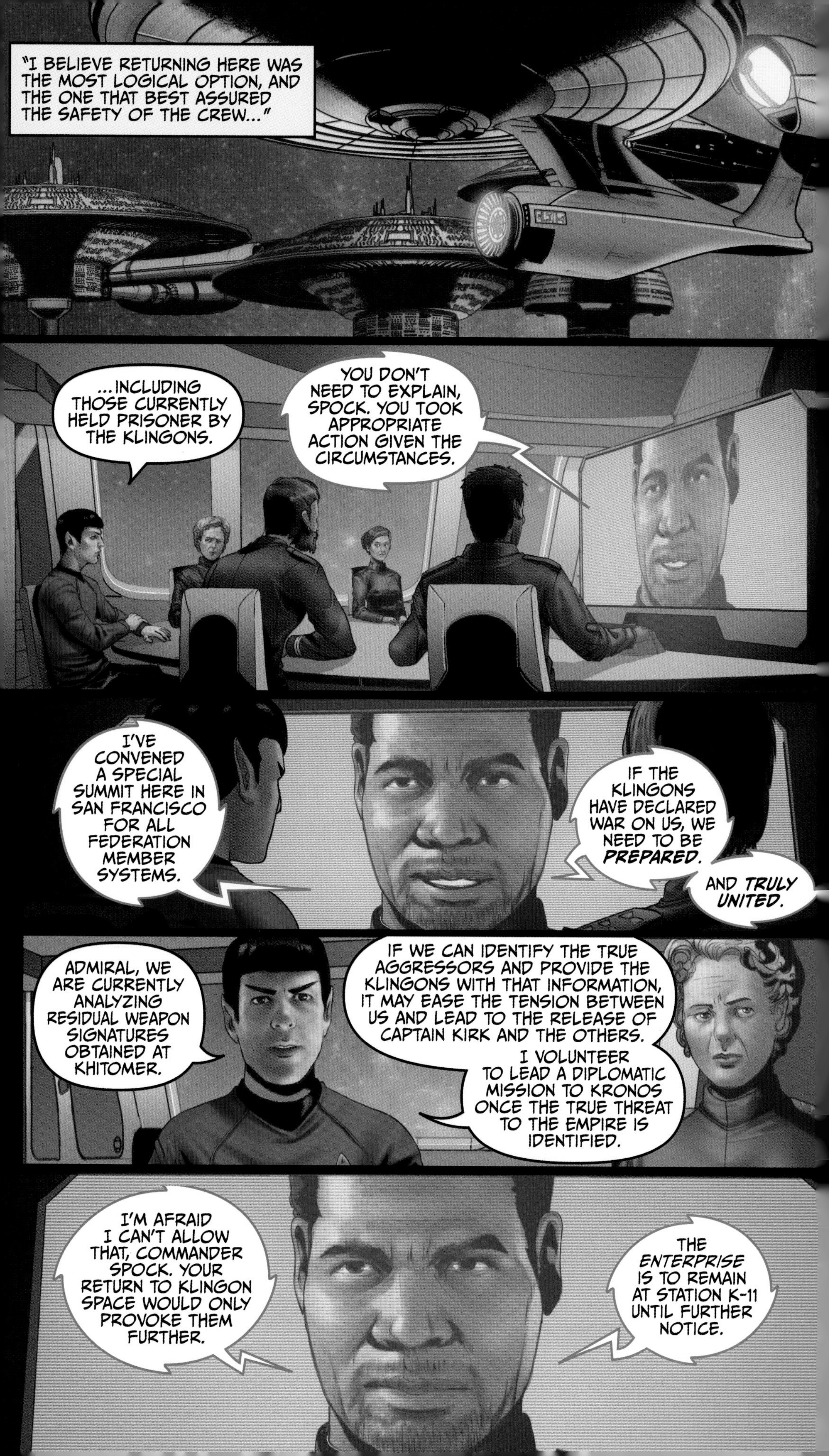
"I BELIEVE RETURNING HERE WAS THE MOST LOGICAL OPTION, AND THE ONE THAT BEST ASSURED THE SAFETY OF THE CREW..."
...INCLUDING THOSE CURRENTLY HELD PRISONER BY THE KLINGONS.
YOU DON'T NEED TO EXPLAIN, SPOCK. YOU TOOK APPROPRIATE ACTION GIVEN THE CIRCUMSTANCES.
I'VE CONVENED A SPECIAL SUMMIT HERE IN SAN FRANCISCO FOR ALL FEDERATION MEMBER SYSTEMS.
IF THE KLINGONS HAVE DECLARED WAR ON US, WE NEED TO BE *PREPARED*.
AND *TRULY UNITED*.
ADMIRAL, WE ARE CURRENTLY ANALYZING RESIDUAL WEAPON SIGNATURES OBTAINED AT KHITOMER.
IF WE CAN IDENTIFY THE TRUE AGGRESSORS AND PROVIDE THE KLINGONS WITH THAT INFORMATION, IT MAY EASE THE TENSION BETWEEN US AND LEAD TO THE RELEASE OF CAPTAIN KIRK AND THE OTHERS.
I VOLUNTEER TO LEAD A DIPLOMATIC MISSION TO KRONOS ONCE THE TRUE THREAT TO THE EMPIRE IS IDENTIFIED.
I'M AFRAID I CAN'T ALLOW THAT, COMMANDER SPOCK. YOUR RETURN TO KLINGON SPACE WOULD ONLY PROVOKE THEM FURTHER.
THE *ENTERPRISE* IS TO REMAIN AT STATION K-11 UNTIL FURTHER NOTICE.

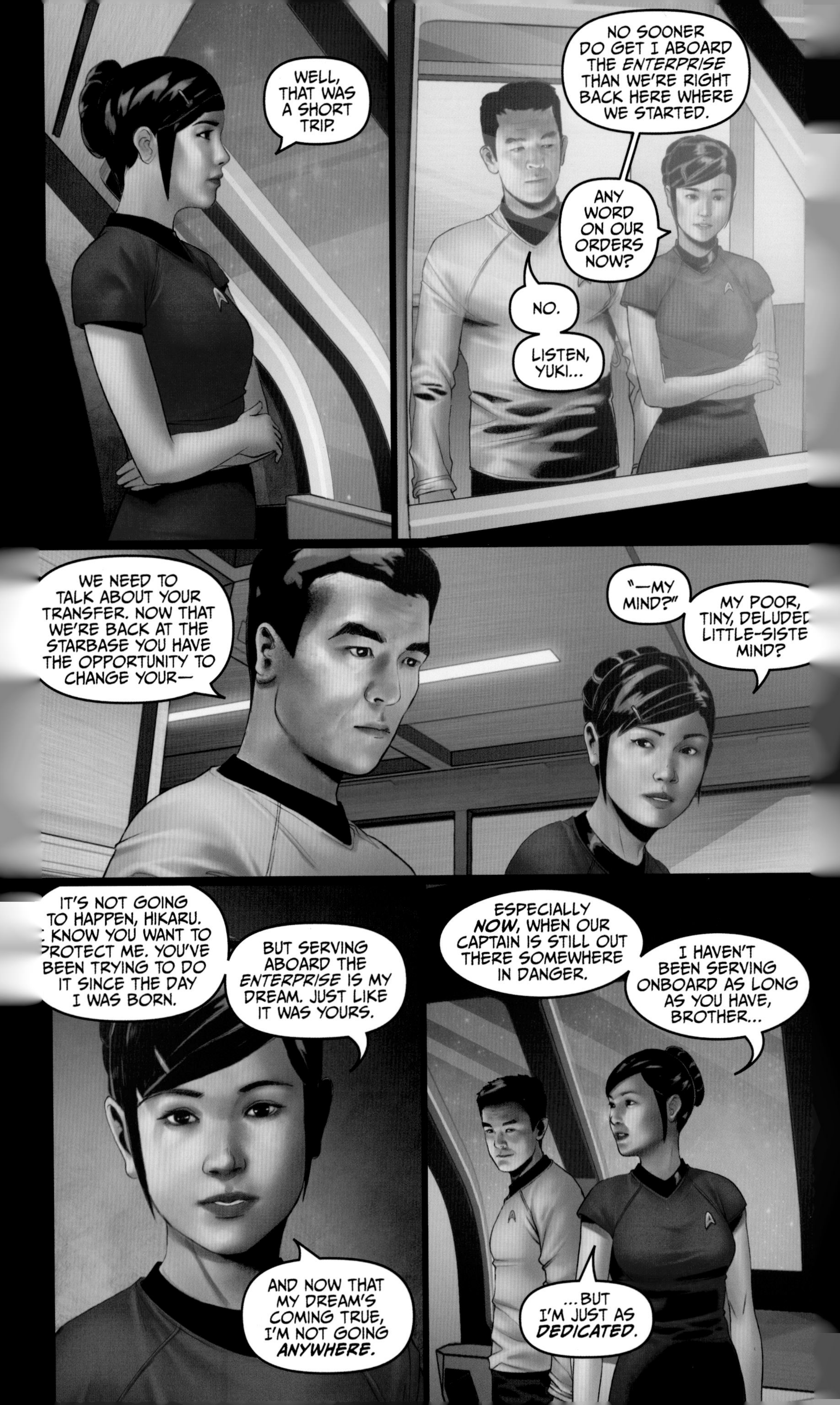
WELL, THAT WAS A SHORT TRIP.
NO SOONER DO GET I ABOARD THE *ENTERPRISE* THAN WE'RE RIGHT BACK HERE WHERE WE STARTED.
ANY WORD ON OUR ORDERS NOW?
NO.
LISTEN, YUKI...
WE NEED TO TALK ABOUT YOUR TRANSFER. NOW THAT WE'RE BACK AT THE STARBASE YOU HAVE THE OPPORTUNITY TO CHANGE YOUR—
"—MY MIND?"
MY POOR, TINY, DELUDED LITTLE-SISTE MIND?
IT'S NOT GOING TO HAPPEN, HIKARU. KNOW YOU WANT TO PROTECT ME. YOU'VE BEEN TRYING TO DO IT SINCE THE DAY I WAS BORN.
BUT SERVING ABOARD THE *ENTERPRISE* IS MY DREAM. JUST LIKE IT WAS YOURS.
AND NOW THAT MY DREAM'S COMING TRUE, I'M NOT GOING ***ANYWHERE***.
ESPECIALLY ***NOW***, WHEN OUR CAPTAIN IS STILL OUT THERE SOMEWHERE IN DANGER.
I HAVEN'T BEEN SERVING ONBOARD AS LONG AS YOU HAVE, BROTHER...
...BUT I'M JUST AS ***DEDICATED***.

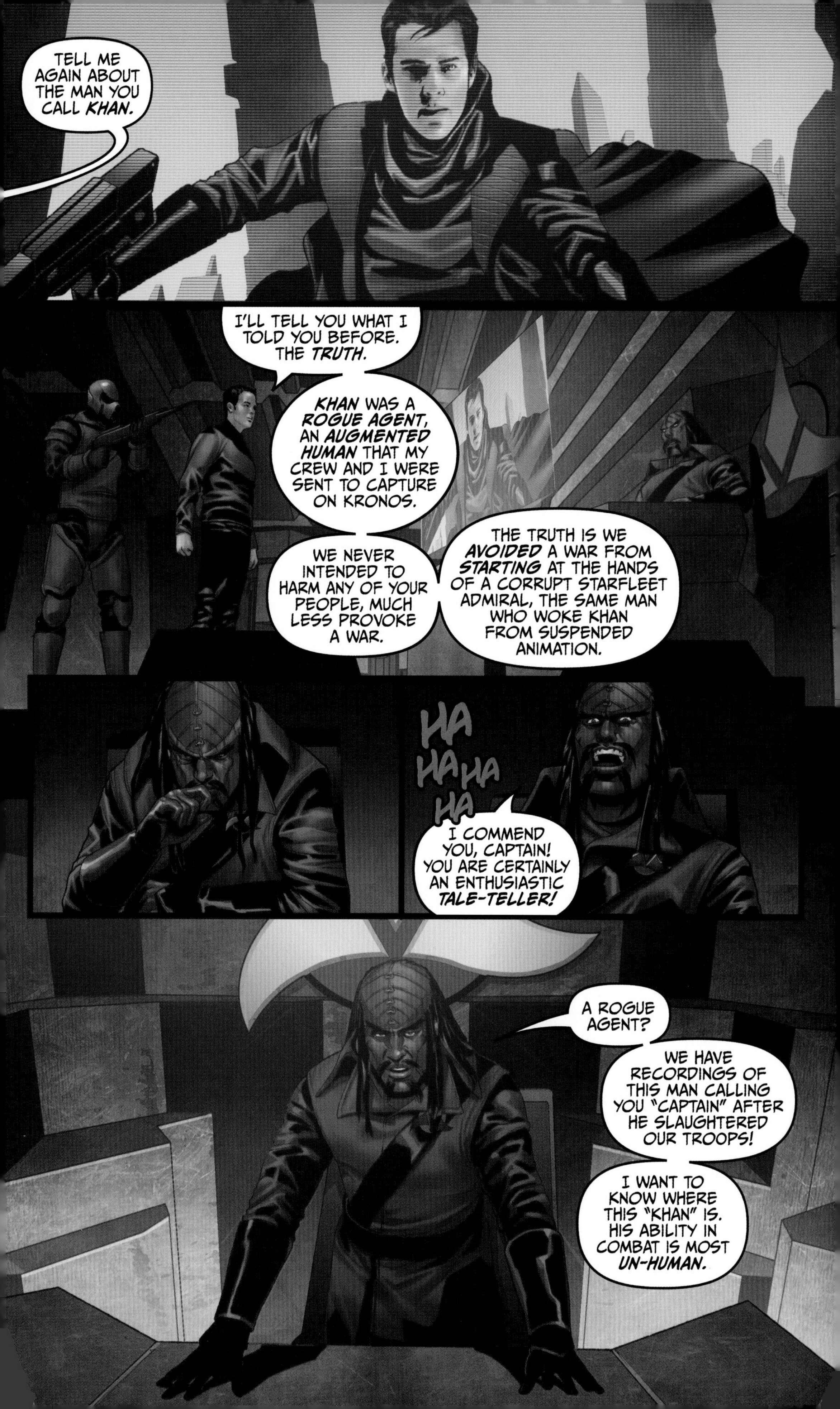
TELL ME AGAIN ABOUT THE MAN YOU CALL KHAN.
I'LL TELL YOU WHAT I TOLD YOU BEFORE. THE TRUTH.
KHAN WAS A ROGUE AGENT, AN AUGMENTED HUMAN THAT MY CREW AND I WERE SENT TO CAPTURE ON KRONOS.
WE NEVER INTENDED TO HARM ANY OF YOUR PEOPLE, MUCH LESS PROVOKE A WAR.
THE TRUTH IS WE AVOIDED A WAR FROM STARTING AT THE HANDS OF A CORRUPT STARFLEET ADMIRAL, THE SAME MAN WHO WOKE KHAN FROM SUSPENDED ANIMATION.
HA HA HA HA
I COMMEND YOU, CAPTAIN! YOU ARE CERTAINLY AN ENTHUSIASTIC TALE-TELLER!
A ROGUE AGENT?
WE HAVE RECORDINGS OF THIS MAN CALLING YOU "CAPTAIN" AFTER HE SLAUGHTERED OUR TROOPS!
I WANT TO KNOW WHERE THIS "KHAN" IS. HIS ABILITY IN COMBAT IS MOST UN-HUMAN.

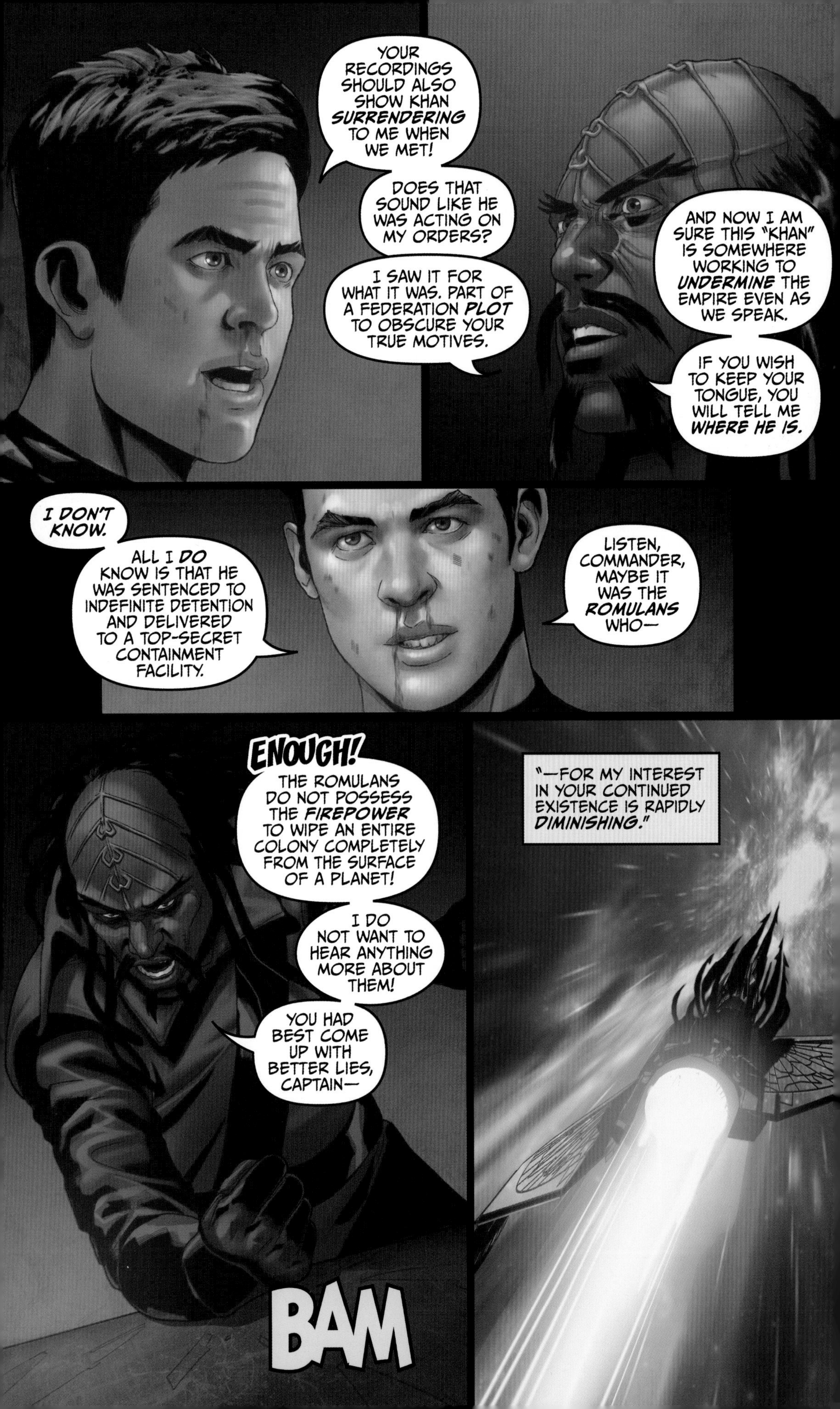

YOUR RECORDINGS SHOULD ALSO SHOW KHAN SURRENDERING TO ME WHEN WE MET!
DOES THAT SOUND LIKE HE WAS ACTING ON MY ORDERS?
I SAW IT FOR WHAT IT WAS. PART OF A FEDERATION PLOT TO OBSCURE YOUR TRUE MOTIVES.
AND NOW I AM SURE THIS "KHAN" IS SOMEWHERE WORKING TO UNDERMINE THE EMPIRE EVEN AS WE SPEAK.
IF YOU WISH TO KEEP YOUR TONGUE, YOU WILL TELL ME WHERE HE IS.
I DON'T KNOW.
ALL I DO KNOW IS THAT HE WAS SENTENCED TO INDEFINITE DETENTION AND DELIVERED TO A TOP-SECRET CONTAINMENT FACILITY.
LISTEN, COMMANDER, MAYBE IT WAS THE ROMULANS WHO—
ENOUGH!
THE ROMULANS DO NOT POSSESS THE FIREPOWER TO WIPE AN ENTIRE COLONY COMPLETELY FROM THE SURFACE OF A PLANET!
I DO NOT WANT TO HEAR ANYTHING MORE ABOUT THEM!
YOU HAD BEST COME UP WITH BETTER LIES, CAPTAIN—
BAM
"—FOR MY INTEREST IN YOUR CONTINUED EXISTENCE IS RAPIDLY DIMINISHING."

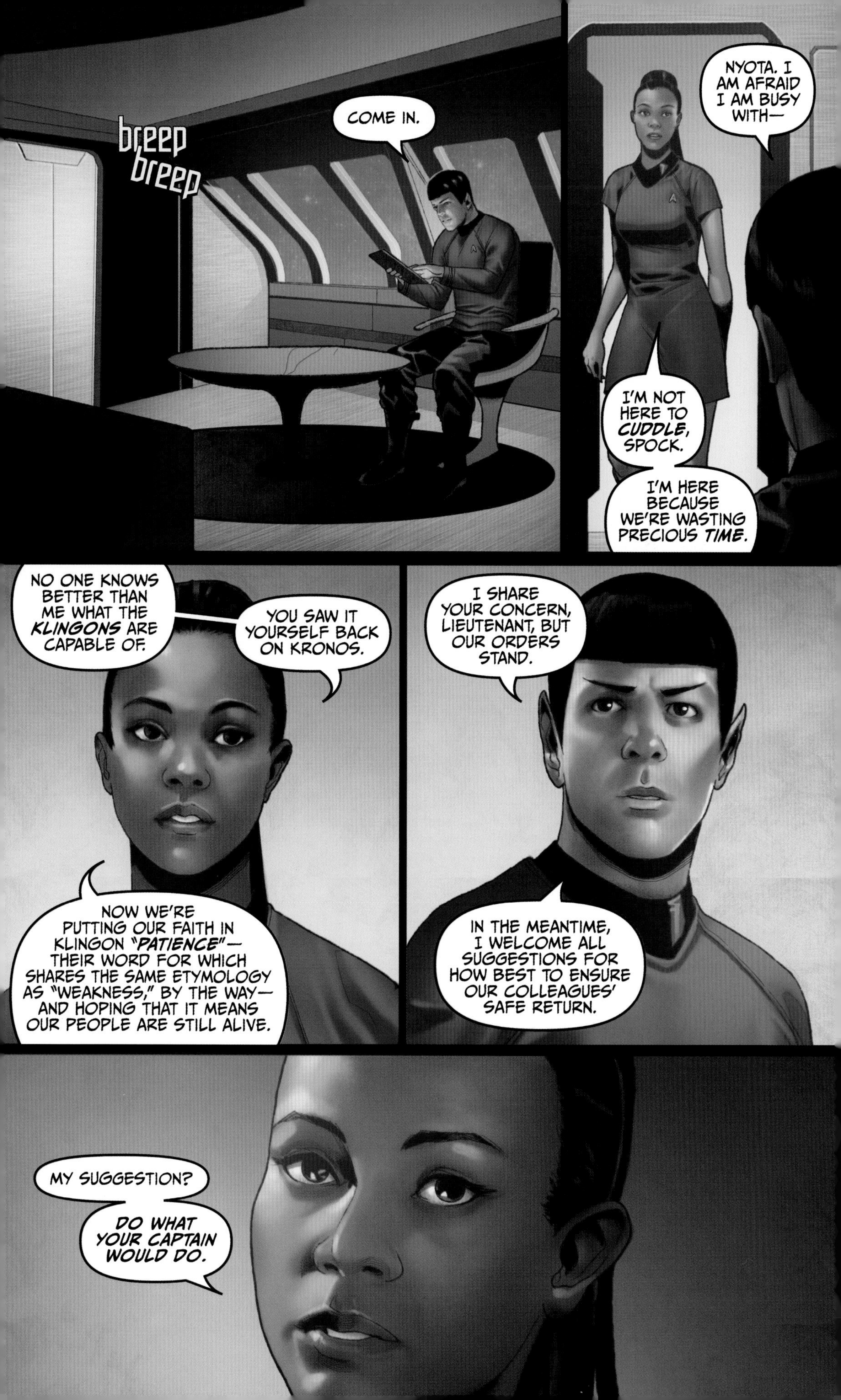
breep breep
COME IN.
NYOTA. I AM AFRAID I AM BUSY WITH—
I'M NOT HERE TO CUDDLE, SPOCK.
I'M HERE BECAUSE WE'RE WASTING PRECIOUS TIME.
NO ONE KNOWS BETTER THAN ME WHAT THE KLINGONS ARE CAPABLE OF.
YOU SAW IT YOURSELF BACK ON KRONOS.
NOW WE'RE PUTTING OUR FAITH IN KLINGON "PATIENCE"— THEIR WORD FOR WHICH SHARES THE SAME ETYMOLOGY AS "WEAKNESS," BY THE WAY— AND HOPING THAT IT MEANS OUR PEOPLE ARE STILL ALIVE.
I SHARE YOUR CONCERN, LIEUTENANT, BUT OUR ORDERS STAND.
IN THE MEANTIME, I WELCOME ALL SUGGESTIONS FOR HOW BEST TO ENSURE OUR COLLEAGUES' SAFE RETURN.
MY SUGGESTION?
DO WHAT YOUR CAPTAIN WOULD DO.

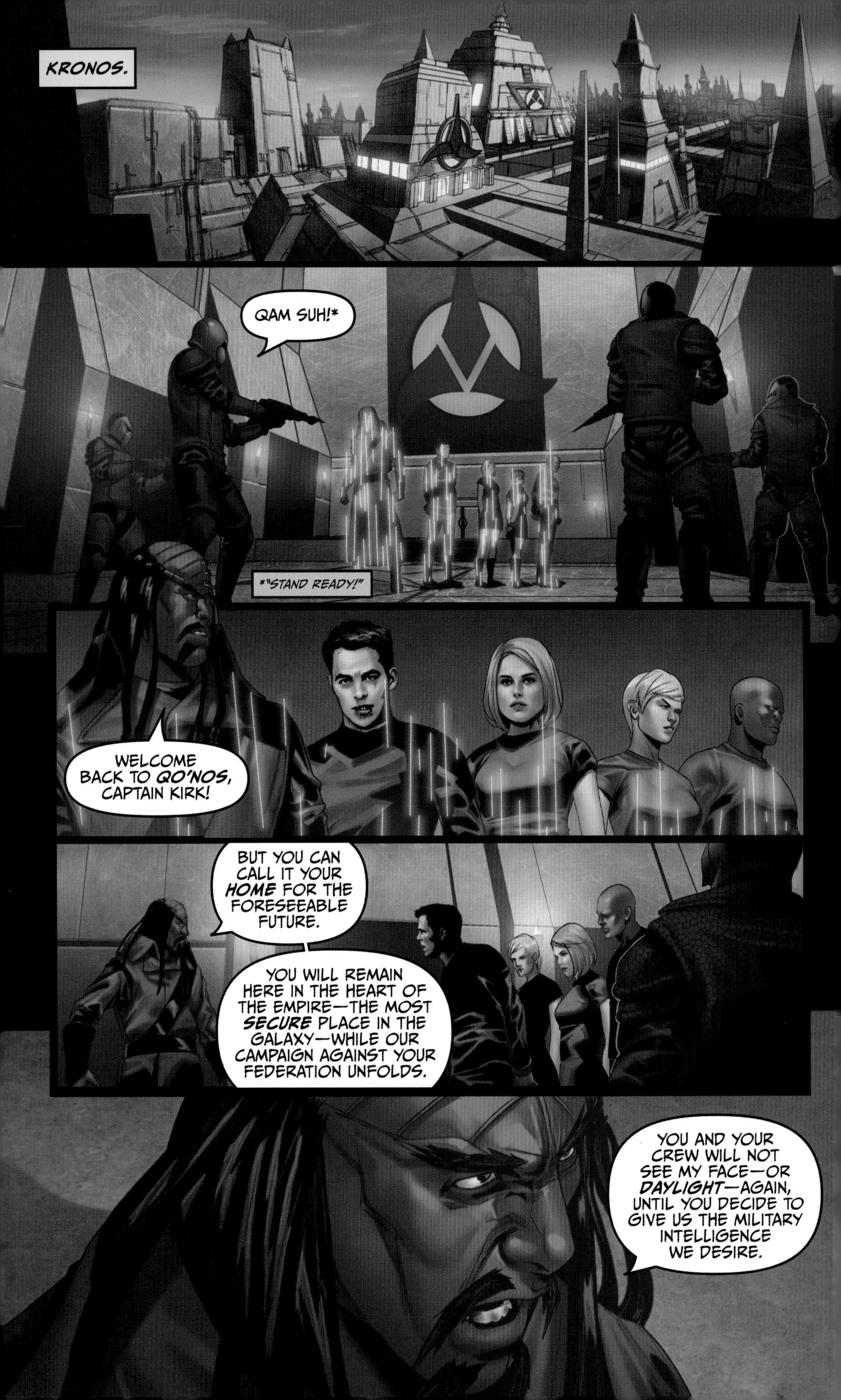
KRONOS.
QAM SUH!*
*"STAND READY!"
WELCOME BACK TO *QO'NOS*, CAPTAIN KIRK!
BUT YOU CAN CALL IT YOUR *HOME* FOR THE FORESEEABLE FUTURE.
YOU WILL REMAIN HERE IN THE HEART OF THE EMPIRE—THE MOST *SECURE* PLACE IN THE GALAXY—WHILE OUR CAMPAIGN AGAINST YOUR FEDERATION UNFOLDS.
YOU AND YOUR CREW WILL NOT SEE MY FACE—OR *DAYLIGHT*—AGAIN, UNTIL YOU DECIDE TO GIVE US THE MILITARY INTELLIGENCE WE DESIRE.

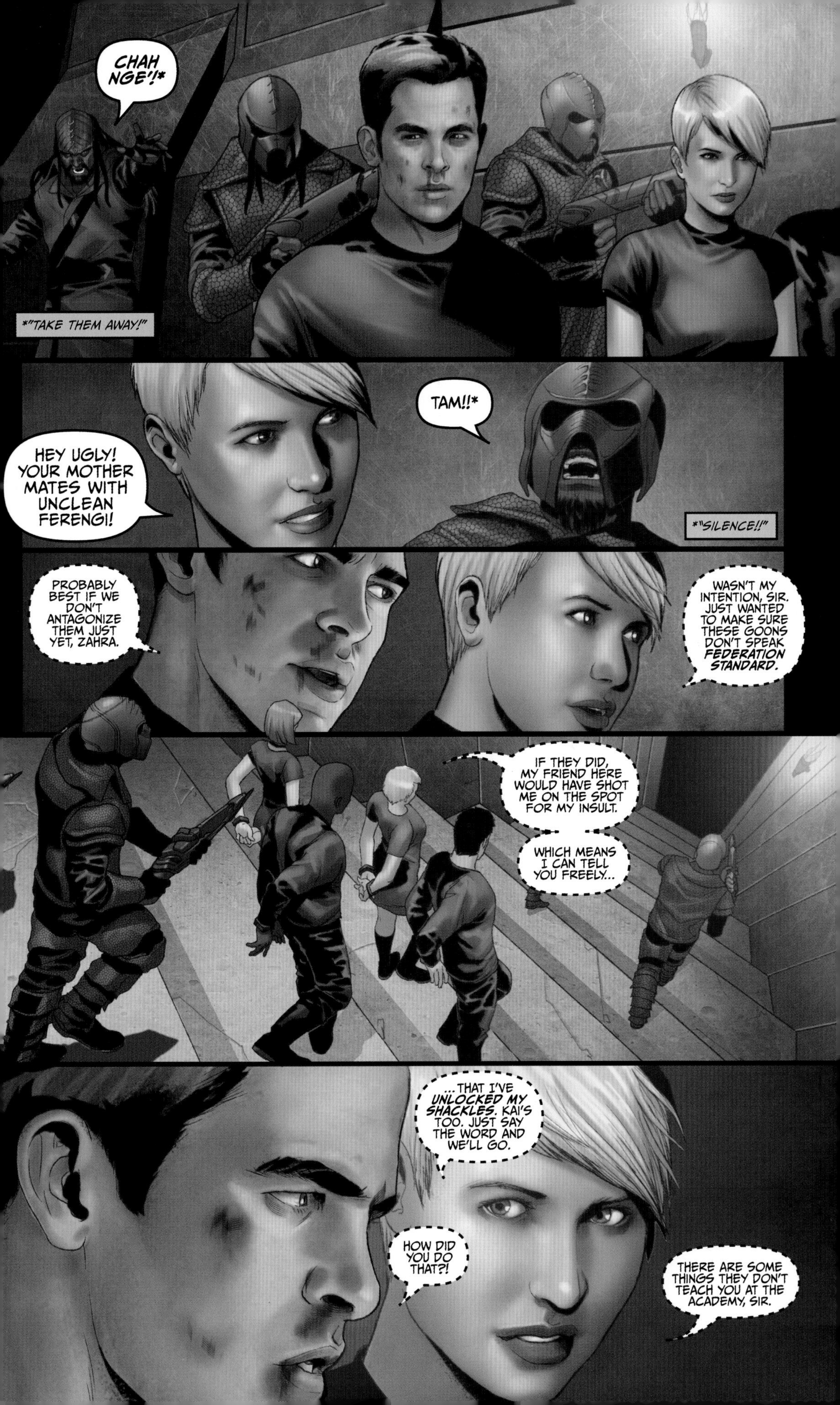
CHAH NGE'!*
*"TAKE THEM AWAY!"
HEY UGLY! YOUR MOTHER MATES WITH UNCLEAN FERENGI!
TAM!!*
*"SILENCE!!"
PROBABLY BEST IF WE DON'T ANTAGONIZE THEM JUST YET, ZAHRA.
WASN'T MY INTENTION, SIR. JUST WANTED TO MAKE SURE THESE GOONS DON'T SPEAK FEDERATION STANDARD.
IF THEY DID, MY FRIEND HERE WOULD HAVE SHOT ME ON THE SPOT FOR MY INSULT.
WHICH MEANS I CAN TELL YOU FREELY...
...THAT I'VE UNLOCKED MY SHACKLES. KAI'S TOO. JUST SAY THE WORD AND WE'LL GO.
HOW DID YOU DO THAT?!
THERE ARE SOME THINGS THEY DON'T TEACH YOU AT THE ACADEMY, SIR.

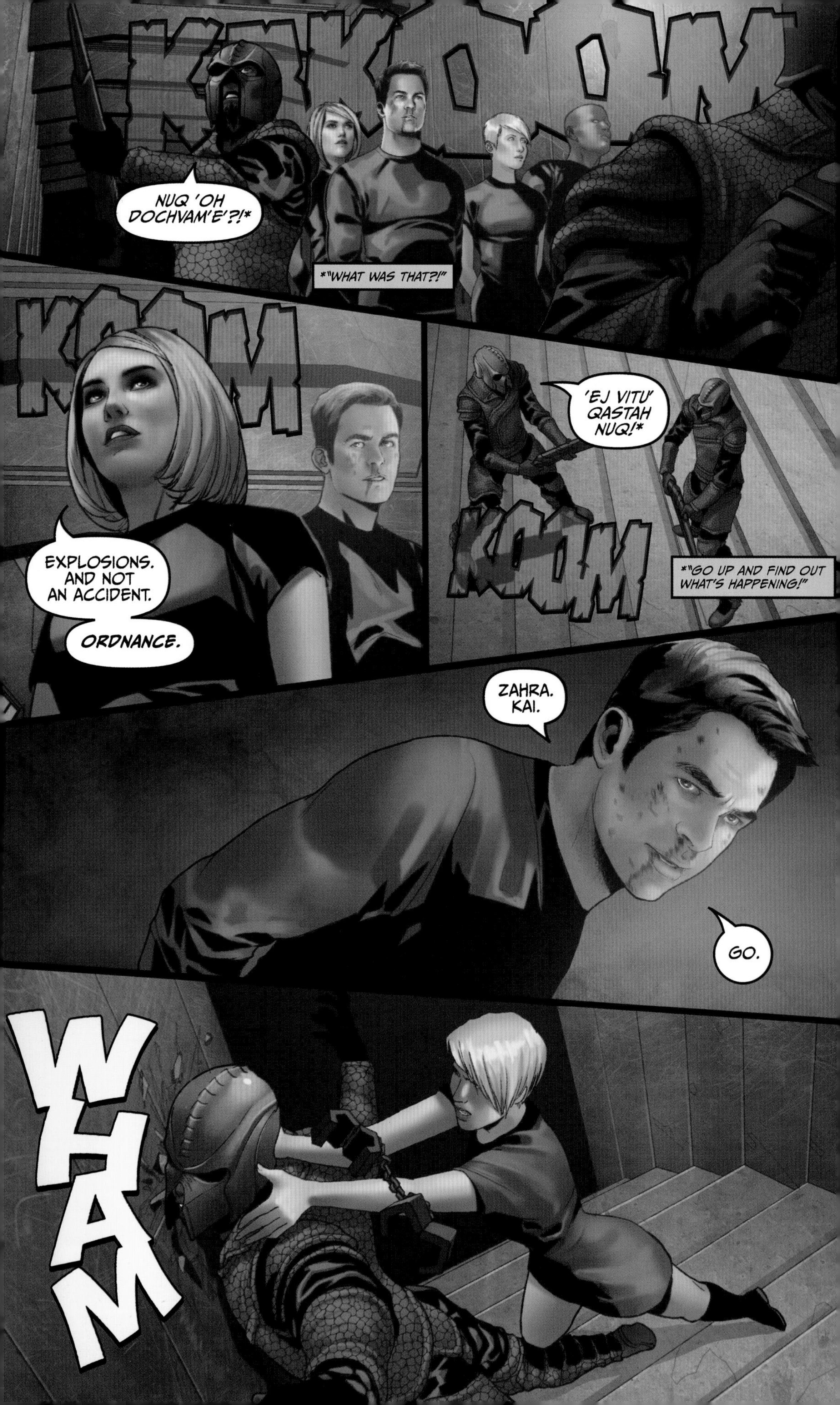
KA-KOOM
NUQ 'OH DOCHVAM'E'?!*
*"WHAT WAS THAT?!"
KOOM
EXPLOSIONS. AND NOT AN ACCIDENT.
ORDNANCE.
'EJ VITU' QASTAH NUQ!*
KOOM
*"GO UP AND FIND OUT WHAT'S HAPPENING!"
ZAHRA. KAI.
GO.
WHAM

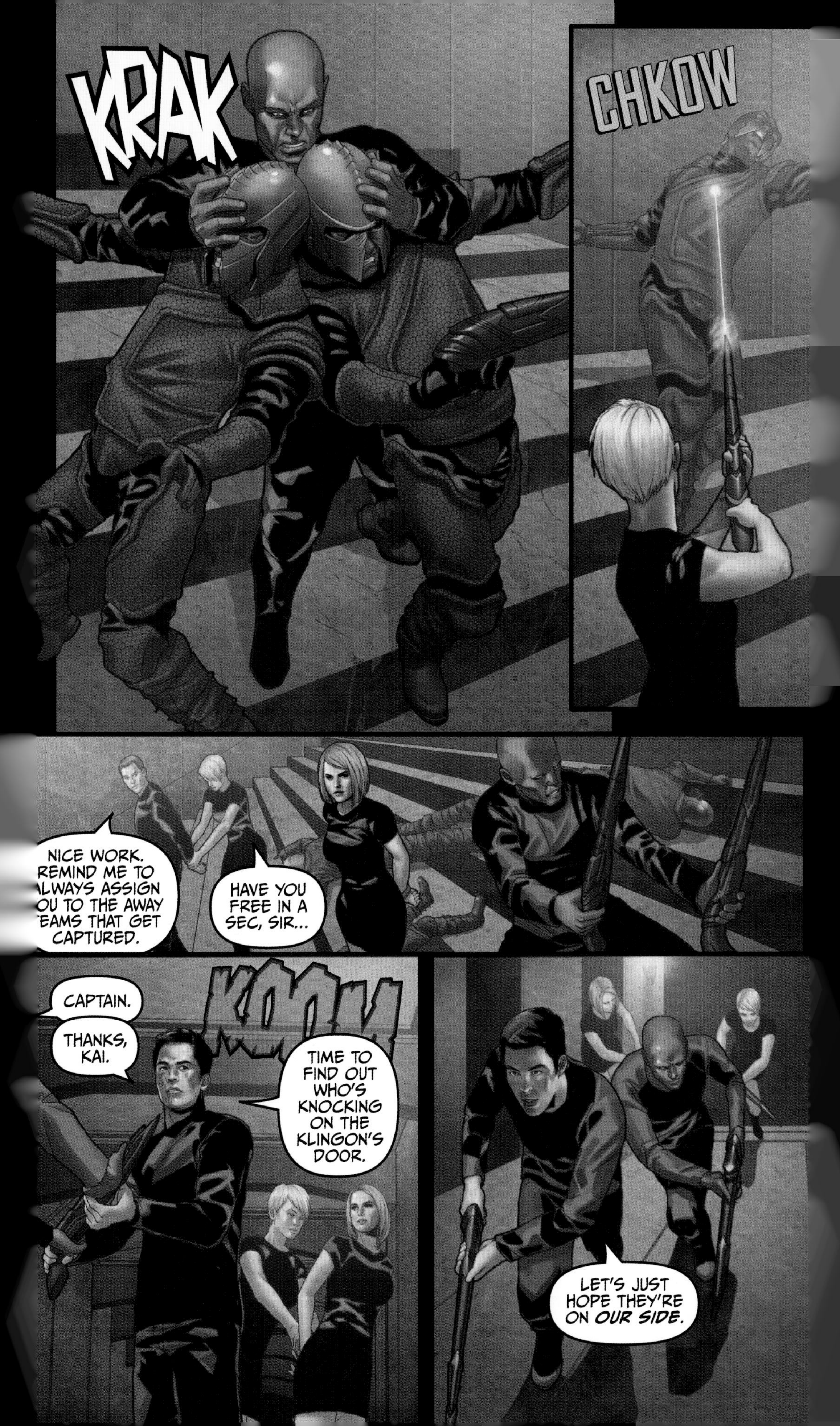
KRAK
CHKOW
NICE WORK. REMIND ME TO ALWAYS ASSIGN YOU TO THE AWAY TEAMS THAT GET CAPTURED.
HAVE YOU FREE IN A SEC, SIR...
CAPTAIN.
THANKS, KAI.
TIME TO FIND OUT WHO'S KNOCKING ON THE KLINGON'S DOOR.
LET'S JUST HOPE THEY'RE ON *OUR SIDE*.

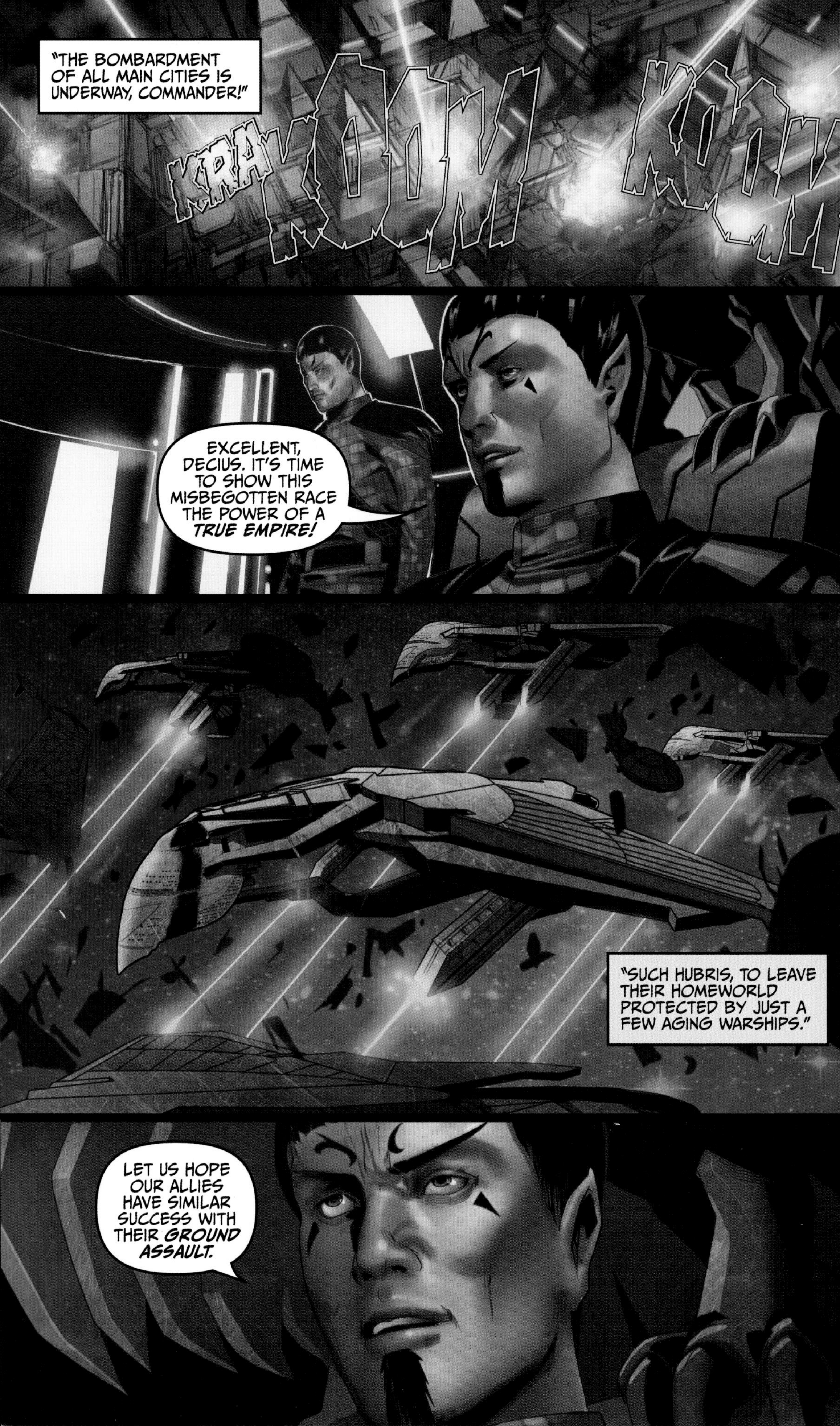
"THE BOMBARDMENT OF ALL MAIN CITIES IS UNDERWAY, COMMANDER!"
KRAKOOM
EXCELLENT, DECIUS. IT'S TIME TO SHOW THIS MISBEGOTTEN RACE THE POWER OF A TRUE EMPIRE!
"SUCH HUBRIS, TO LEAVE THEIR HOMEWORLD PROTECTED BY JUST A FEW AGING WARSHIPS."
LET US HOPE OUR ALLIES HAVE SIMILAR SUCCESS WITH THEIR GROUND ASSAULT.

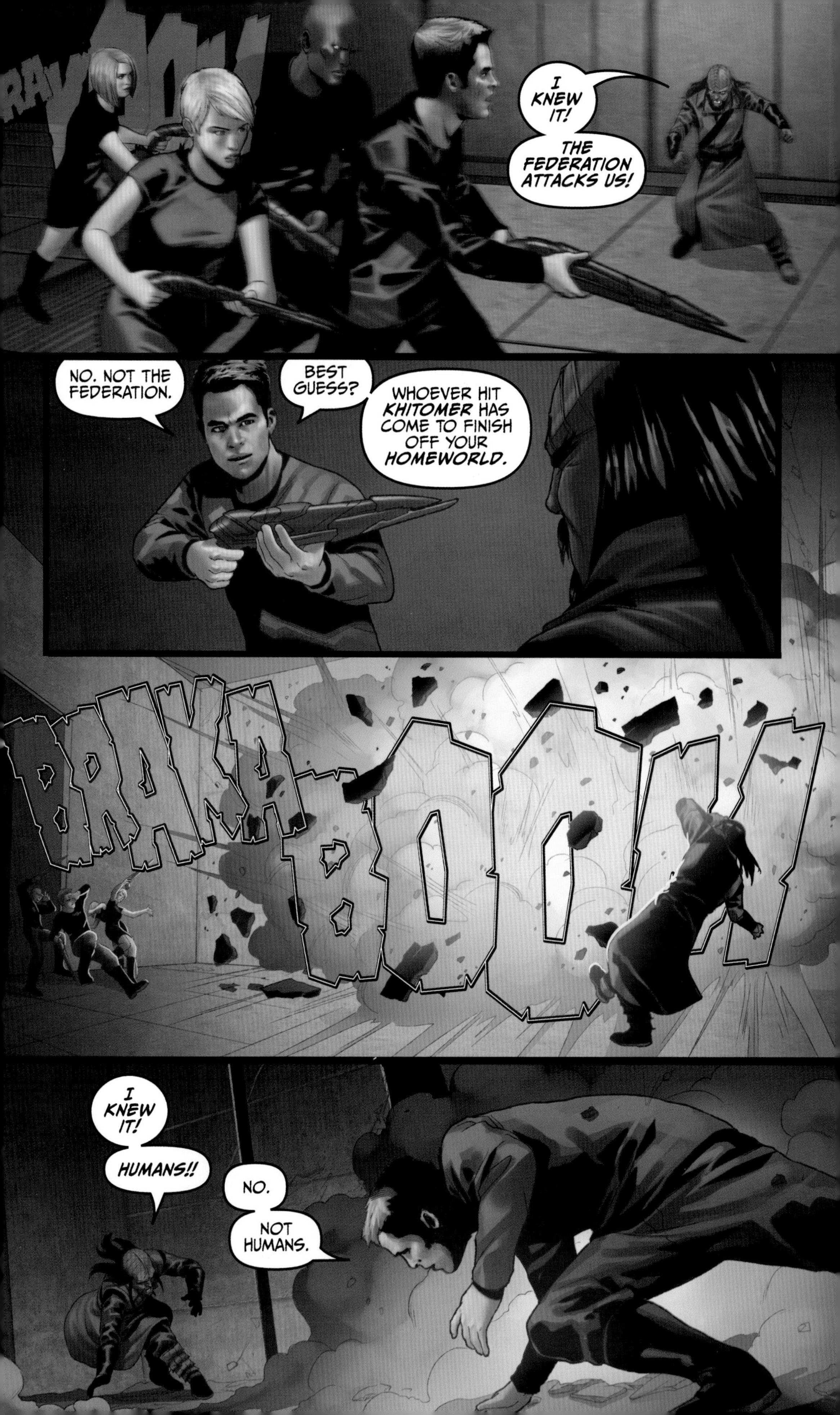
RAWOW!
I KNEW IT!
THE FEDERATION ATTACKS US!
NO. NOT THE FEDERATION.
BEST GUESS?
WHOEVER HIT *KHITOMER* HAS COME TO FINISH OFF YOUR *HOMEWORLD.*
BRAKA-BOOM
I KNEW IT!
HUMANS!!
NO.
NOT HUMANS.

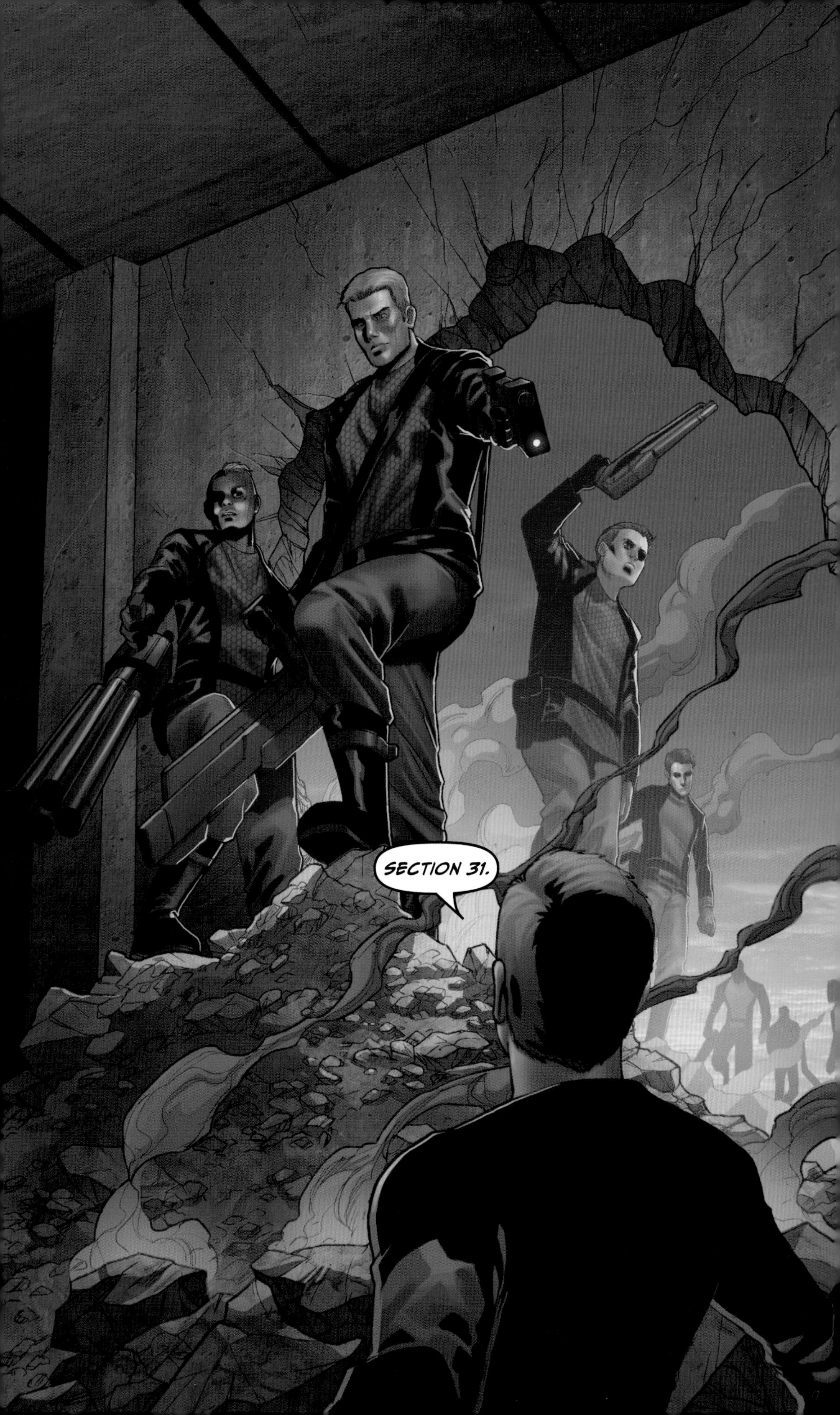
SECTION 31.

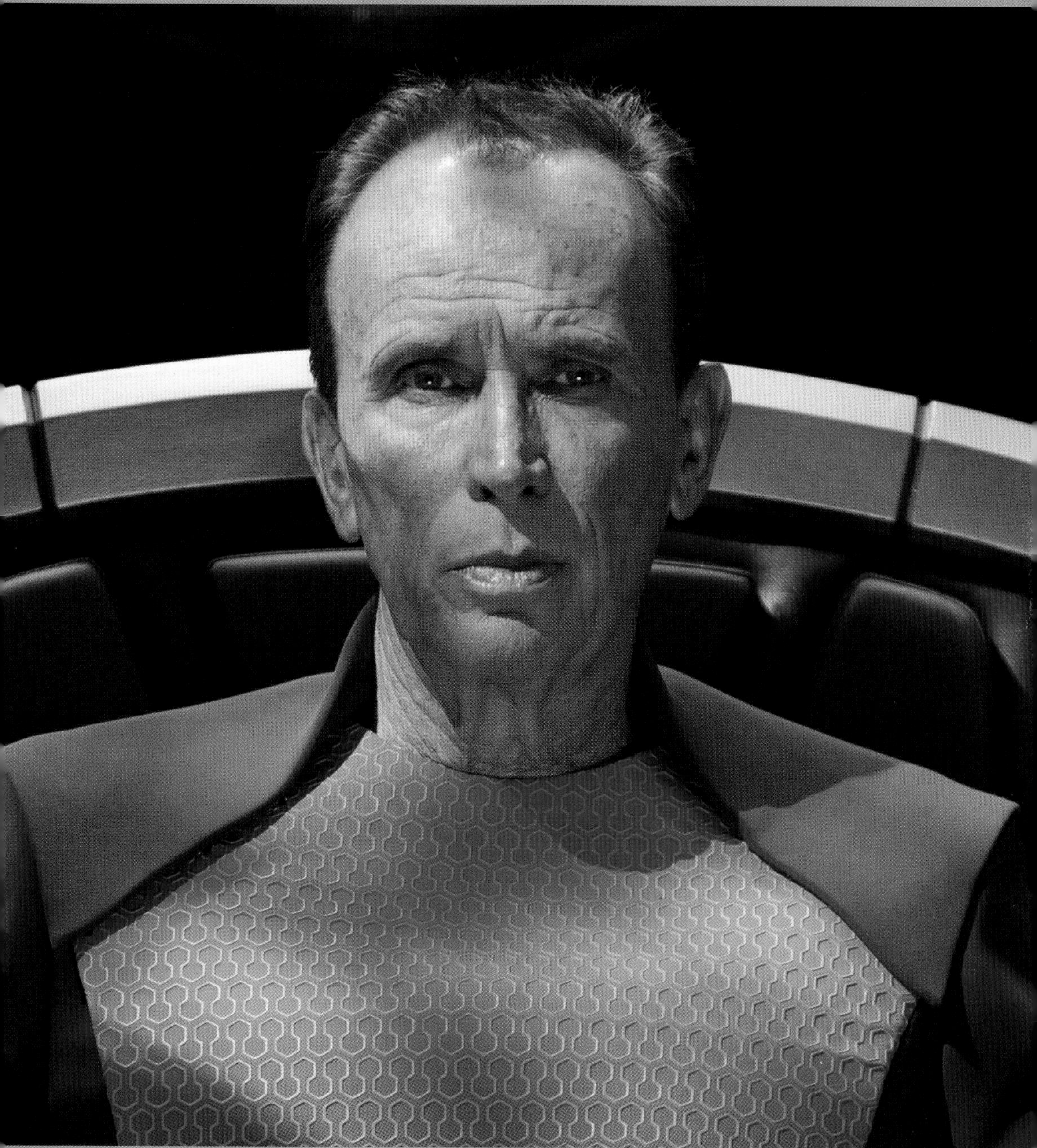

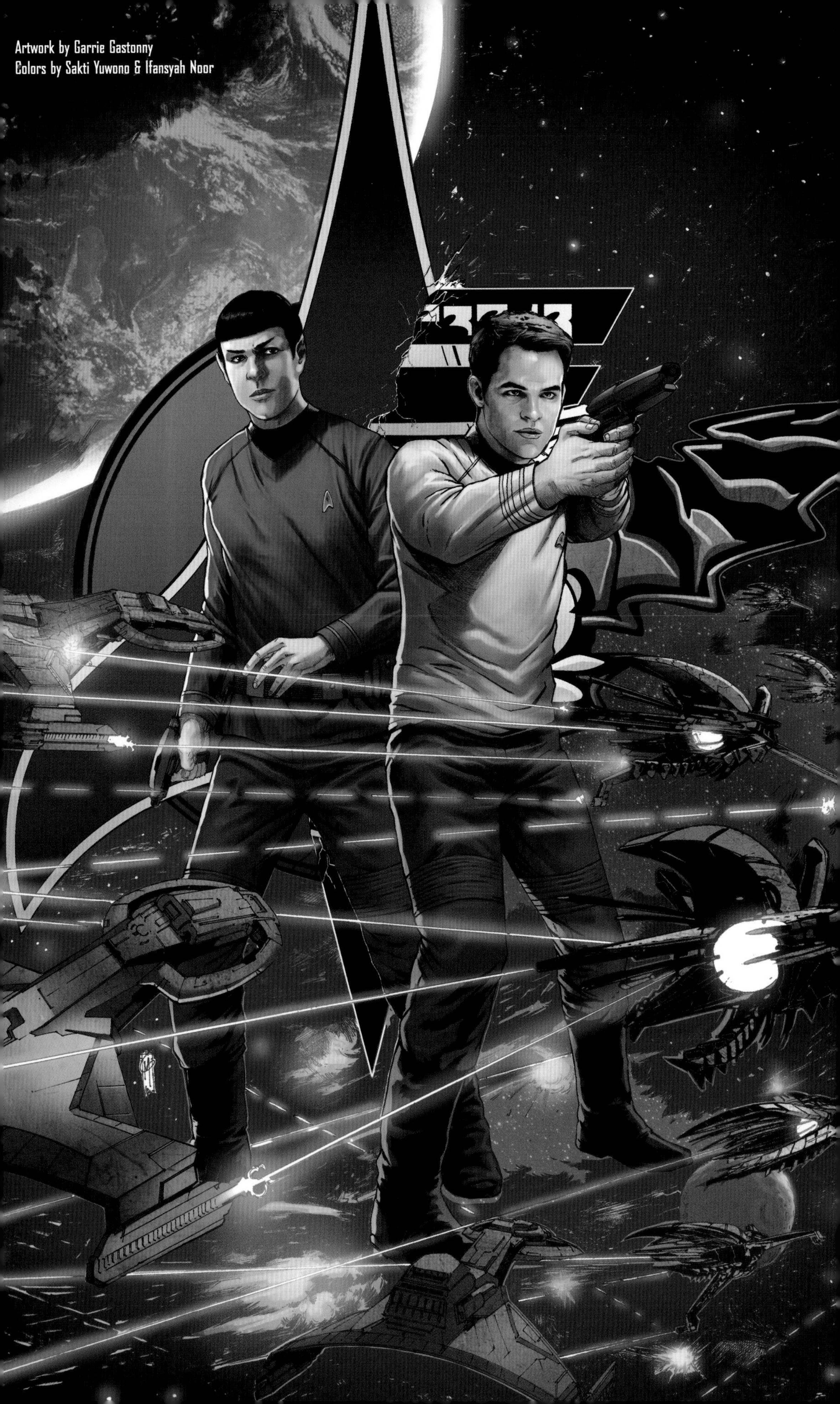

Artwork by Garrie Gastonny
Colors by Sakti Yuwono & Ifansyah Noor

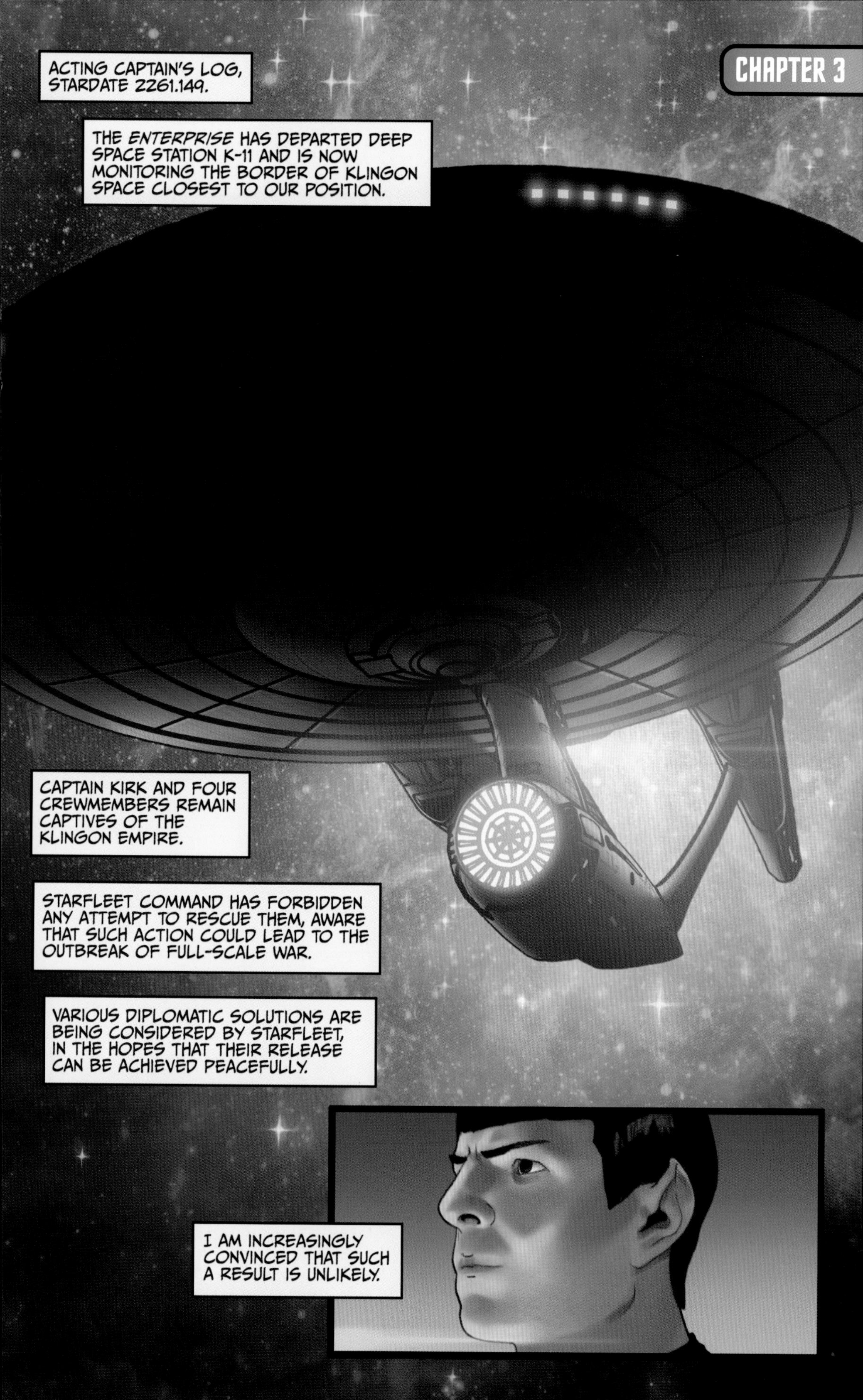
CHAPTER 3
ACTING CAPTAIN'S LOG, STARDATE 2261.149.
THE *ENTERPRISE* HAS DEPARTED DEEP SPACE STATION K-11 AND IS NOW MONITORING THE BORDER OF KLINGON SPACE CLOSEST TO OUR POSITION.
CAPTAIN KIRK AND FOUR CREWMEMBERS REMAIN CAPTIVES OF THE KLINGON EMPIRE.
STARFLEET COMMAND HAS FORBIDDEN ANY ATTEMPT TO RESCUE THEM, AWARE THAT SUCH ACTION COULD LEAD TO THE OUTBREAK OF FULL-SCALE WAR.
VARIOUS DIPLOMATIC SOLUTIONS ARE BEING CONSIDERED BY STARFLEET, IN THE HOPES THAT THEIR RELEASE CAN BE ACHIEVED PEACEFULLY.
I AM INCREASINGLY CONVINCED THAT SUCH A RESULT IS UNLIKELY.

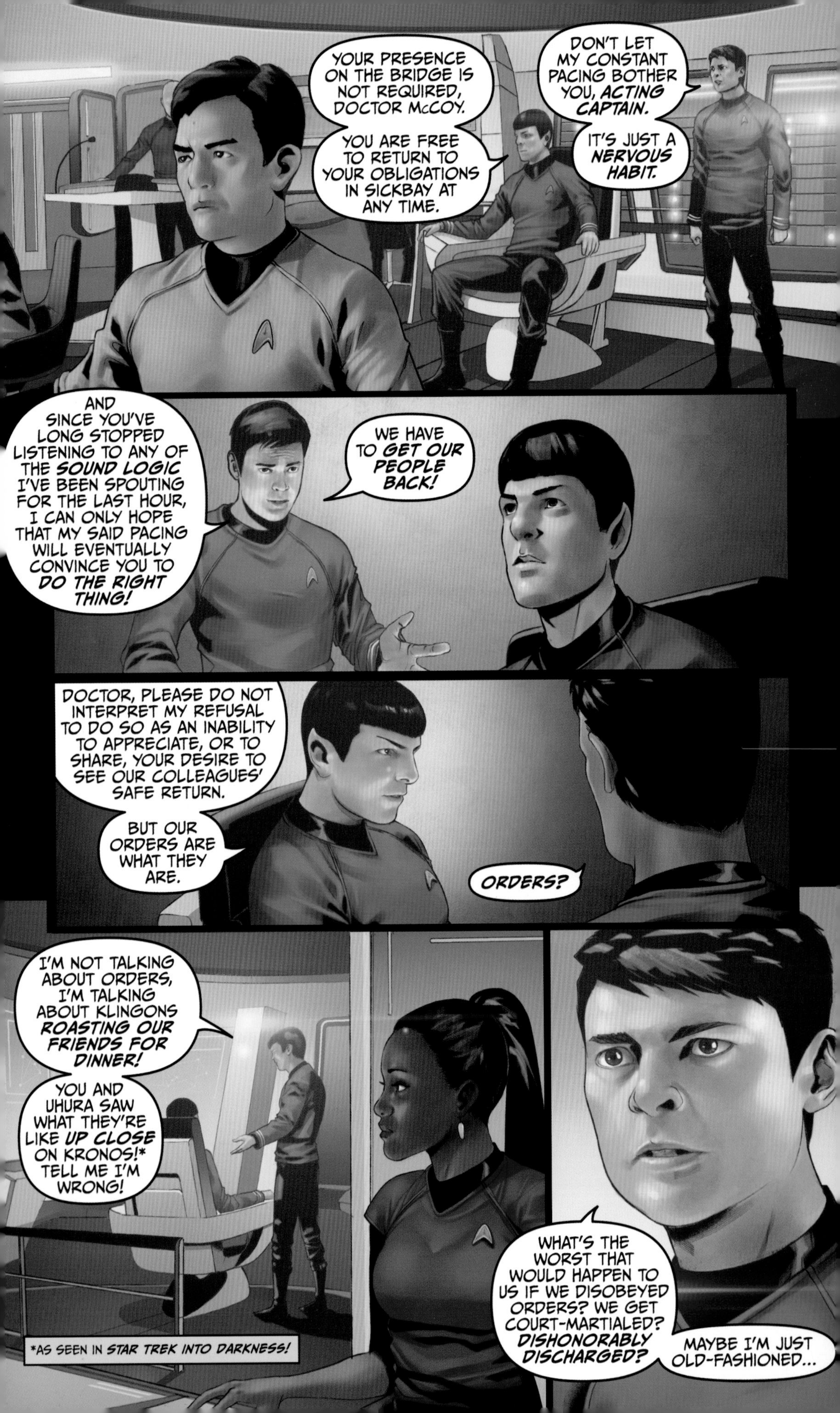

YOUR PRESENCE ON THE BRIDGE IS NOT REQUIRED, DOCTOR McCOY.
YOU ARE FREE TO RETURN TO YOUR OBLIGATIONS IN SICKBAY AT ANY TIME.
DON'T LET MY CONSTANT PACING BOTHER YOU, *ACTING CAPTAIN.*
IT'S JUST A *NERVOUS HABIT.*
AND SINCE YOU'VE LONG STOPPED LISTENING TO ANY OF THE *SOUND LOGIC* I'VE BEEN SPOUTING FOR THE LAST HOUR, I CAN ONLY HOPE THAT MY SAID PACING WILL EVENTUALLY CONVINCE YOU TO *DO THE RIGHT THING!*
WE HAVE TO *GET OUR PEOPLE BACK!*
DOCTOR, PLEASE DO NOT INTERPRET MY REFUSAL TO DO SO AS AN INABILITY TO APPRECIATE, OR TO SHARE, YOUR DESIRE TO SEE OUR COLLEAGUES' SAFE RETURN.
BUT OUR ORDERS ARE WHAT THEY ARE.
ORDERS?
I'M NOT TALKING ABOUT ORDERS, I'M TALKING ABOUT KLINGONS *ROASTING OUR FRIENDS FOR DINNER!*
YOU AND UHURA SAW WHAT THEY'RE LIKE *UP CLOSE* ON KRONOS!* TELL ME I'M WRONG!
*AS SEEN IN *STAR TREK INTO DARKNESS!*
WHAT'S THE WORST THAT WOULD HAPPEN TO US IF WE DISOBEYED ORDERS? WE GET COURT-MARTIALED? *DISHONORABLY DISCHARGED?*
MAYBE I'M JUST OLD-FASHIONED...

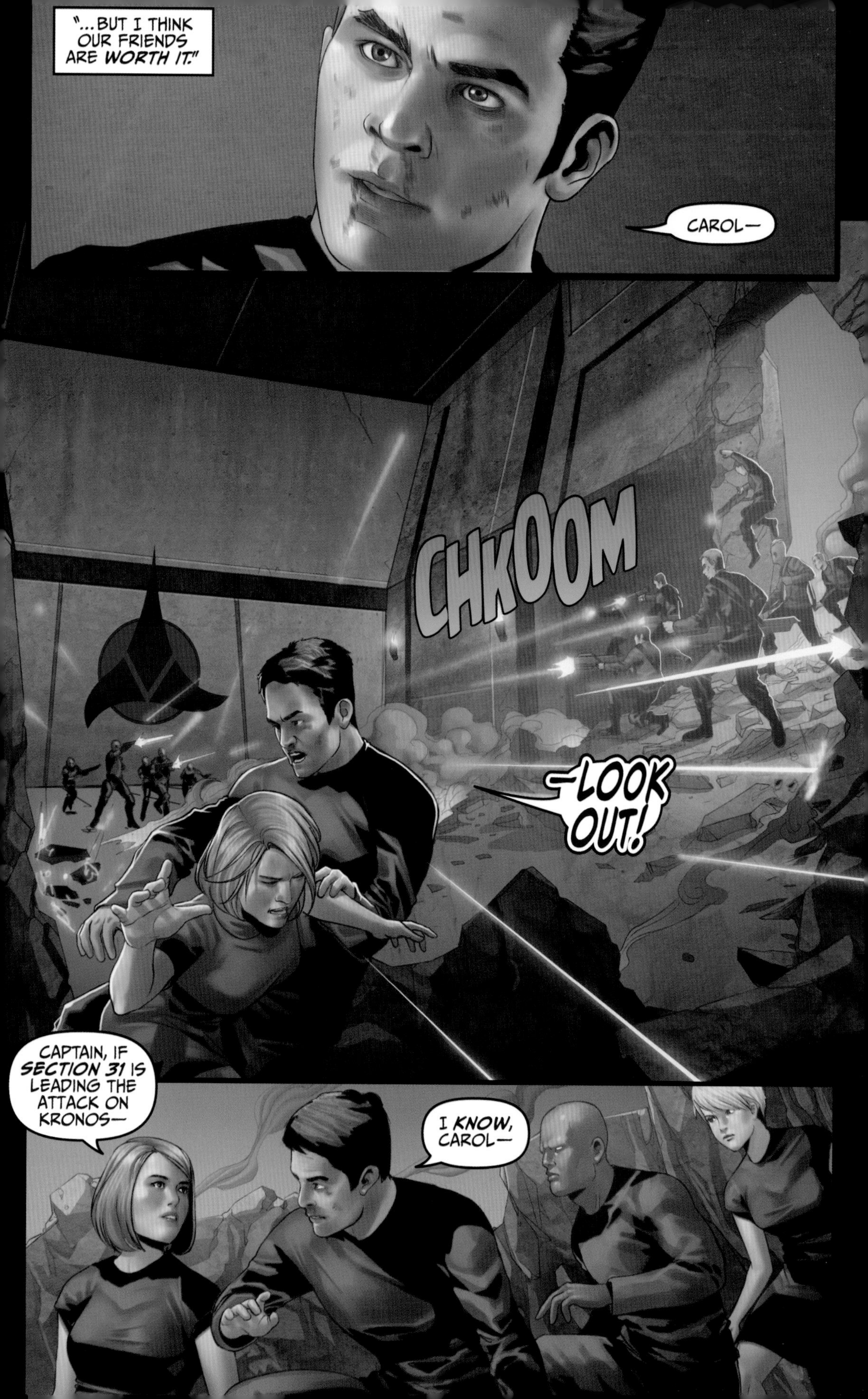
"...BUT I THINK OUR FRIENDS ARE WORTH IT."
CAROL—
CHKOOM
—LOOK OUT!
CAPTAIN, IF SECTION 31 IS LEADING THE ATTACK ON KRONOS—
I KNOW, CAROL—

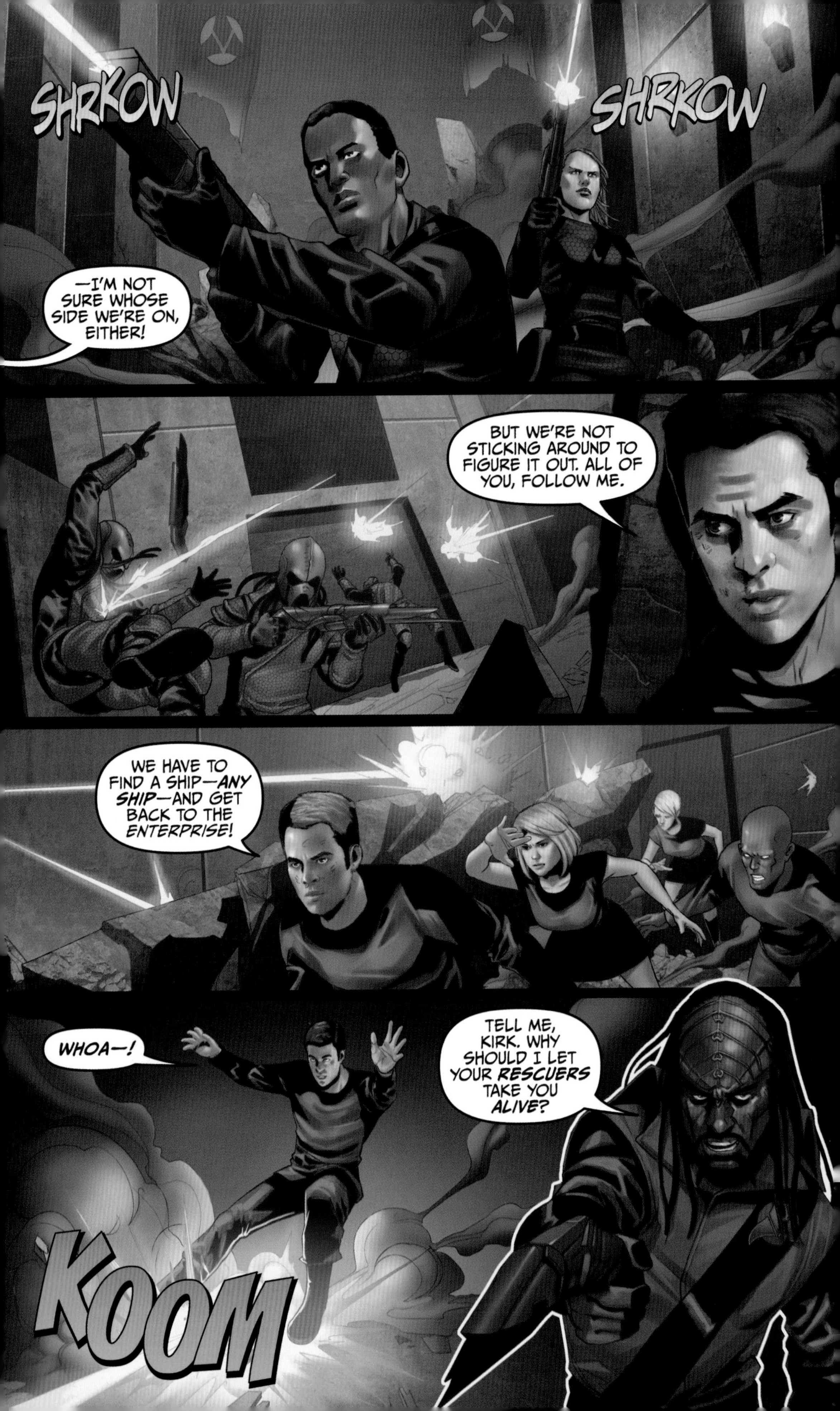
SHRKOW
SHRKOW
—I'M NOT SURE WHOSE SIDE WE'RE ON, EITHER!
BUT WE'RE NOT STICKING AROUND TO FIGURE IT OUT. ALL OF YOU, FOLLOW ME.
WE HAVE TO FIND A SHIP—*ANY SHIP*—AND GET BACK TO THE *ENTERPRISE*!
WHOA—!
TELL ME, KIRK. WHY SHOULD I LET YOUR ***RESCUERS*** TAKE YOU *ALIVE*?
KOOM

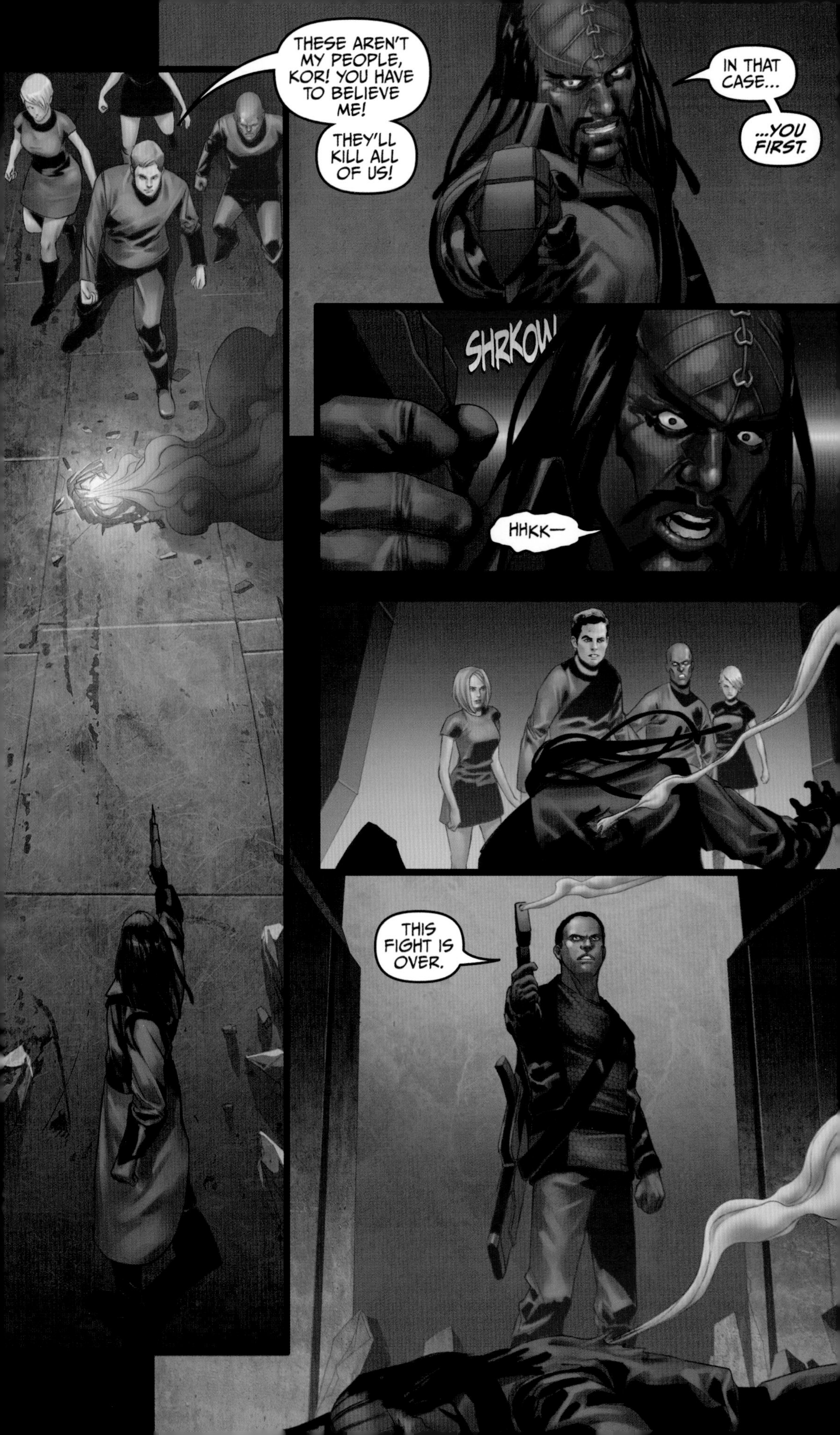
THESE AREN'T MY PEOPLE, KOR! YOU HAVE TO BELIEVE ME!
THEY'LL KILL ALL OF US!
IN THAT CASE...
...YOU FIRST.
SHRKOW!
HHKK—
THIS FIGHT IS OVER.

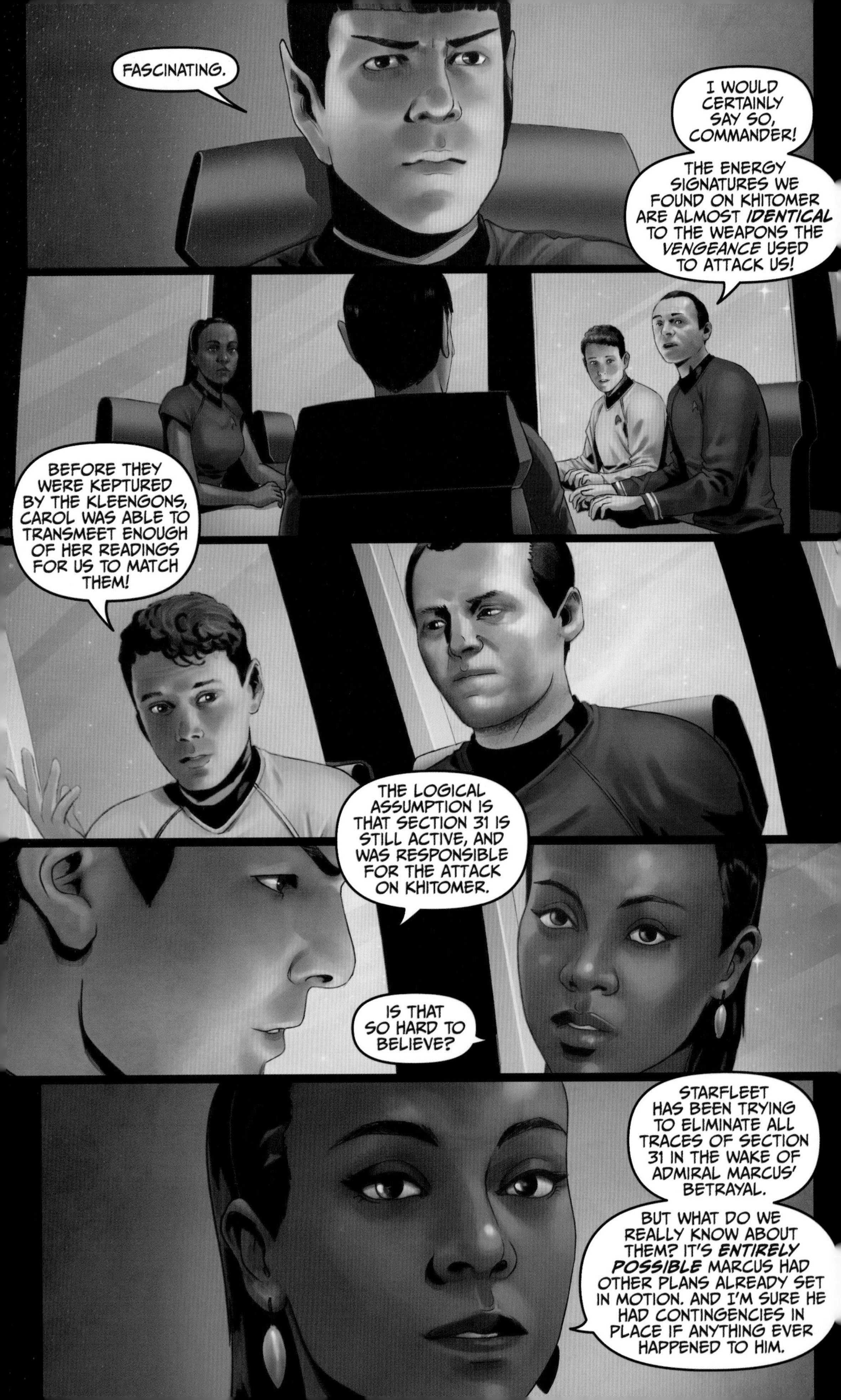

FASCINATING.
I WOULD CERTAINLY SAY SO, COMMANDER!
THE ENERGY SIGNATURES WE FOUND ON KHITOMER ARE ALMOST *IDENTICAL* TO THE WEAPONS THE *VENGEANCE* USED TO ATTACK US!
BEFORE THEY WERE KEPTURED BY THE KLEENGONS, CAROL WAS ABLE TO TRANSMEET ENOUGH OF HER READINGS FOR US TO MATCH THEM!
THE LOGICAL ASSUMPTION IS THAT SECTION 31 IS STILL ACTIVE, AND WAS RESPONSIBLE FOR THE ATTACK ON KHITOMER.
IS THAT SO HARD TO BELIEVE?
STARFLEET HAS BEEN TRYING TO ELIMINATE ALL TRACES OF SECTION 31 IN THE WAKE OF ADMIRAL MARCUS' BETRAYAL.
BUT WHAT DO WE REALLY KNOW ABOUT THEM? IT'S *ENTIRELY POSSIBLE* MARCUS HAD OTHER PLANS ALREADY SET IN MOTION. AND I'M SURE HE HAD CONTINGENCIES IN PLACE IF ANYTHING EVER HAPPENED TO HIM.

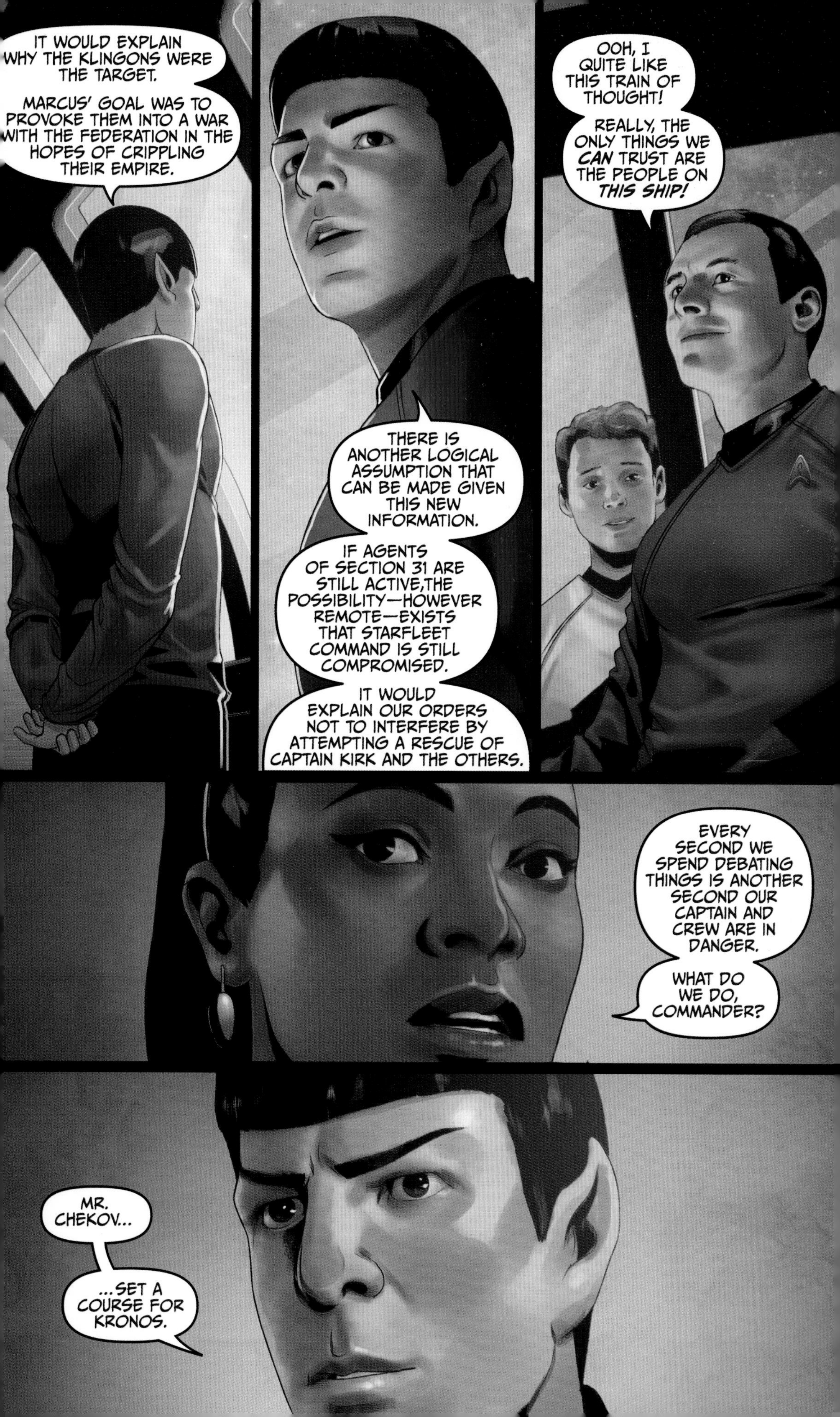
IT WOULD EXPLAIN WHY THE KLINGONS WERE THE TARGET.
MARCUS' GOAL WAS TO PROVOKE THEM INTO A WAR WITH THE FEDERATION IN THE HOPES OF CRIPPLING THEIR EMPIRE.
THERE IS ANOTHER LOGICAL ASSUMPTION THAT CAN BE MADE GIVEN THIS NEW INFORMATION.
IF AGENTS OF SECTION 31 ARE STILL ACTIVE,THE POSSIBILITY—HOWEVER REMOTE—EXISTS THAT STARFLEET COMMAND IS STILL COMPROMISED.
IT WOULD EXPLAIN OUR ORDERS NOT TO INTERFERE BY ATTEMPTING A RESCUE OF CAPTAIN KIRK AND THE OTHERS.
OOH, I QUITE LIKE THIS TRAIN OF THOUGHT!
REALLY, THE ONLY THINGS WE *CAN* TRUST ARE THE PEOPLE ON *THIS SHIP!*
EVERY SECOND WE SPEND DEBATING THINGS IS ANOTHER SECOND OUR CAPTAIN AND CREW ARE IN DANGER.
WHAT DO WE DO, COMMANDER?
MR. CHEKOV...
...SET A COURSE FOR KRONOS.

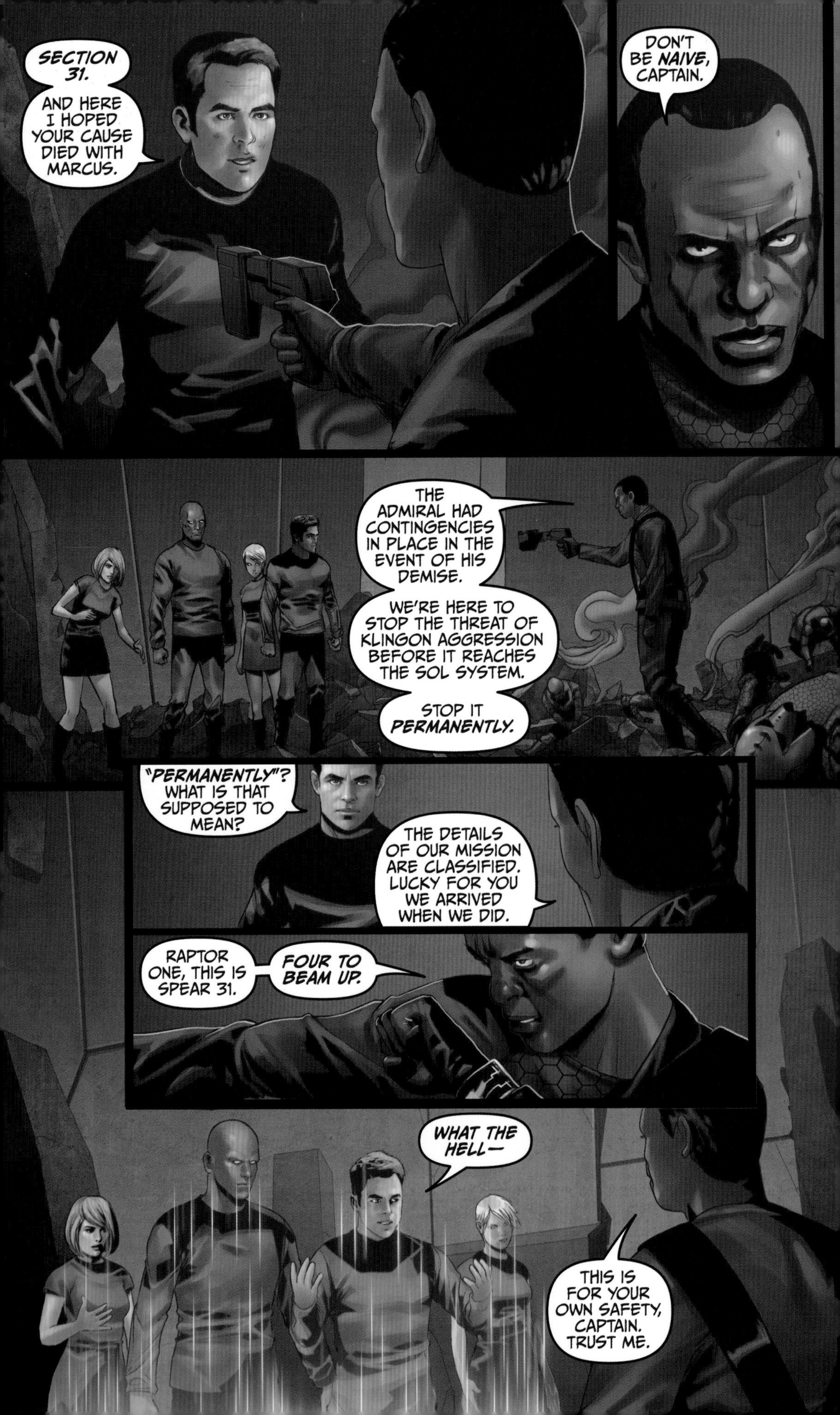
SECTION 31.
AND HERE I HOPED YOUR CAUSE DIED WITH MARCUS.
DON'T BE NAIVE, CAPTAIN.
THE ADMIRAL HAD CONTINGENCIES IN PLACE IN THE EVENT OF HIS DEMISE.
WE'RE HERE TO STOP THE THREAT OF KLINGON AGGRESSION BEFORE IT REACHES THE SOL SYSTEM.
STOP IT PERMANENTLY.
"PERMANENTLY"? WHAT IS THAT SUPPOSED TO MEAN?
THE DETAILS OF OUR MISSION ARE CLASSIFIED. LUCKY FOR YOU WE ARRIVED WHEN WE DID.
RAPTOR ONE, THIS IS SPEAR 31.
FOUR TO BEAM UP.
WHAT THE HELL—
THIS IS FOR YOUR OWN SAFETY, CAPTAIN. TRUST ME.

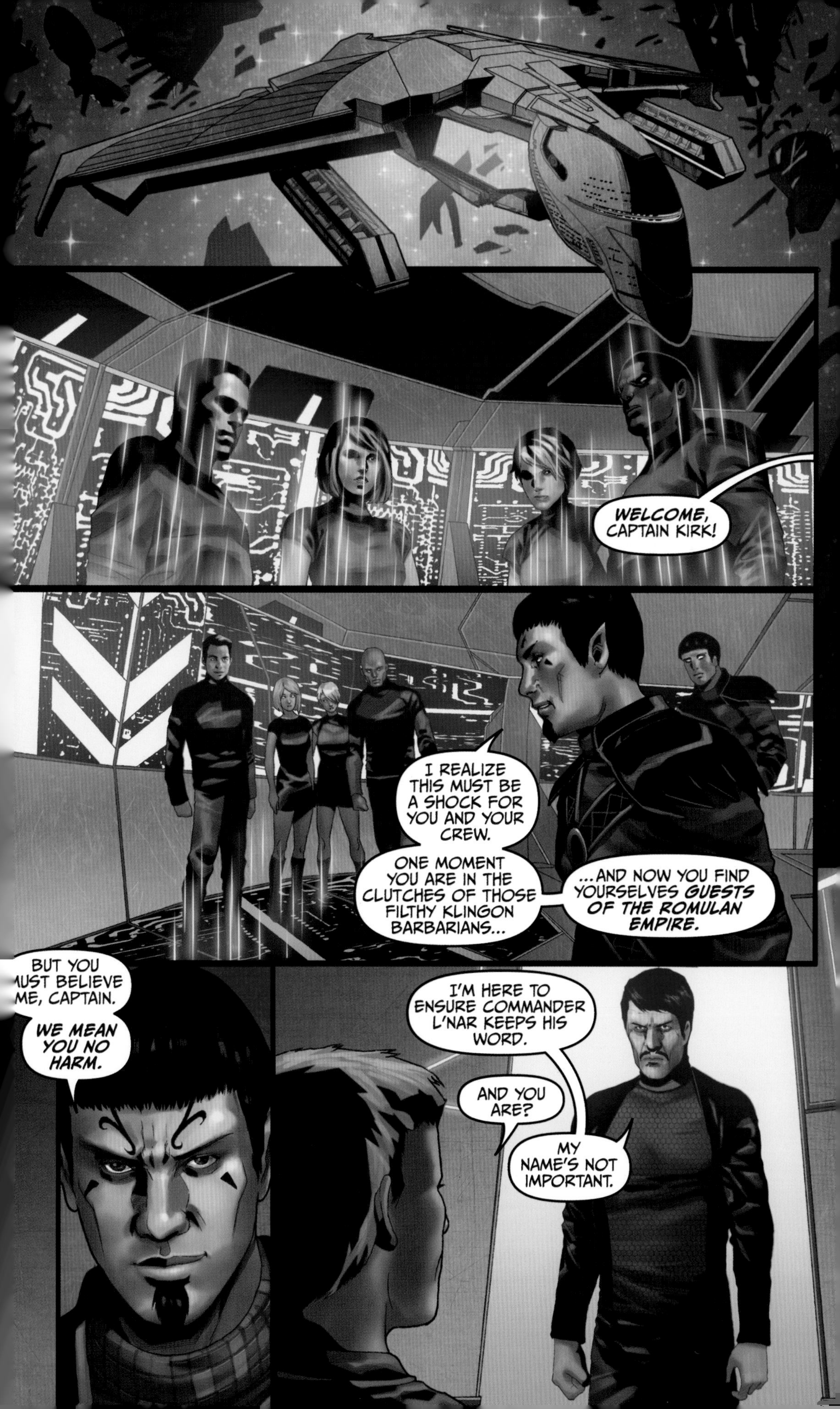
WELCOME, CAPTAIN KIRK!
I REALIZE THIS MUST BE A SHOCK FOR YOU AND YOUR CREW.
ONE MOMENT YOU ARE IN THE CLUTCHES OF THOSE FILTHY KLINGON BARBARIANS...
...AND NOW YOU FIND YOURSELVES *GUESTS OF THE ROMULAN EMPIRE.*
BUT YOU MUST BELIEVE ME, CAPTAIN.
WE MEAN YOU NO HARM.
I'M HERE TO ENSURE COMMANDER L'NAR KEEPS HIS WORD.
AND YOU ARE?
MY NAME'S NOT IMPORTANT.

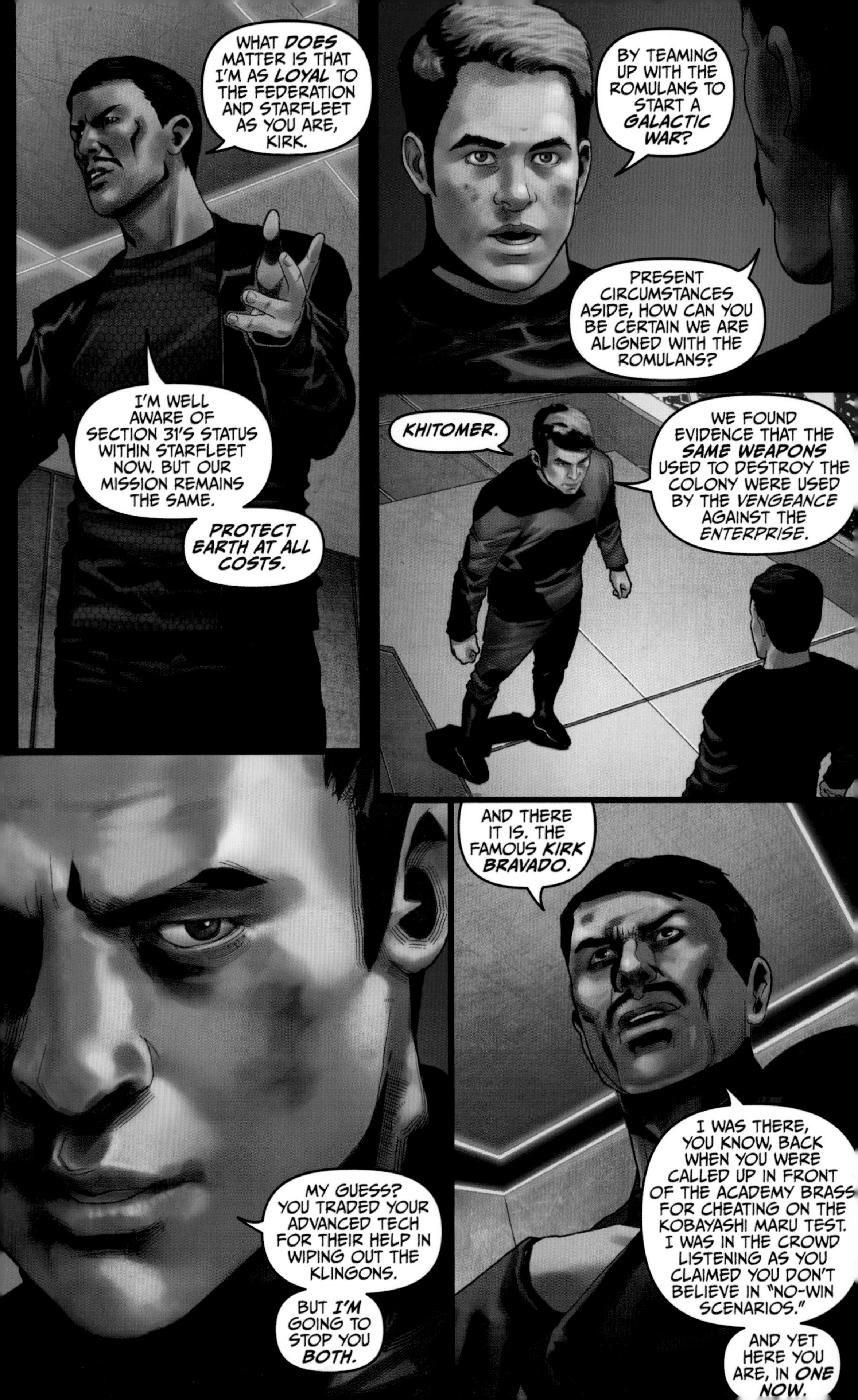

WHAT DOES MATTER IS THAT I'M AS LOYAL TO THE FEDERATION AND STARFLEET AS YOU ARE, KIRK.
I'M WELL AWARE OF SECTION 31'S STATUS WITHIN STARFLEET NOW. BUT OUR MISSION REMAINS THE SAME.
PROTECT EARTH AT ALL COSTS.
BY TEAMING UP WITH THE ROMULANS TO START A GALACTIC WAR?
PRESENT CIRCUMSTANCES ASIDE, HOW CAN YOU BE CERTAIN WE ARE ALIGNED WITH THE ROMULANS?
KHITOMER.
WE FOUND EVIDENCE THAT THE SAME WEAPONS USED TO DESTROY THE COLONY WERE USED BY THE VENGEANCE AGAINST THE ENTERPRISE.
MY GUESS? YOU TRADED YOUR ADVANCED TECH FOR THEIR HELP IN WIPING OUT THE KLINGONS.
BUT I'M GOING TO STOP YOU BOTH.
AND THERE IT IS. THE FAMOUS KIRK BRAVADO.
I WAS THERE, YOU KNOW, BACK WHEN YOU WERE CALLED UP IN FRONT OF THE ACADEMY BRASS FOR CHEATING ON THE KOBAYASHI MARU TEST. I WAS IN THE CROWD LISTENING AS YOU CLAIMED YOU DON'T BELIEVE IN "NO-WIN SCENARIOS."
AND YET HERE YOU ARE, IN ONE NOW.

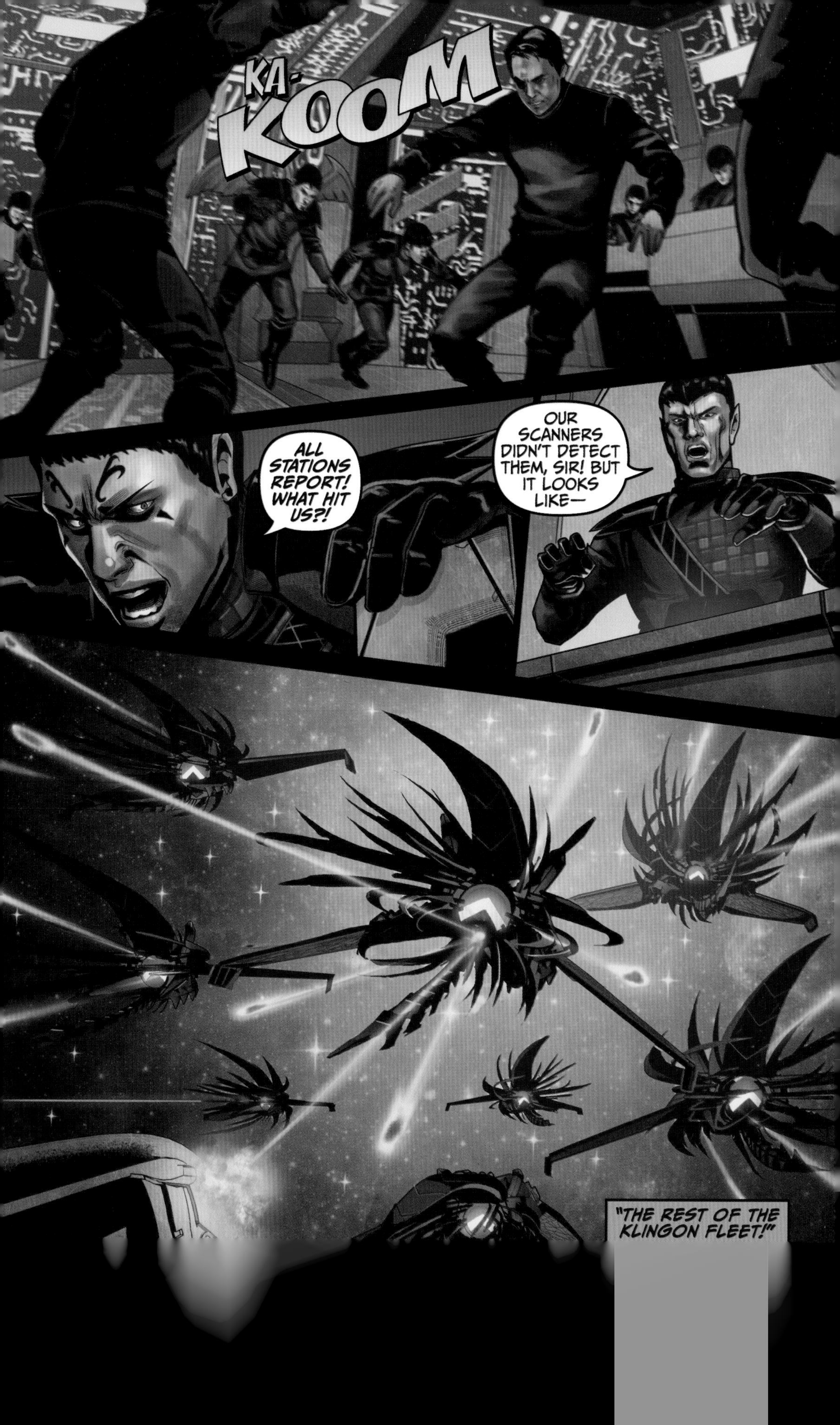
KA-KOOM
ALL STATIONS REPORT! WHAT HIT US?!
OUR SCANNERS DIDN'T DETECT THEM, SIR! BUT IT LOOKS LIKE—
"THE REST OF THE KLINGON FLEET!"

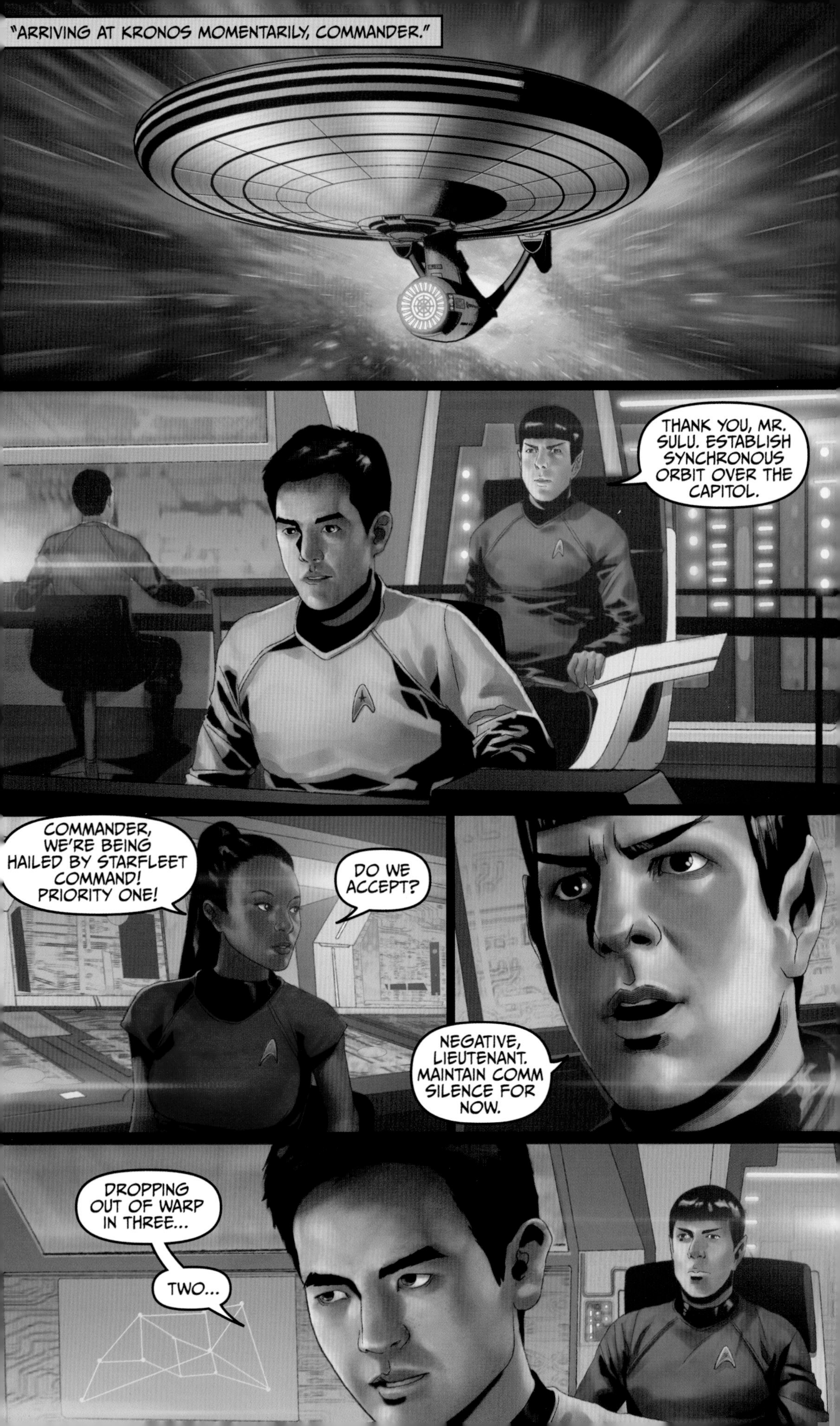
"ARRIVING AT KRONOS MOMENTARILY, COMMANDER."
THANK YOU, MR. SULU. ESTABLISH SYNCHRONOUS ORBIT OVER THE CAPITOL.
COMMANDER, WE'RE BEING HAILED BY STARFLEET COMMAND! PRIORITY ONE!
DO WE ACCEPT?
NEGATIVE, LIEUTENANT. MAINTAIN COMM SILENCE FOR NOW.
DROPPING OUT OF WARP IN THREE...
TWO...

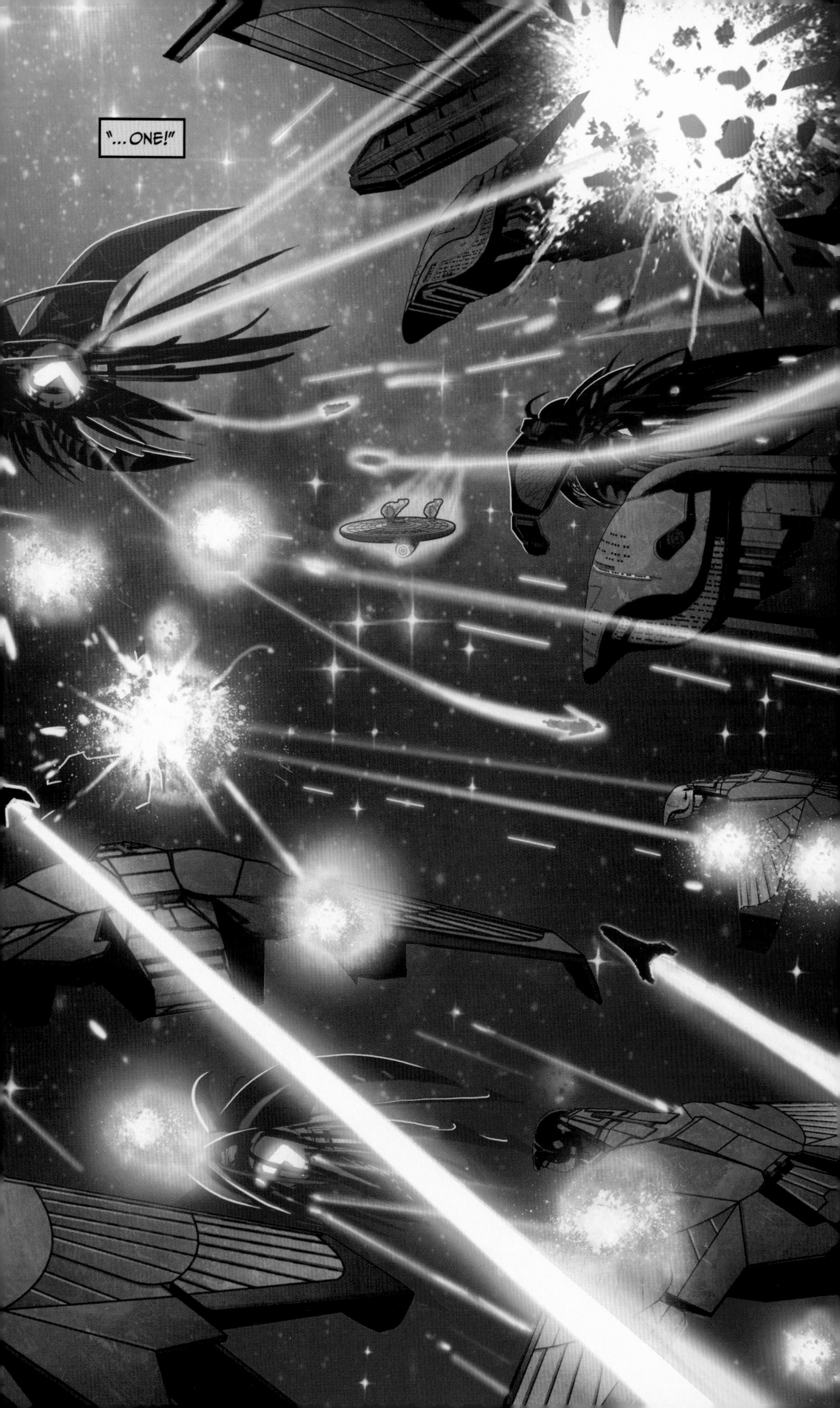
"...ONE!"

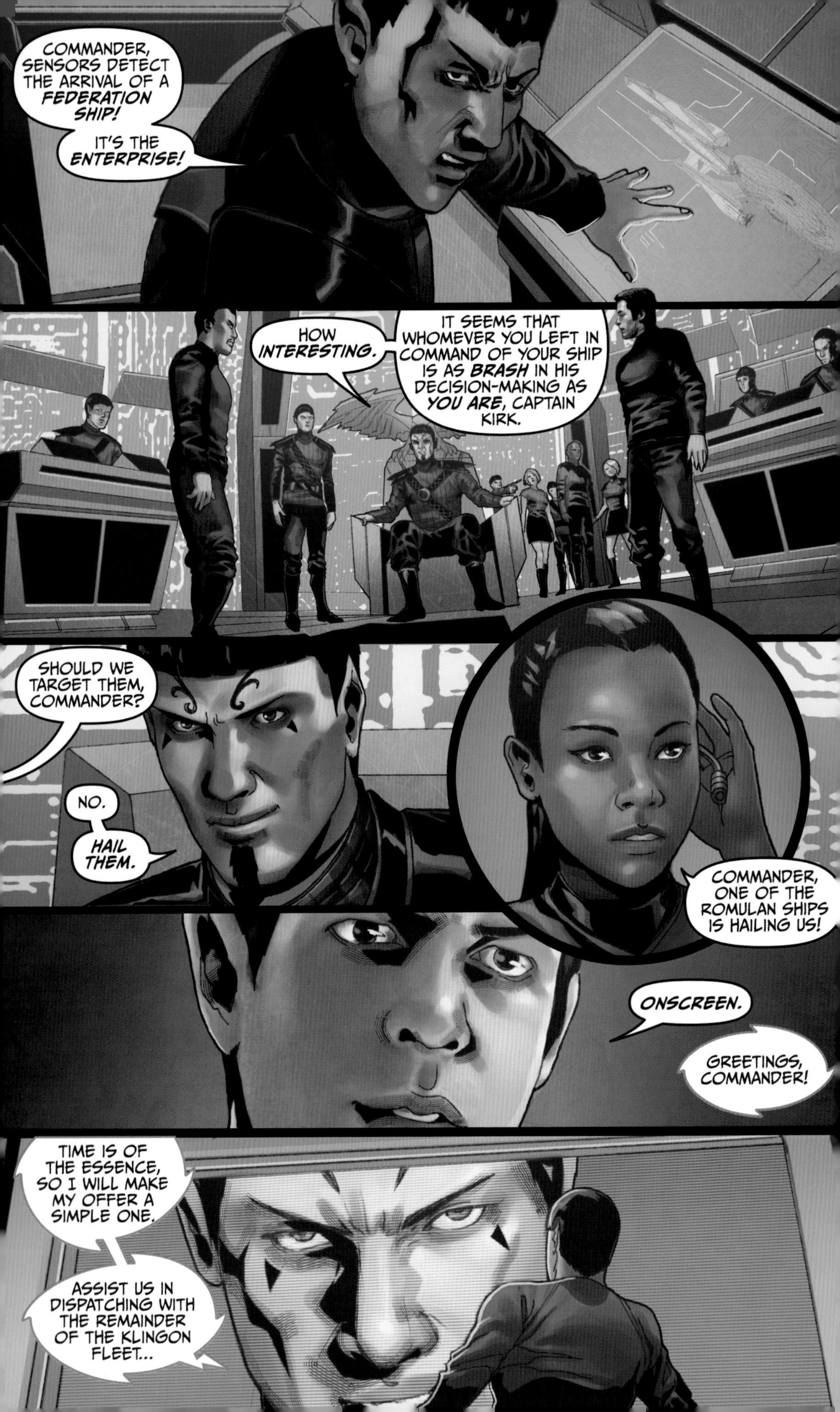
COMMANDER, SENSORS DETECT THE ARRIVAL OF A FEDERATION SHIP!
IT'S THE ENTERPRISE!
HOW INTERESTING.
IT SEEMS THAT WHOMEVER YOU LEFT IN COMMAND OF YOUR SHIP IS AS BRASH IN HIS DECISION-MAKING AS YOU ARE, CAPTAIN KIRK.
SHOULD WE TARGET THEM, COMMANDER?
NO.
HAIL THEM.
COMMANDER, ONE OF THE ROMULAN SHIPS IS HAILING US!
ONSCREEN.
GREETINGS, COMMANDER!
TIME IS OF THE ESSENCE, SO I WILL MAKE MY OFFER A SIMPLE ONE.
ASSIST US IN DISPATCHING WITH THE REMAINDER OF THE KLINGON FLEET...

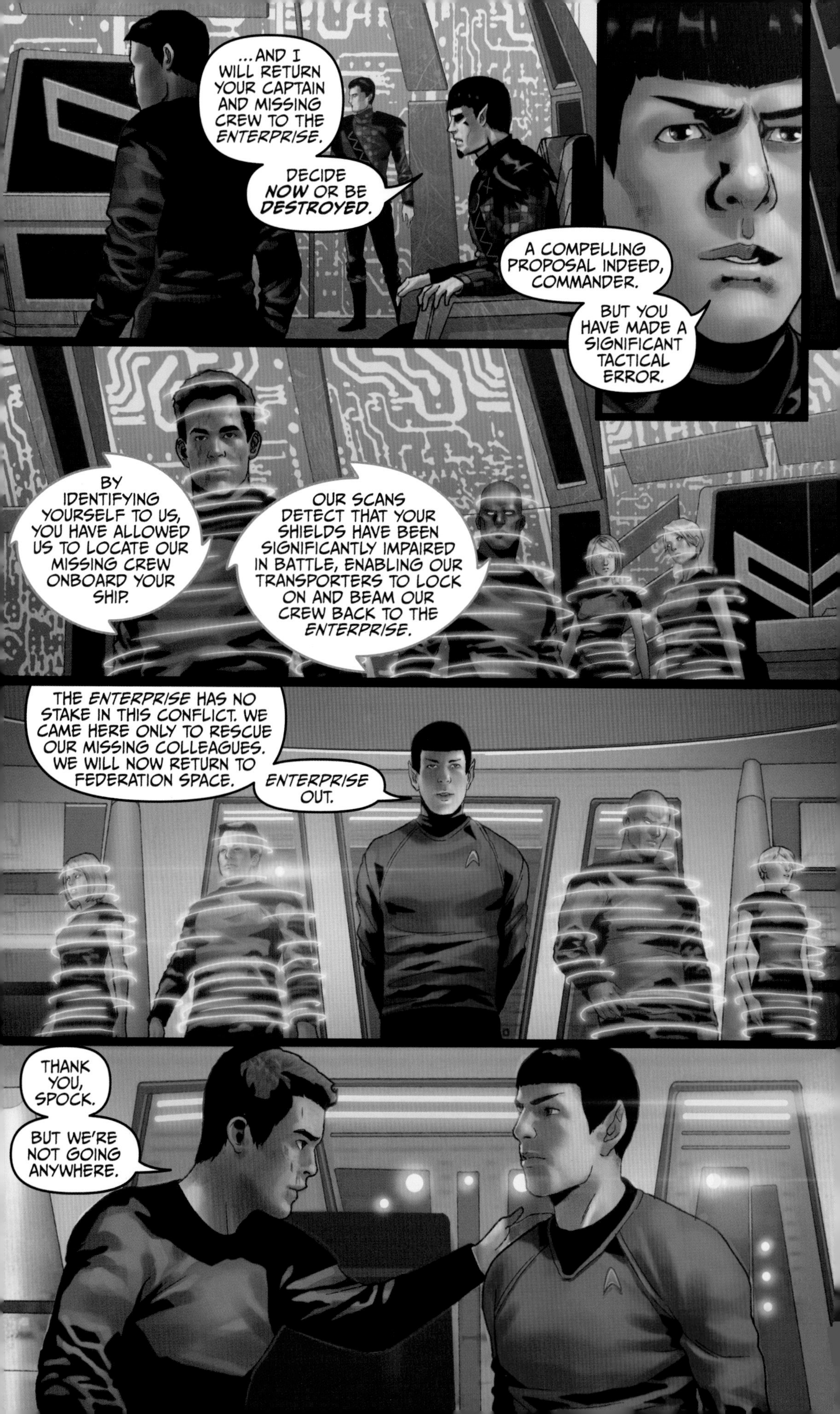
...AND I WILL RETURN YOUR CAPTAIN AND MISSING CREW TO THE ENTERPRISE.
DECIDE NOW OR BE DESTROYED.
A COMPELLING PROPOSAL INDEED, COMMANDER.
BUT YOU HAVE MADE A SIGNIFICANT TACTICAL ERROR.
BY IDENTIFYING YOURSELF TO US, YOU HAVE ALLOWED US TO LOCATE OUR MISSING CREW ONBOARD YOUR SHIP.
OUR SCANS DETECT THAT YOUR SHIELDS HAVE BEEN SIGNIFICANTLY IMPAIRED IN BATTLE, ENABLING OUR TRANSPORTERS TO LOCK ON AND BEAM OUR CREW BACK TO THE ENTERPRISE.
THE ENTERPRISE HAS NO STAKE IN THIS CONFLICT. WE CAME HERE ONLY TO RESCUE OUR MISSING COLLEAGUES. WE WILL NOW RETURN TO FEDERATION SPACE.
ENTERPRISE OUT.
THANK YOU, SPOCK.
BUT WE'RE NOT GOING ANYWHERE.

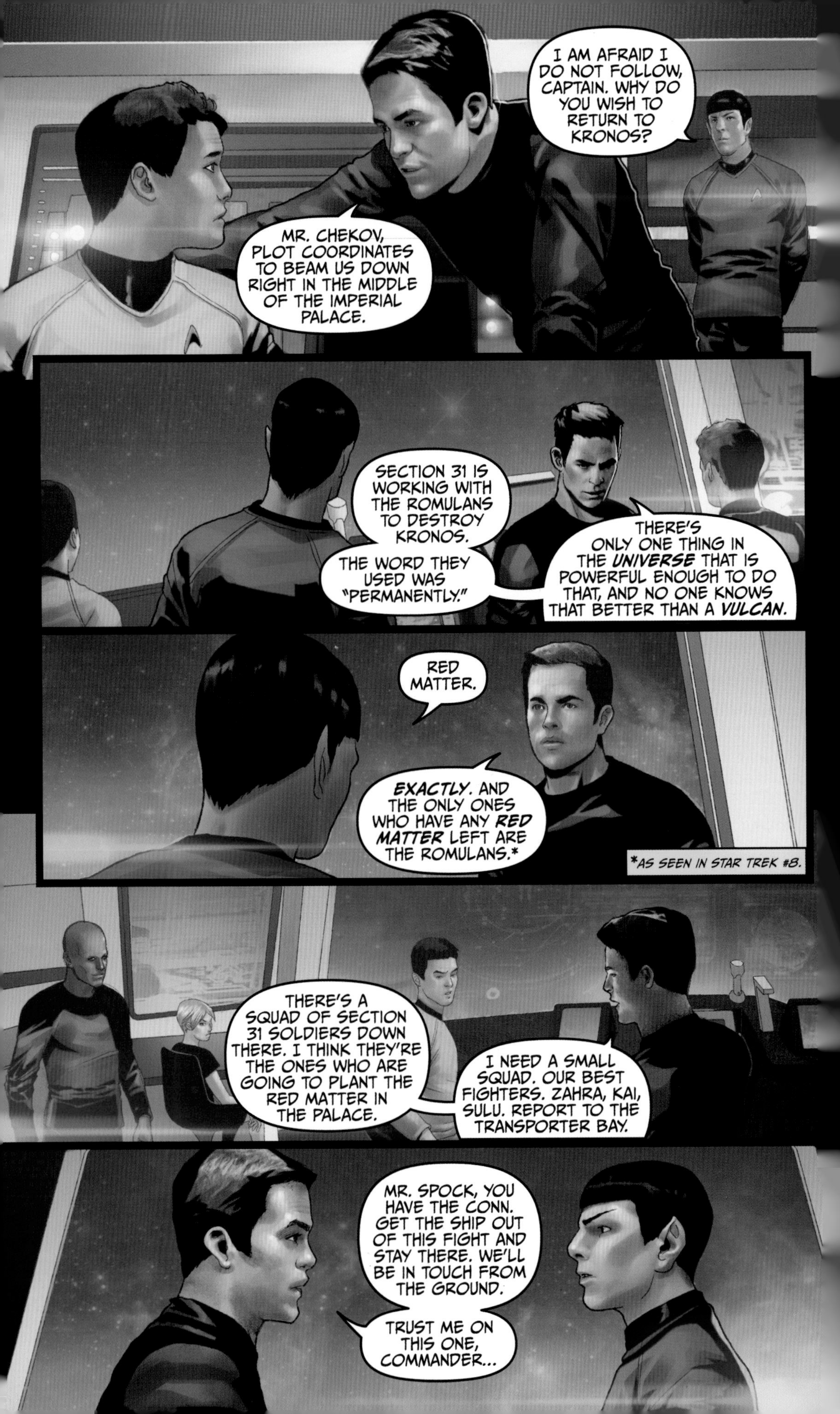
I AM AFRAID I DO NOT FOLLOW, CAPTAIN. WHY DO YOU WISH TO RETURN TO KRONOS?
MR. CHEKOV, PLOT COORDINATES TO BEAM US DOWN RIGHT IN THE MIDDLE OF THE IMPERIAL PALACE.
SECTION 31 IS WORKING WITH THE ROMULANS TO DESTROY KRONOS.
THE WORD THEY USED WAS "PERMANENTLY."
THERE'S ONLY ONE THING IN THE UNIVERSE THAT IS POWERFUL ENOUGH TO DO THAT, AND NO ONE KNOWS THAT BETTER THAN A VULCAN.
RED MATTER.
EXACTLY. AND THE ONLY ONES WHO HAVE ANY RED MATTER LEFT ARE THE ROMULANS.*
*AS SEEN IN STAR TREK #8.
THERE'S A SQUAD OF SECTION 31 SOLDIERS DOWN THERE. I THINK THEY'RE THE ONES WHO ARE GOING TO PLANT THE RED MATTER IN THE PALACE.
I NEED A SMALL SQUAD. OUR BEST FIGHTERS. ZAHRA, KAI, SULU. REPORT TO THE TRANSPORTER BAY.
MR. SPOCK, YOU HAVE THE CONN. GET THE SHIP OUT OF THIS FIGHT AND STAY THERE. WE'LL BE IN TOUCH FROM THE GROUND.
TRUST ME ON THIS ONE, COMMANDER...

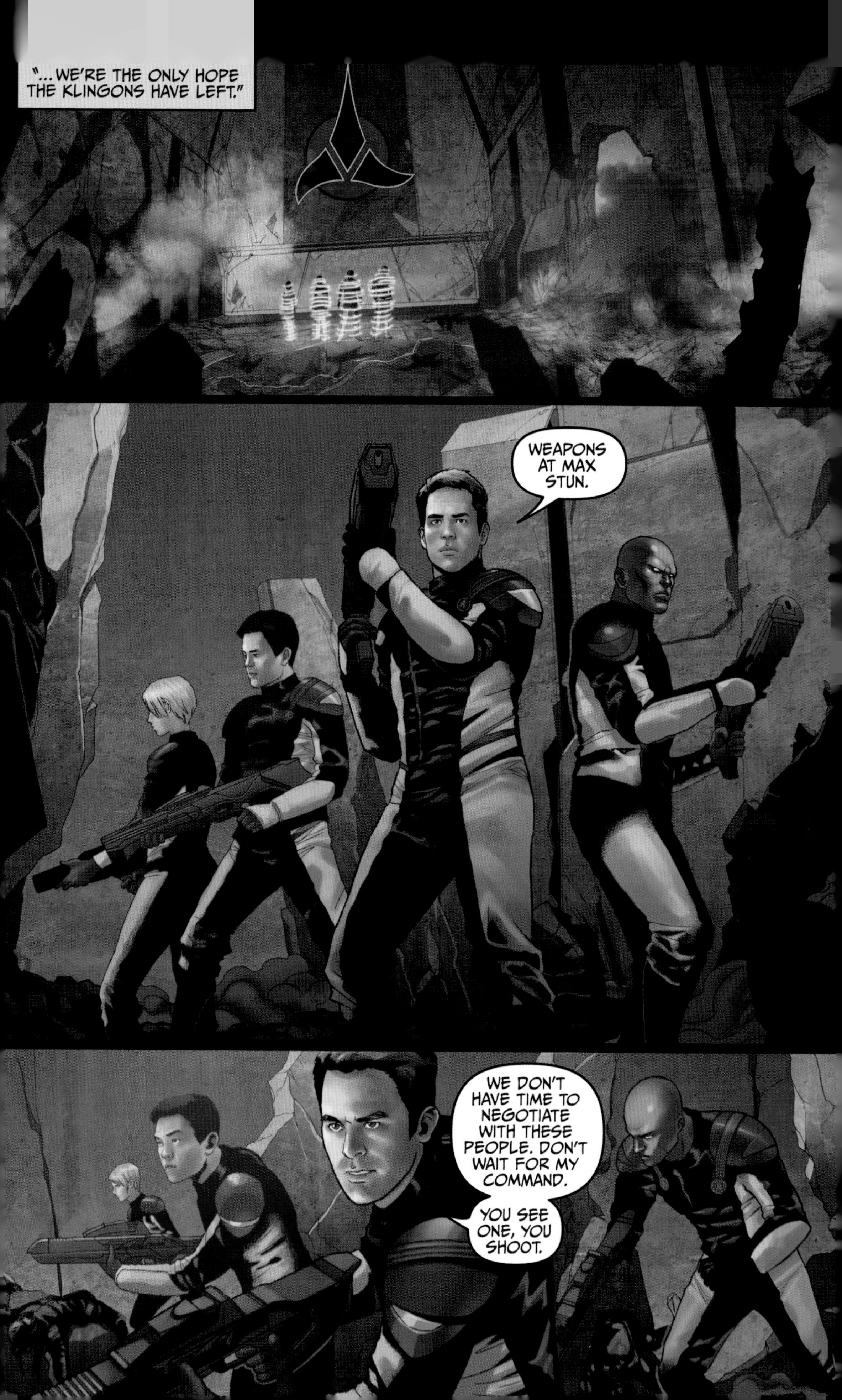

"...WE'RE THE ONLY HOPE THE KLINGONS HAVE LEFT."
WEAPONS AT MAX STUN.
WE DON'T HAVE TIME TO NEGOTIATE WITH THESE PEOPLE. DON'T WAIT FOR MY COMMAND.
YOU SEE ONE, YOU SHOOT.

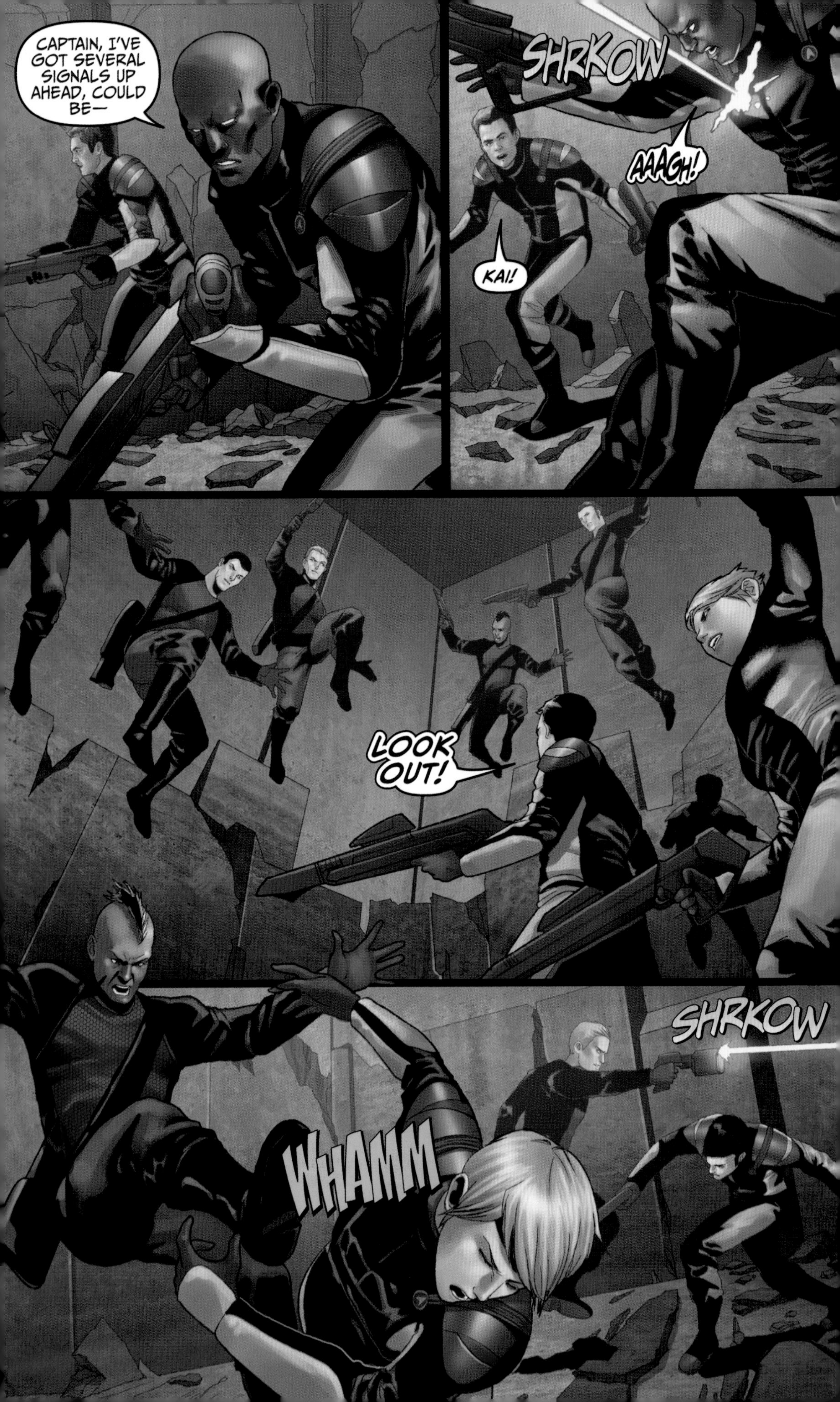

CAPTAIN, I'VE GOT SEVERAL SIGNALS UP AHEAD, COULD BE—
SHRKOW
AAAGH!
KAI!
LOOK OUT!
SHRKOW
WHAMM

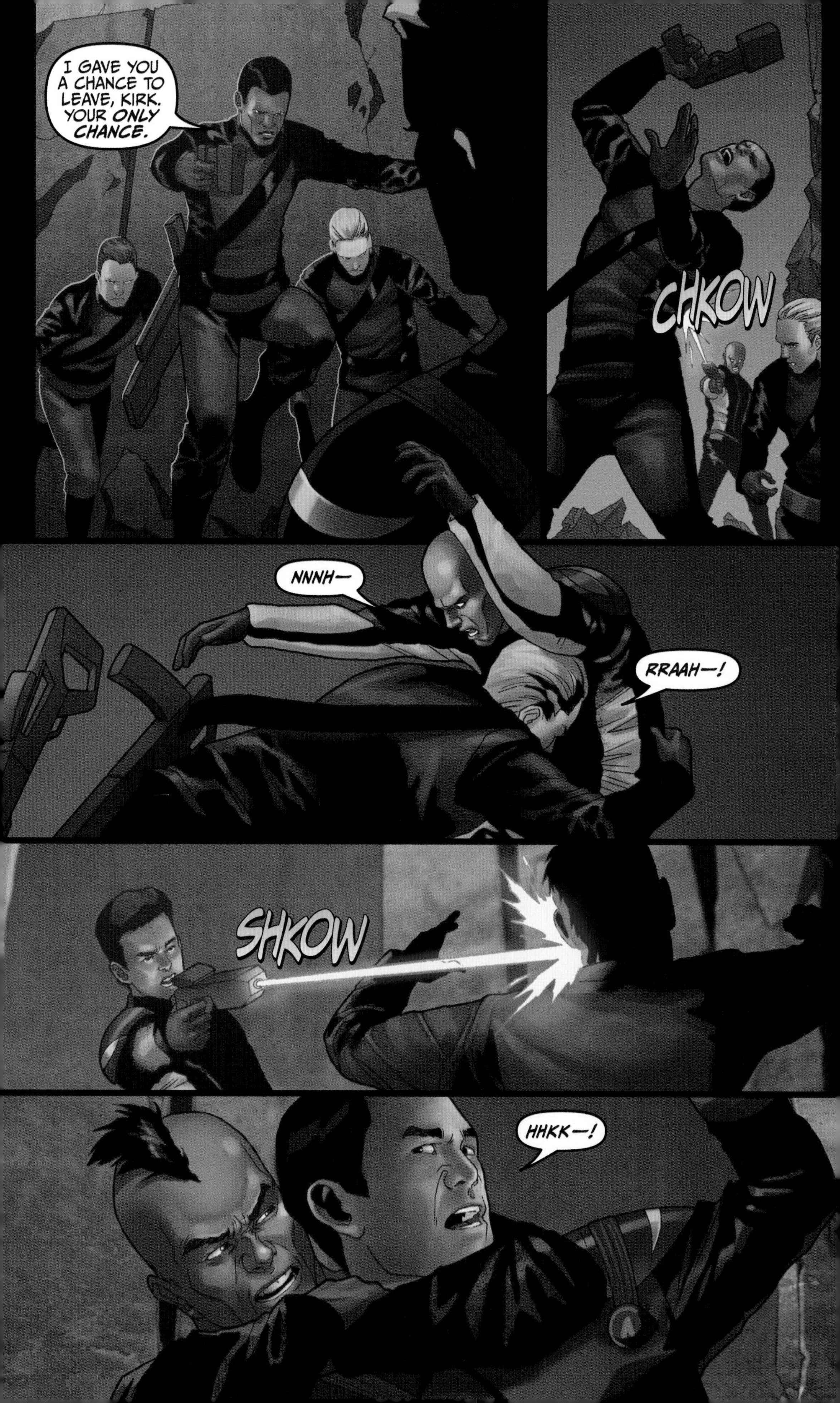
I GAVE YOU A CHANCE TO LEAVE, KIRK. YOUR *ONLY CHANCE.*
CHKOW
NNNH—
RRAAH—!
SHKOW
HHKK—!

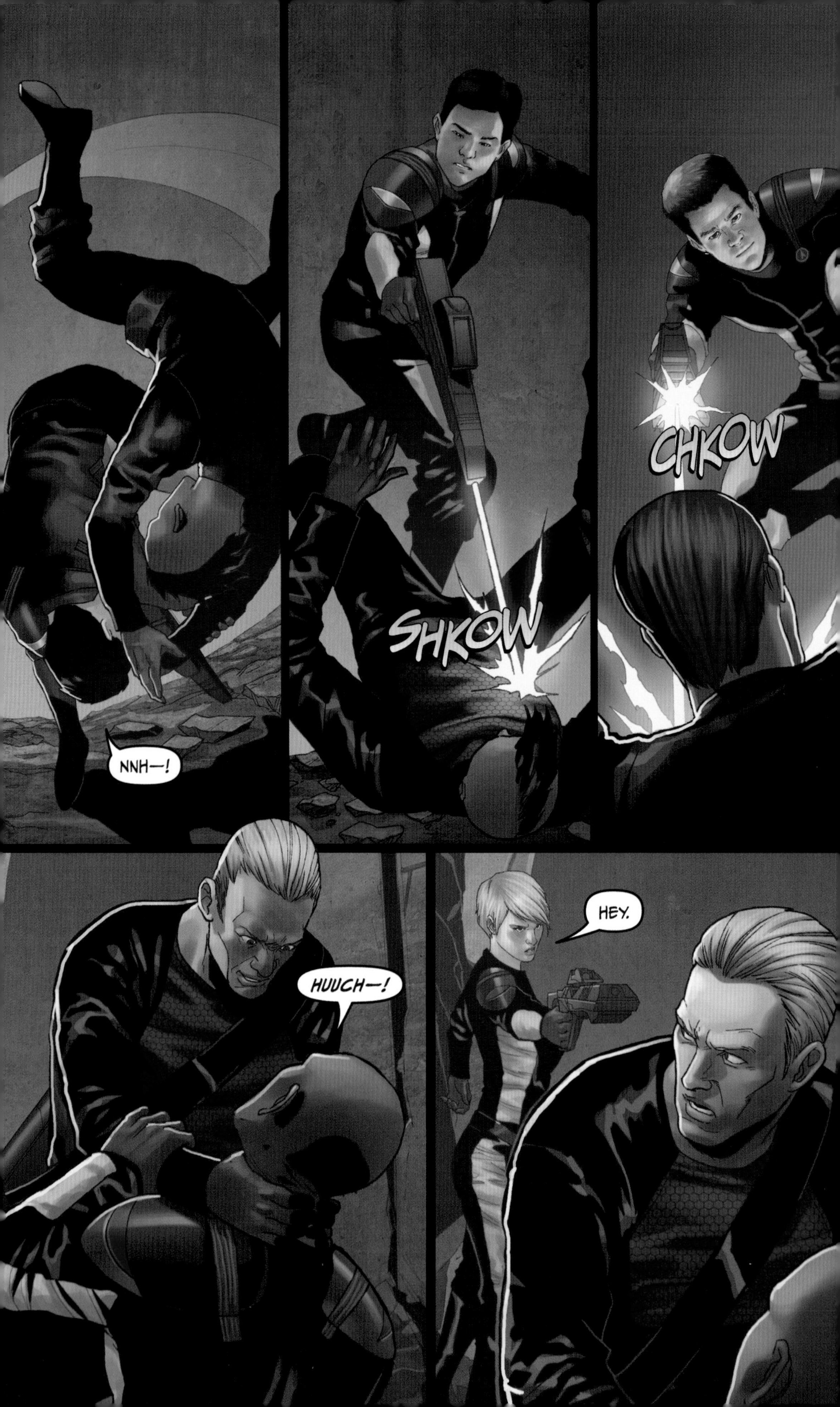
NNH—!
SHKOW
CHKOW
HUUCH—!
HEY.

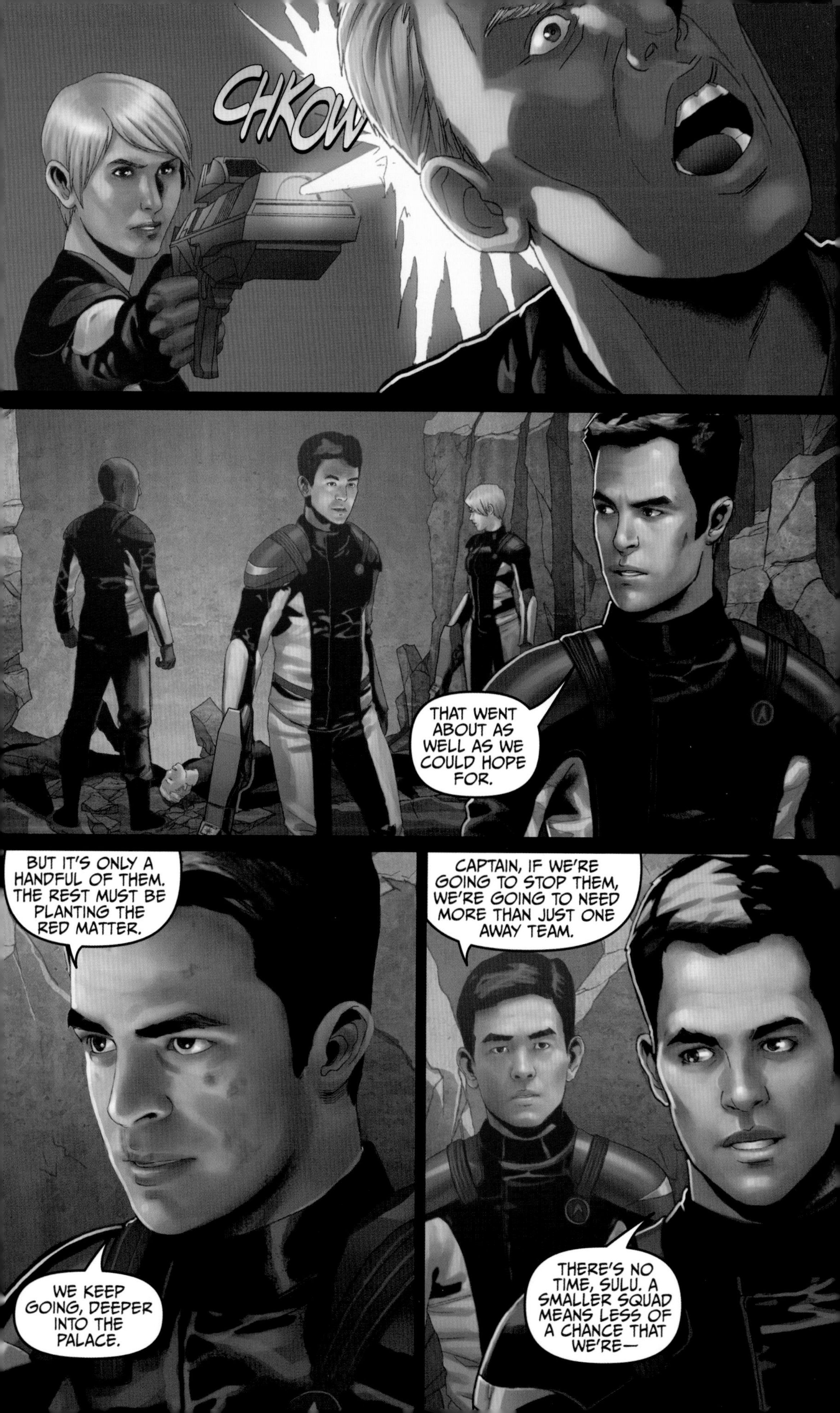
CHKOW
THAT WENT ABOUT AS WELL AS WE COULD HOPE FOR.
BUT IT'S ONLY A HANDFUL OF THEM. THE REST MUST BE PLANTING THE RED MATTER.
WE KEEP GOING, DEEPER INTO THE PALACE.
CAPTAIN, IF WE'RE GOING TO STOP THEM, WE'RE GOING TO NEED MORE THAN JUST ONE AWAY TEAM.
THERE'S NO TIME, SULU. A SMALLER SQUAD MEANS LESS OF A CHANCE THAT WE'RE—

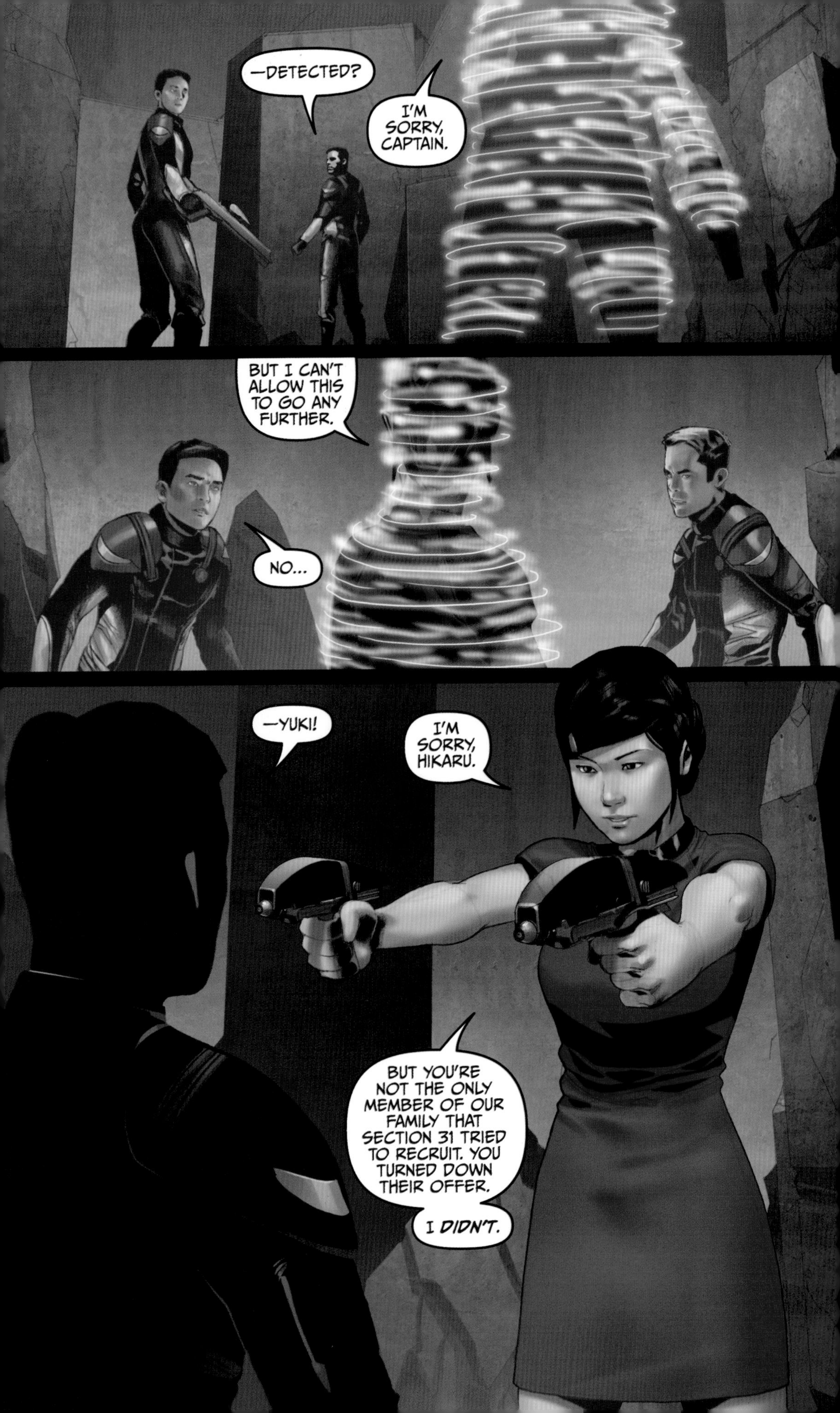
—DETECTED?
I'M SORRY, CAPTAIN.
BUT I CAN'T ALLOW THIS TO GO ANY FURTHER.
NO...
—YUKI!
I'M SORRY, HIKARU.
BUT YOU'RE NOT THE ONLY MEMBER OF OUR FAMILY THAT SECTION 31 TRIED TO RECRUIT. YOU TURNED DOWN THEIR OFFER.
I *DIDN'T*.

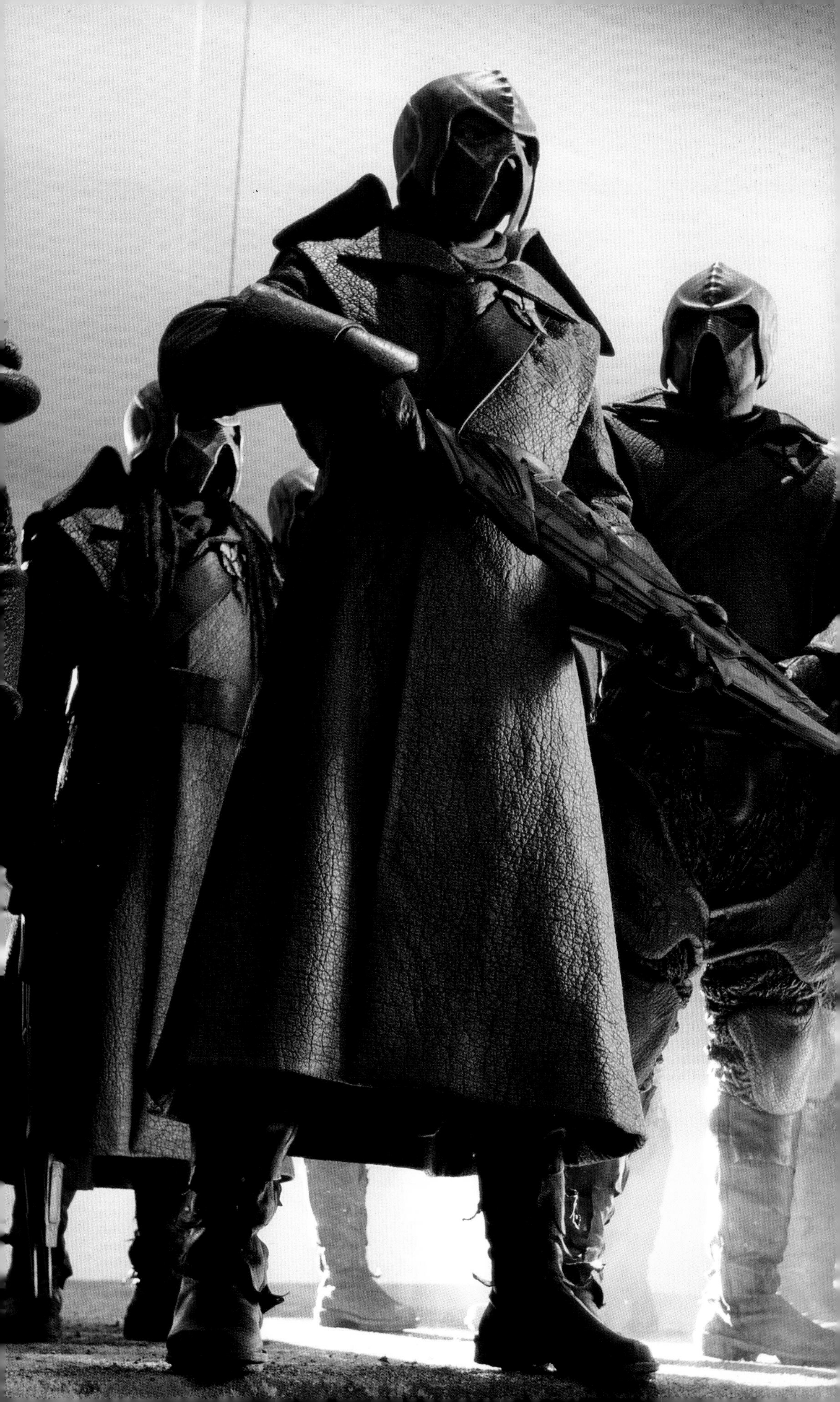

Artwork by Erfan Fajar
Colors by Ifansyah Noor

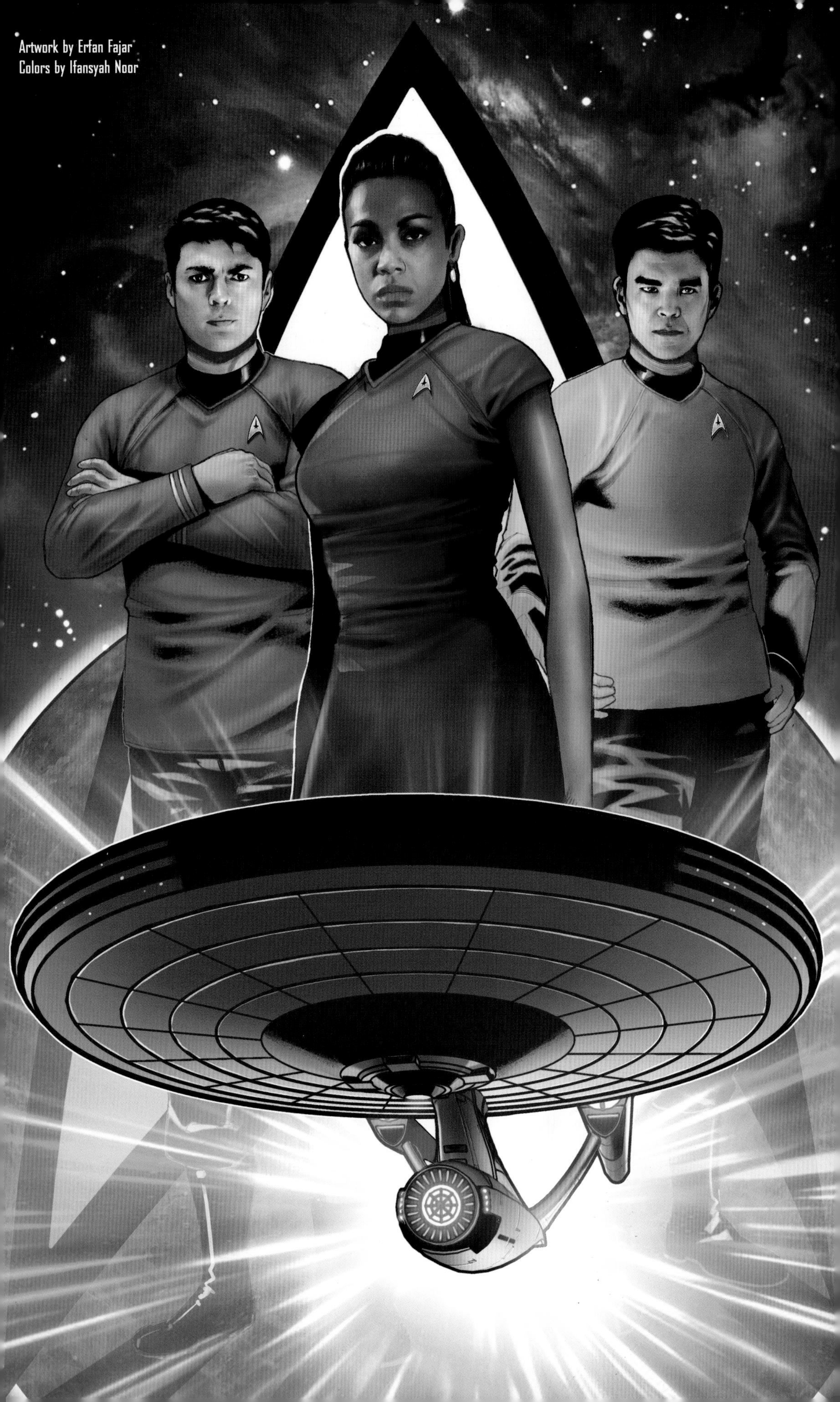

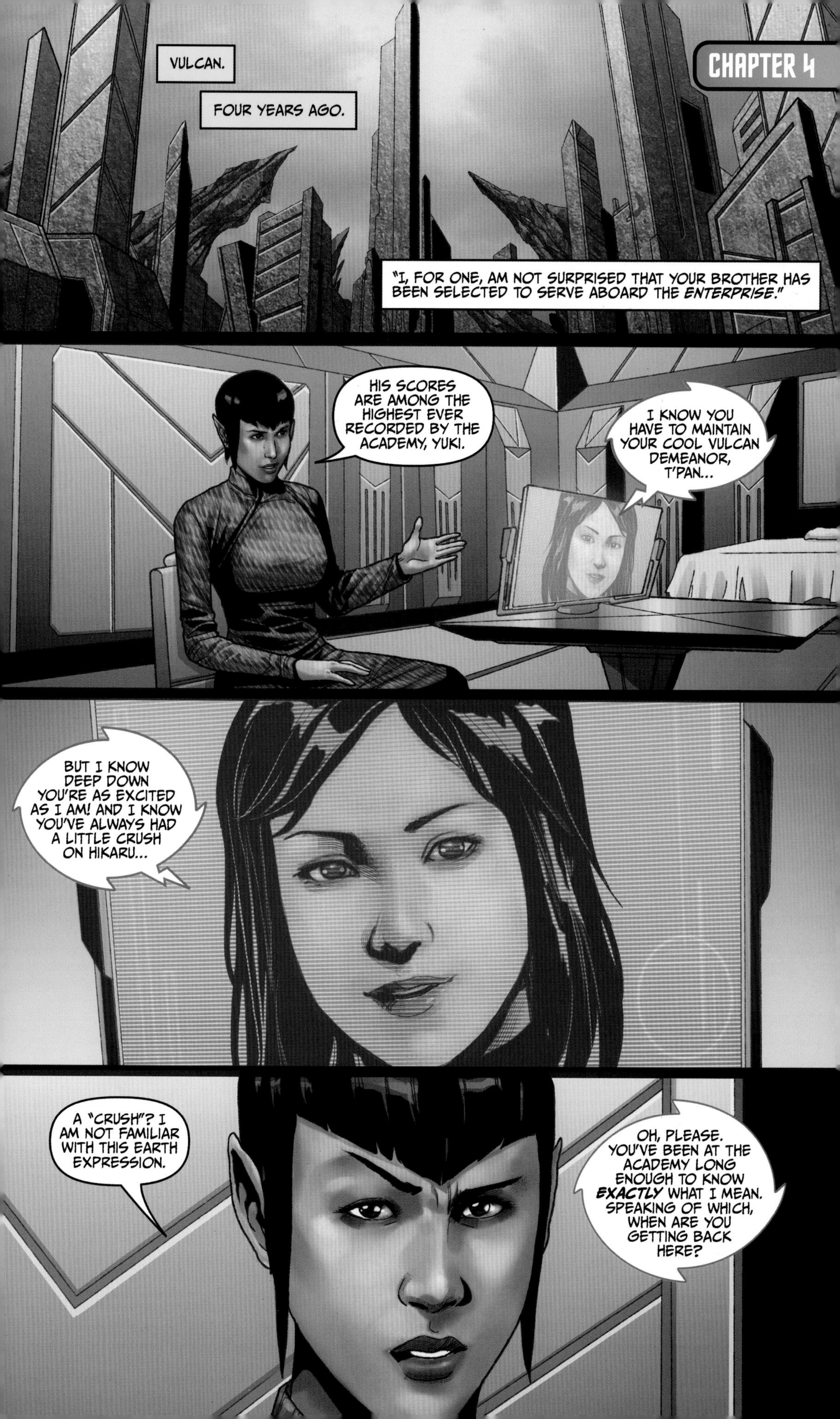
CHAPTER 4
VULCAN.
FOUR YEARS AGO.
"I, FOR ONE, AM NOT SURPRISED THAT YOUR BROTHER HAS BEEN SELECTED TO SERVE ABOARD THE *ENTERPRISE*."
HIS SCORES ARE AMONG THE HIGHEST EVER RECORDED BY THE ACADEMY, YUKI.
I KNOW YOU HAVE TO MAINTAIN YOUR COOL VULCAN DEMEANOR, T'PAN...
BUT I KNOW DEEP DOWN YOU'RE AS EXCITED AS I AM! AND I KNOW YOU'VE ALWAYS HAD A LITTLE CRUSH ON HIKARU...
A "CRUSH"? I AM NOT FAMILIAR WITH THIS EARTH EXPRESSION.
OH, PLEASE. YOU'VE BEEN AT THE ACADEMY LONG ENOUGH TO KNOW **EXACTLY** WHAT I MEAN. SPEAKING OF WHICH, WHEN ARE YOU GETTING BACK HERE?

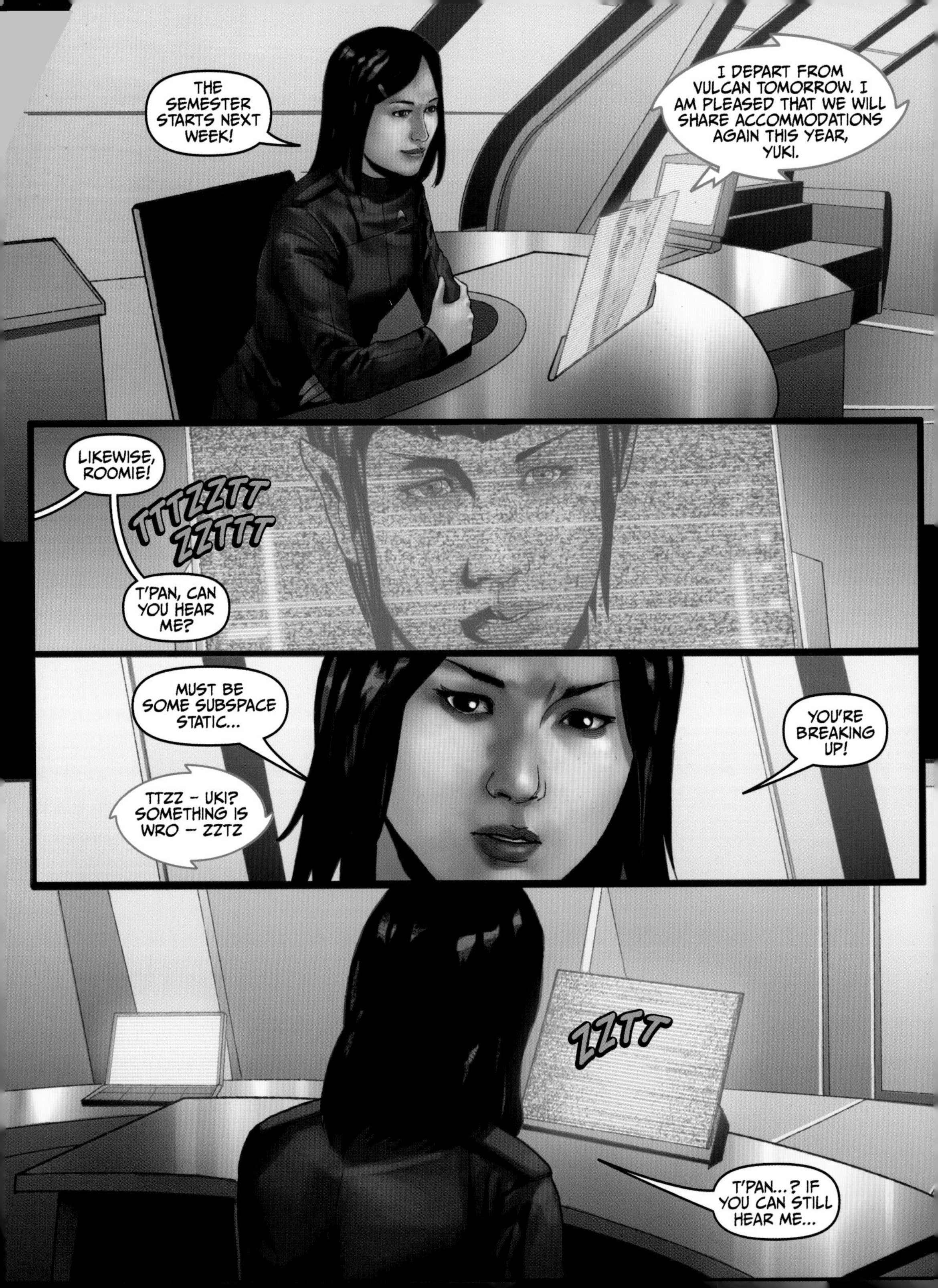
THE SEMESTER STARTS NEXT WEEK!
I DEPART FROM VULCAN TOMORROW. I AM PLEASED THAT WE WILL SHARE ACCOMMODATIONS AGAIN THIS YEAR, YUKI.
LIKEWISE, ROOMIE!
TTTZZTT ZZTTT
T'PAN, CAN YOU HEAR ME?
MUST BE SOME SUBSPACE STATIC...
TTZZ - UKI? SOMETHING IS WRO - ZZTZ
YOU'RE BREAKING UP!
ZZTT
T'PAN...? IF YOU CAN STILL HEAR ME...

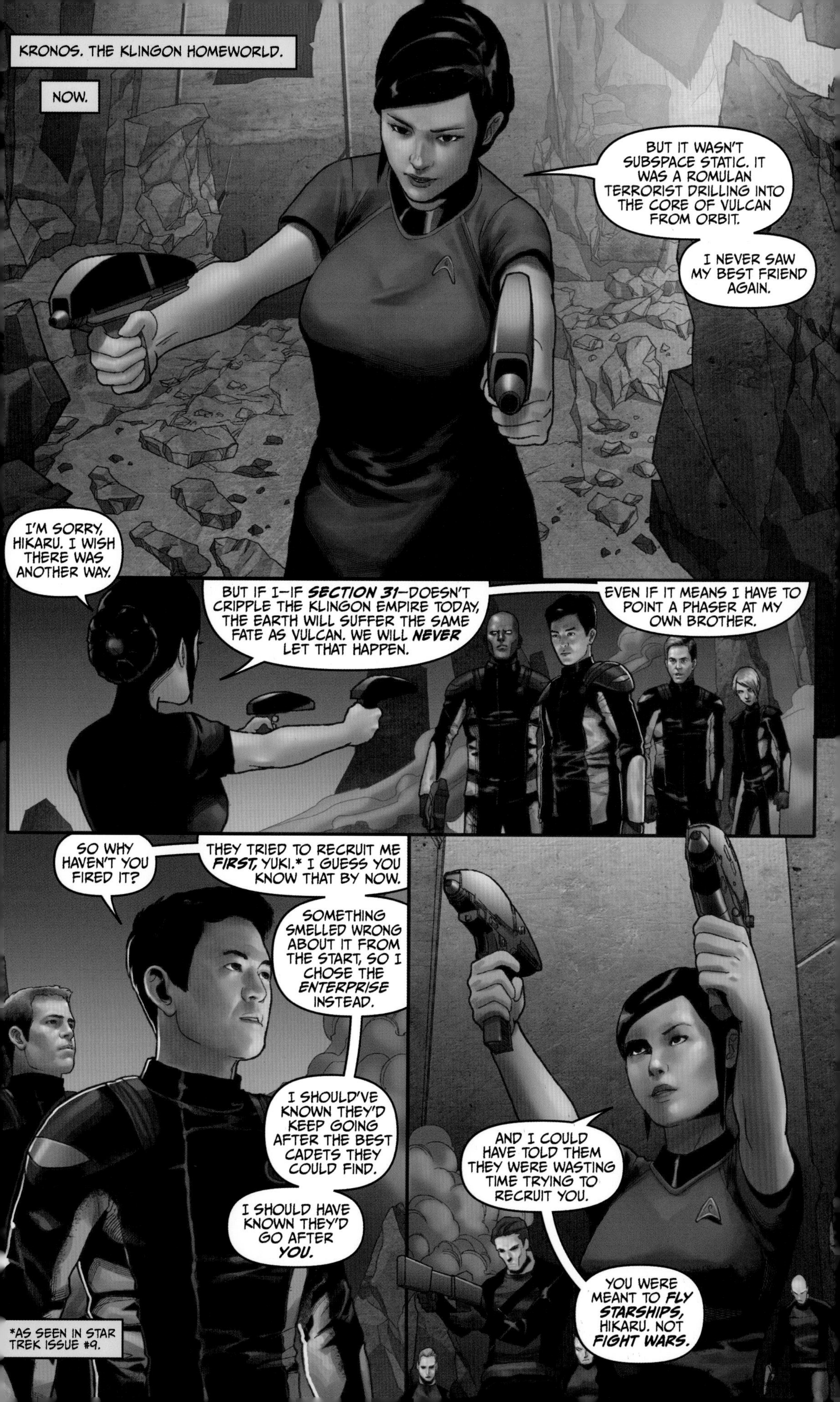
KRONOS. THE KLINGON HOMEWORLD.
NOW.
BUT IT WASN'T SUBSPACE STATIC. IT WAS A ROMULAN TERRORIST DRILLING INTO THE CORE OF VULCAN FROM ORBIT.
I NEVER SAW MY BEST FRIEND AGAIN.
I'M SORRY, HIKARU. I WISH THERE WAS ANOTHER WAY.
BUT IF I—IF SECTION 31—DOESN'T CRIPPLE THE KLINGON EMPIRE TODAY, THE EARTH WILL SUFFER THE SAME FATE AS VULCAN. WE WILL NEVER LET THAT HAPPEN.
EVEN IF IT MEANS I HAVE TO POINT A PHASER AT MY OWN BROTHER.
SO WHY HAVEN'T YOU FIRED IT?
THEY TRIED TO RECRUIT ME FIRST, YUKI.* I GUESS YOU KNOW THAT BY NOW.
SOMETHING SMELLED WRONG ABOUT IT FROM THE START, SO I CHOSE THE ENTERPRISE INSTEAD.
I SHOULD'VE KNOWN THEY'D KEEP GOING AFTER THE BEST CADETS THEY COULD FIND.
I SHOULD HAVE KNOWN THEY'D GO AFTER YOU.
*AS SEEN IN STAR TREK ISSUE #9.
AND I COULD HAVE TOLD THEM THEY WERE WASTING TIME TRYING TO RECRUIT YOU.
YOU WERE MEANT TO FLY STARSHIPS, HIKARU. NOT FIGHT WARS.

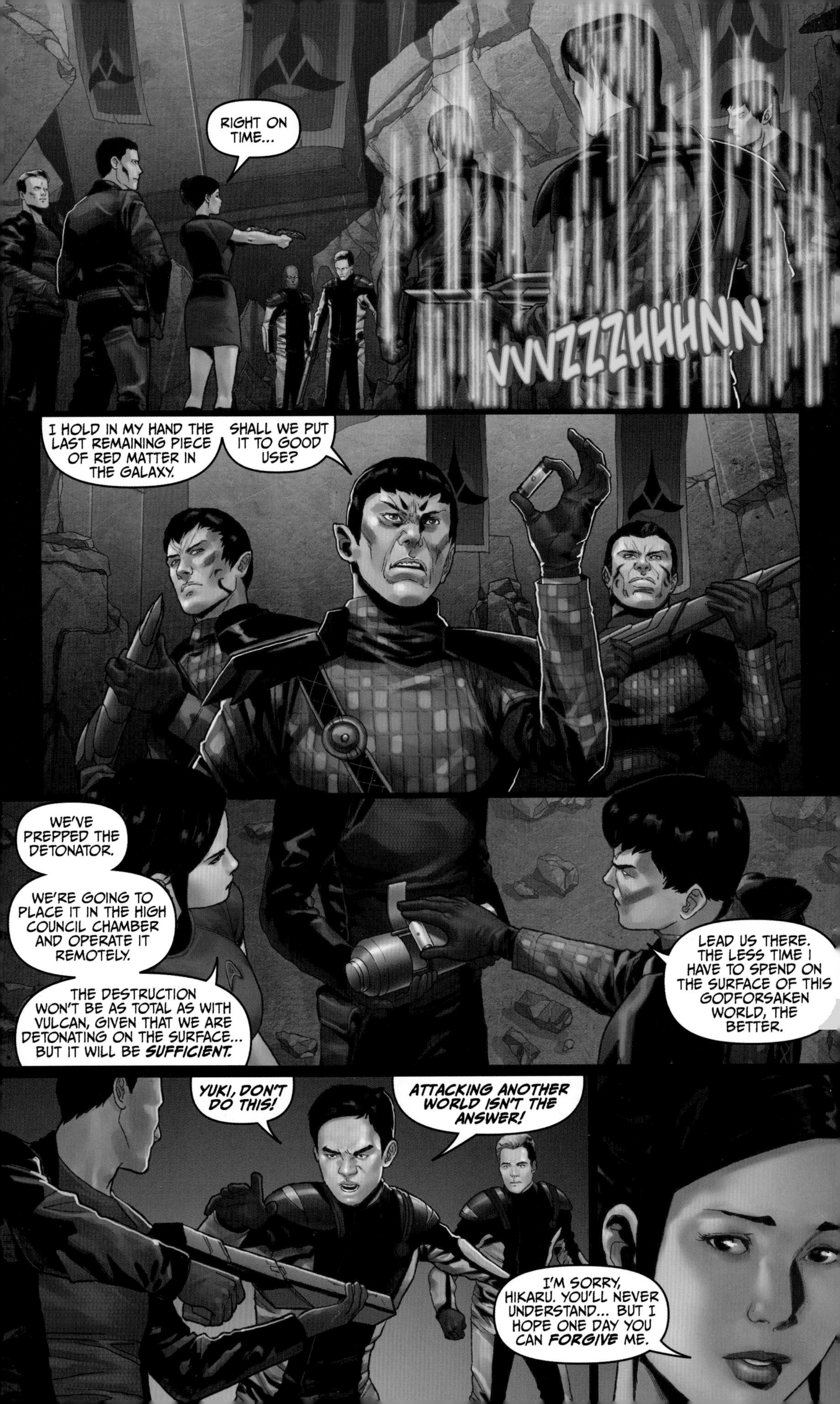

RIGHT ON TIME...
VVVZZZHHHHNN
I HOLD IN MY HAND THE LAST REMAINING PIECE OF RED MATTER IN THE GALAXY.
SHALL WE PUT IT TO GOOD USE?
WE'VE PREPPED THE DETONATOR.
WE'RE GOING TO PLACE IT IN THE HIGH COUNCIL CHAMBER AND OPERATE IT REMOTELY.
THE DESTRUCTION WON'T BE AS TOTAL AS WITH VULCAN, GIVEN THAT WE ARE DETONATING ON THE SURFACE... BUT IT WILL BE SUFFICIENT.
LEAD US THERE. THE LESS TIME I HAVE TO SPEND ON THE SURFACE OF THIS GODFORSAKEN WORLD, THE BETTER.
YUKI, DON'T DO THIS!
ATTACKING ANOTHER WORLD ISN'T THE ANSWER!
I'M SORRY, HIKARU. YOU'LL NEVER UNDERSTAND... BUT I HOPE ONE DAY YOU CAN FORGIVE ME.

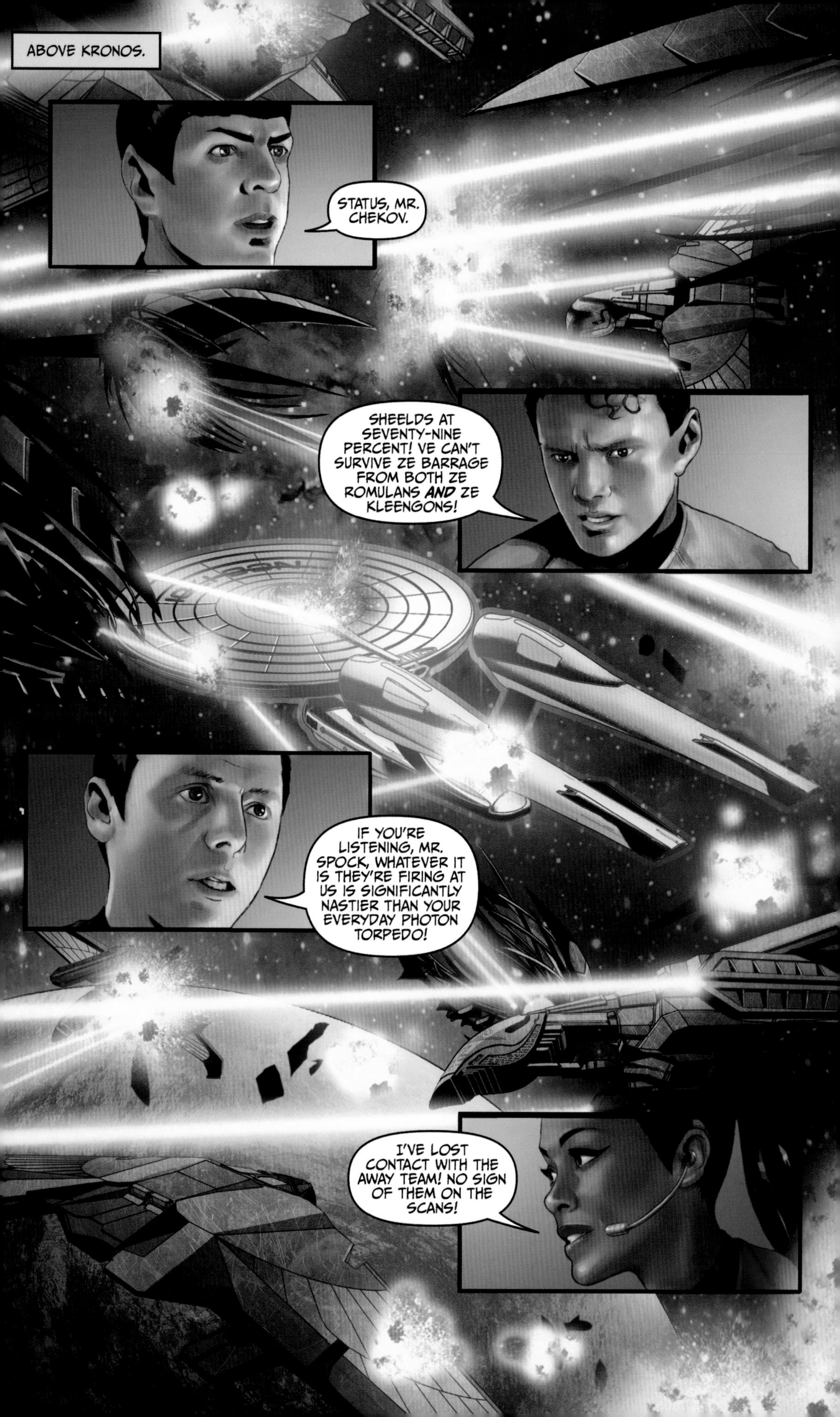
ABOVE KRONOS.
STATUS, MR. CHEKOV.
SHEELDS AT SEVENTY-NINE PERCENT! VE CAN'T SURVIVE ZE BARRAGE FROM BOTH ZE ROMULANS AND ZE KLEENGONS!
IF YOU'RE LISTENING, MR. SPOCK, WHATEVER IT IS THEY'RE FIRING AT US IS SIGNIFICANTLY NASTIER THAN YOUR EVERYDAY PHOTON TORPEDO!
I'VE LOST CONTACT WITH THE AWAY TEAM! NO SIGN OF THEM ON THE SCANS!

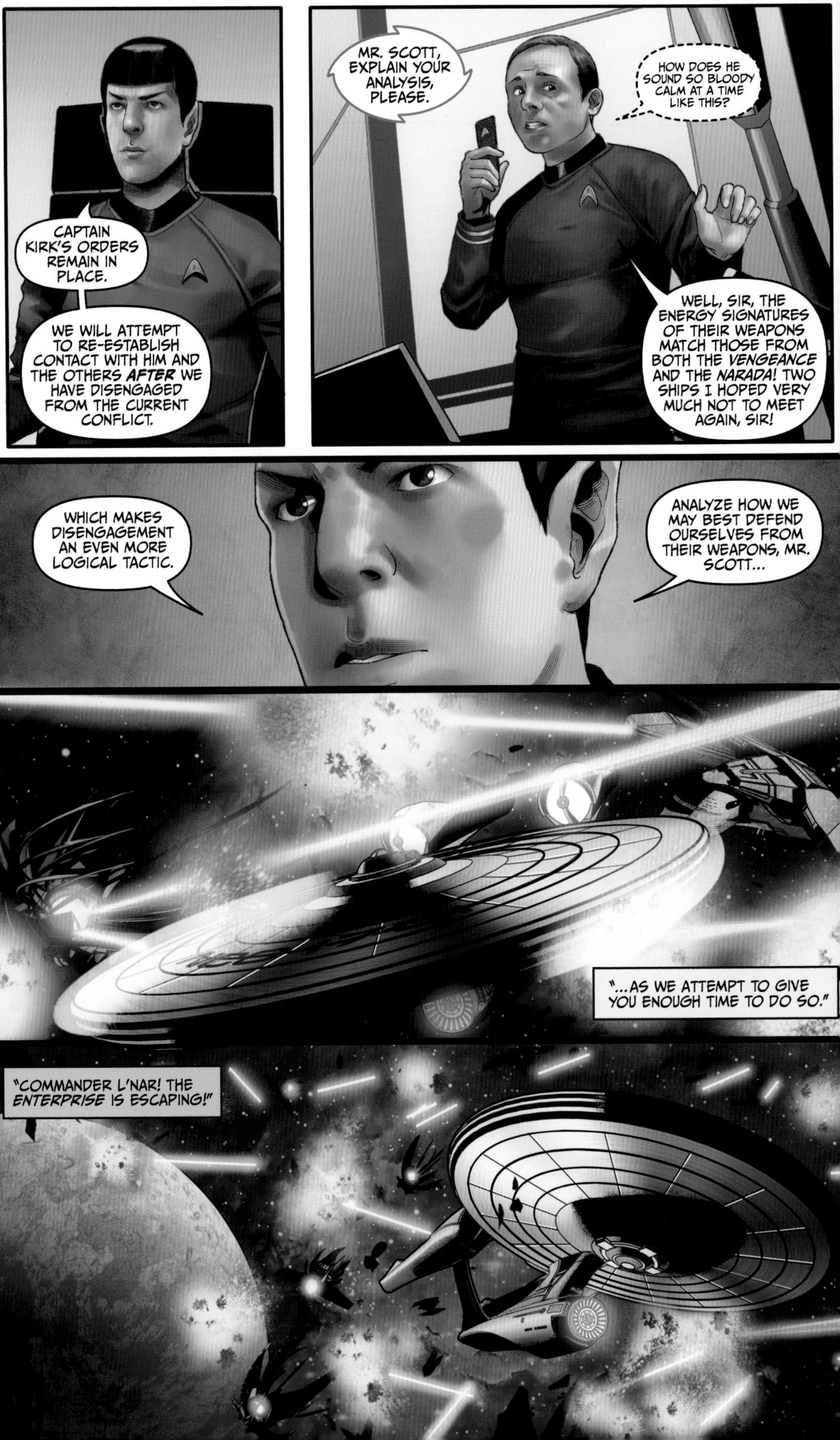
CAPTAIN KIRK'S ORDERS REMAIN IN PLACE.
WE WILL ATTEMPT TO RE-ESTABLISH CONTACT WITH HIM AND THE OTHERS *AFTER* WE HAVE DISENGAGED FROM THE CURRENT CONFLICT.
MR. SCOTT, EXPLAIN YOUR ANALYSIS, PLEASE.
HOW DOES HE SOUND SO BLOODY CALM AT A TIME LIKE THIS?
WELL, SIR, THE ENERGY SIGNATURES OF THEIR WEAPONS MATCH THOSE FROM BOTH THE *VENGEANCE* AND THE *NARADA*! TWO SHIPS I HOPED VERY MUCH NOT TO MEET AGAIN, SIR!
WHICH MAKES DISENGAGEMENT AN EVEN MORE LOGICAL TACTIC.
ANALYZE HOW WE MAY BEST DEFEND OURSELVES FROM THEIR WEAPONS, MR. SCOTT...
"...AS WE ATTEMPT TO GIVE YOU ENOUGH TIME TO DO SO."
"COMMANDER L'NAR! THE *ENTERPRISE* IS ESCAPING!"

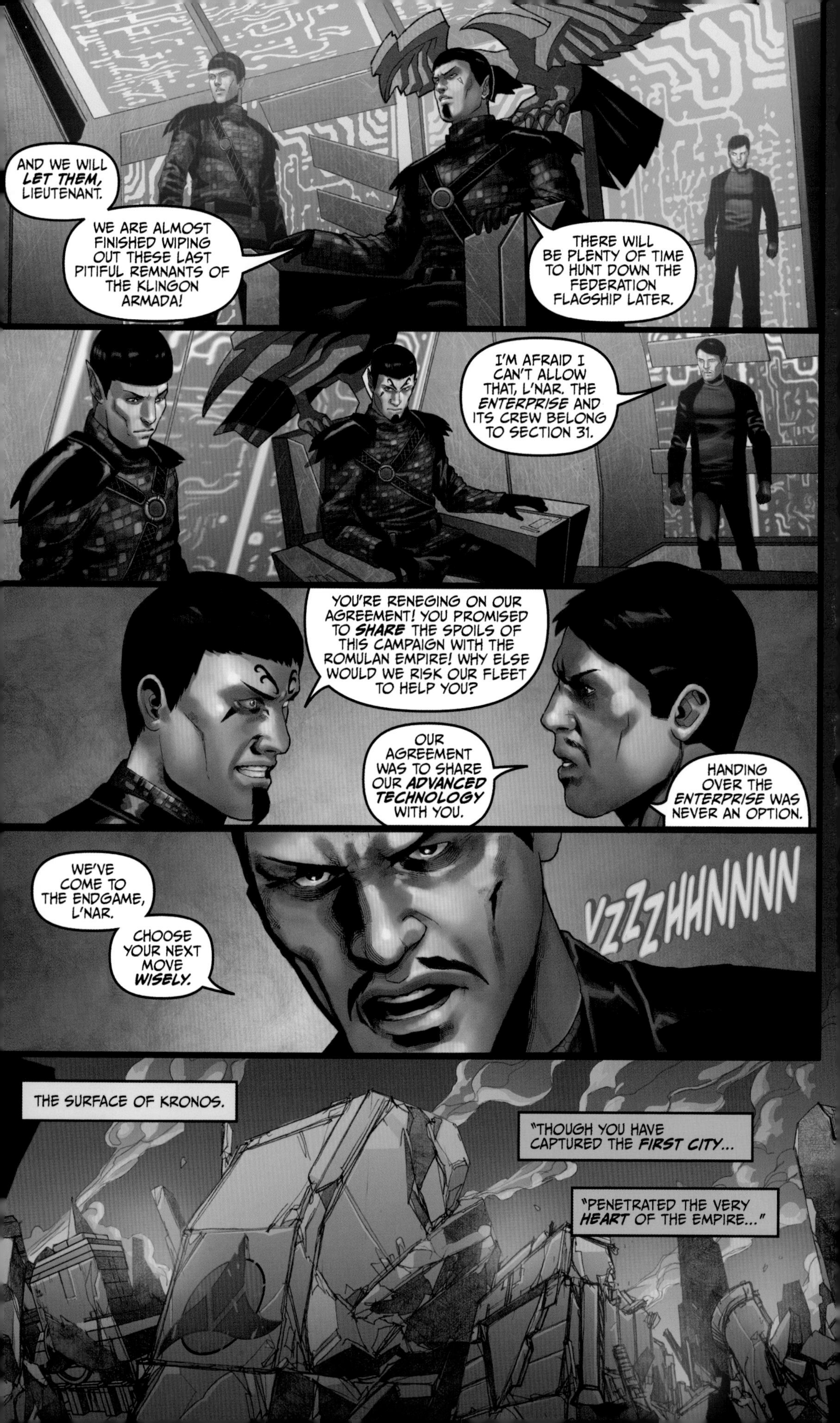

AND WE WILL LET THEM, LIEUTENANT.
WE ARE ALMOST FINISHED WIPING OUT THESE LAST PITIFUL REMNANTS OF THE KLINGON ARMADA!
THERE WILL BE PLENTY OF TIME TO HUNT DOWN THE FEDERATION FLAGSHIP LATER.
I'M AFRAID I CAN'T ALLOW THAT, L'NAR. THE ENTERPRISE AND ITS CREW BELONG TO SECTION 31.
YOU'RE RENEGING ON OUR AGREEMENT! YOU PROMISED TO SHARE THE SPOILS OF THIS CAMPAIGN WITH THE ROMULAN EMPIRE! WHY ELSE WOULD WE RISK OUR FLEET TO HELP YOU?
OUR AGREEMENT WAS TO SHARE OUR ADVANCED TECHNOLOGY WITH YOU.
HANDING OVER THE ENTERPRISE WAS NEVER AN OPTION.
WE'VE COME TO THE ENDGAME, L'NAR.
CHOOSE YOUR NEXT MOVE WISELY.
VZZZHHNNNN
THE SURFACE OF KRONOS.
"THOUGH YOU HAVE CAPTURED THE FIRST CITY...
"PENETRATED THE VERY HEART OF THE EMPIRE..."

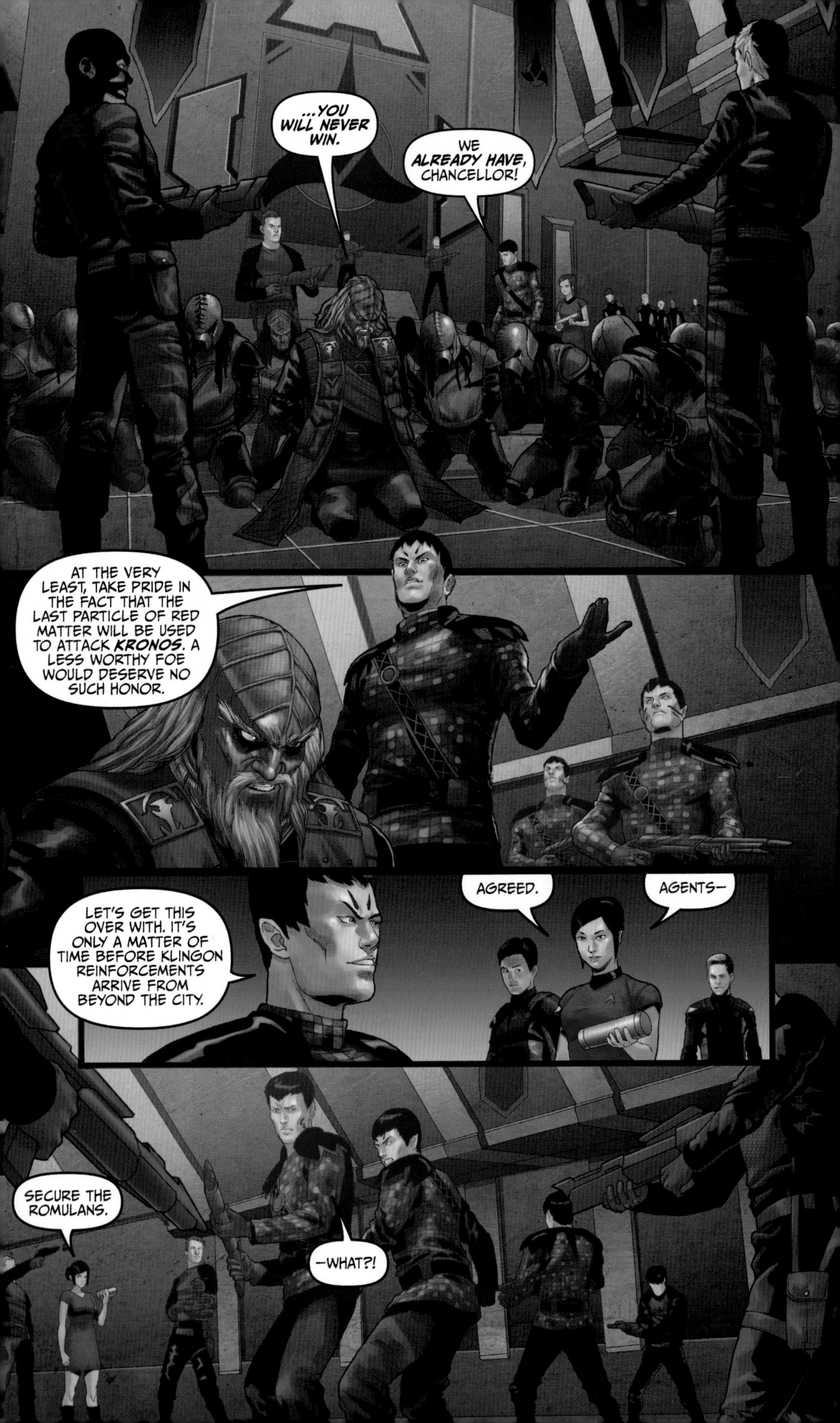
...YOU WILL NEVER WIN.
WE ALREADY HAVE, CHANCELLOR!
AT THE VERY LEAST, TAKE PRIDE IN THE FACT THAT THE LAST PARTICLE OF RED MATTER WILL BE USED TO ATTACK KRONOS. A LESS WORTHY FOE WOULD DESERVE NO SUCH HONOR.
LET'S GET THIS OVER WITH. IT'S ONLY A MATTER OF TIME BEFORE KLINGON REINFORCEMENTS ARRIVE FROM BEYOND THE CITY.
AGREED.
AGENTS—
SECURE THE ROMULANS.
—WHAT?!

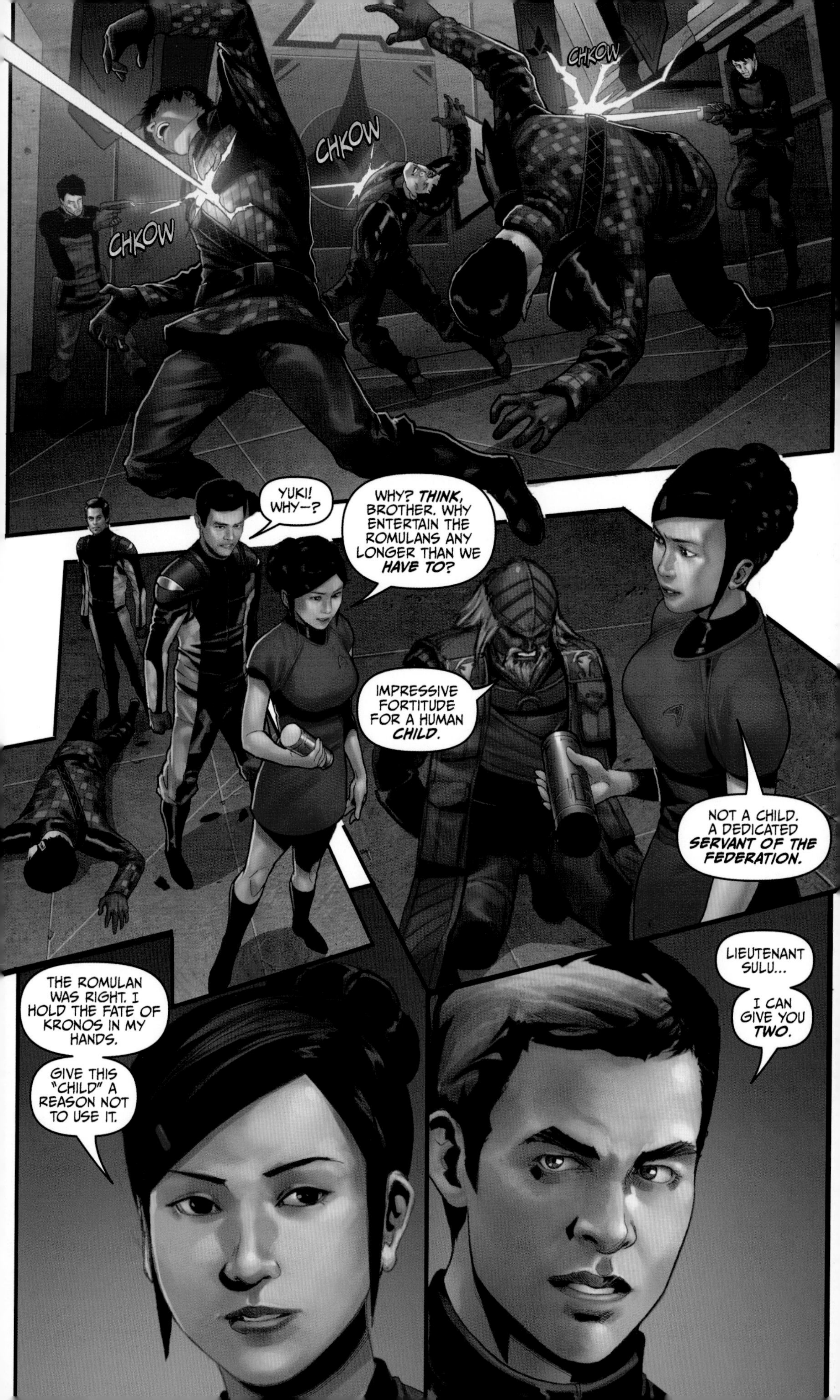
CHKOW
CHKOW
CHKOW
YUKI! WHY--?
WHY? THINK, BROTHER. WHY ENTERTAIN THE ROMULANS ANY LONGER THAN WE HAVE TO?
IMPRESSIVE FORTITUDE FOR A HUMAN CHILD.
NOT A CHILD. A DEDICATED SERVANT OF THE FEDERATION.
THE ROMULAN WAS RIGHT. I HOLD THE FATE OF KRONOS IN MY HANDS.
GIVE THIS "CHILD" A REASON NOT TO USE IT.
LIEUTENANT SULU...
I CAN GIVE YOU TWO.

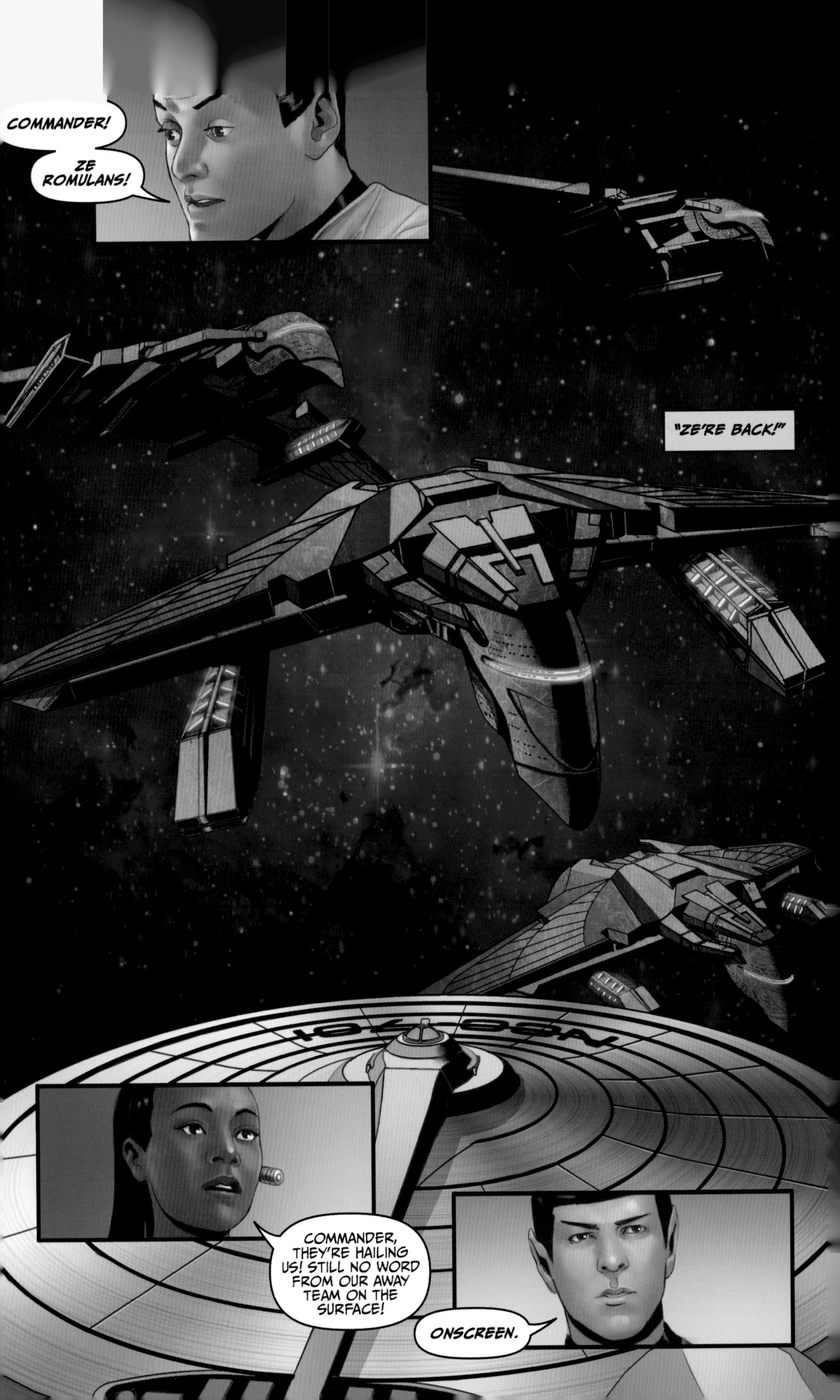
COMMANDER!
ZE ROMULANS!
"ZE'RE BACK!"
COMMANDER, THEY'RE HAILING US! STILL NO WORD FROM OUR AWAY TEAM ON THE SURFACE!
ONSCREEN.

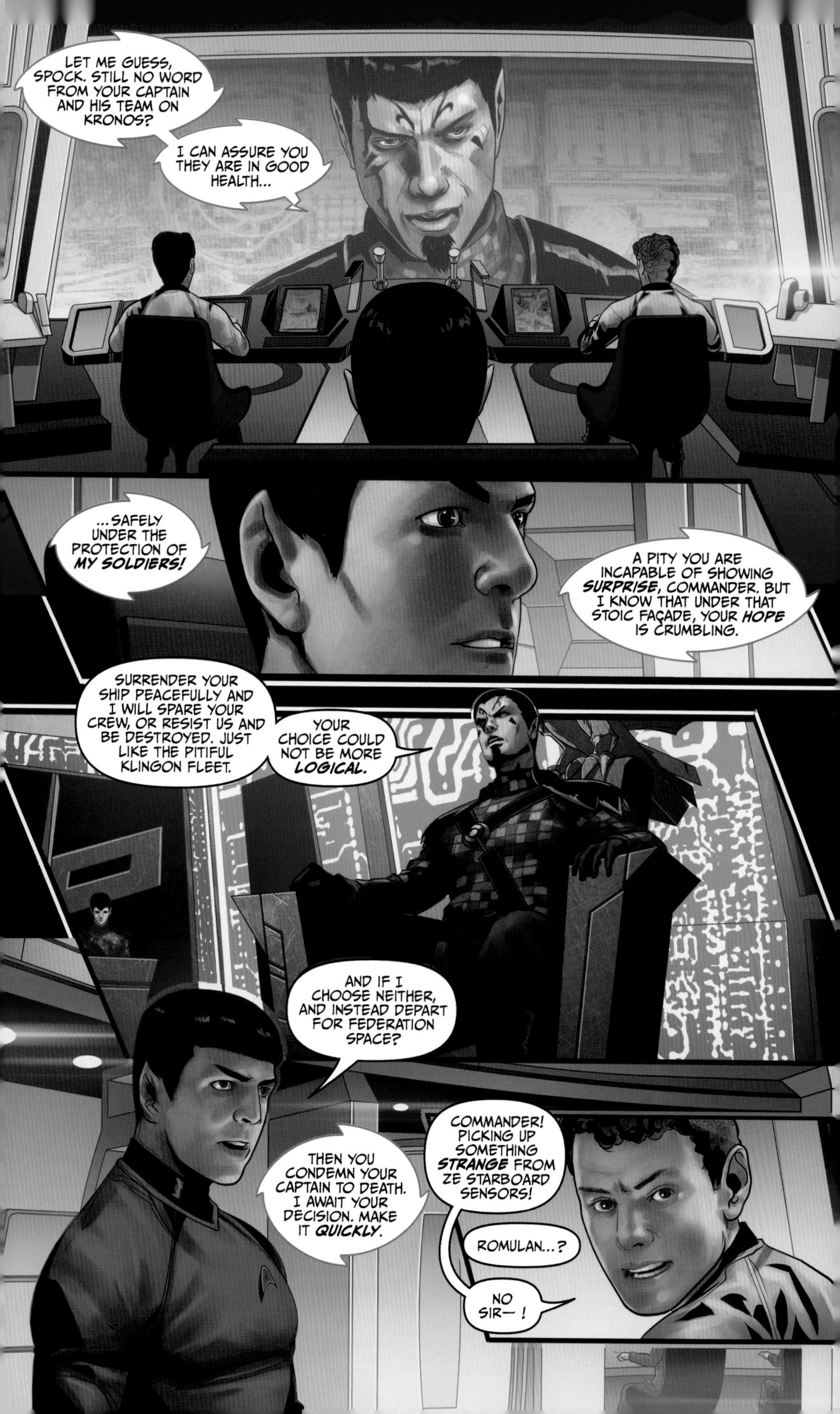
LET ME GUESS, SPOCK. STILL NO WORD FROM YOUR CAPTAIN AND HIS TEAM ON KRONOS?
I CAN ASSURE YOU THEY ARE IN GOOD HEALTH...
...SAFELY UNDER THE PROTECTION OF MY SOLDIERS!
A PITY YOU ARE INCAPABLE OF SHOWING SURPRISE, COMMANDER. BUT I KNOW THAT UNDER THAT STOIC FAÇADE, YOUR HOPE IS CRUMBLING.
SURRENDER YOUR SHIP PEACEFULLY AND I WILL SPARE YOUR CREW, OR RESIST US AND BE DESTROYED. JUST LIKE THE PITIFUL KLINGON FLEET.
YOUR CHOICE COULD NOT BE MORE LOGICAL.
AND IF I CHOOSE NEITHER, AND INSTEAD DEPART FOR FEDERATION SPACE?
THEN YOU CONDEMN YOUR CAPTAIN TO DEATH. I AWAIT YOUR DECISION. MAKE IT QUICKLY.
COMMANDER! PICKING UP SOMETHING STRANGE FROM ZE STARBOARD SENSORS!
ROMULAN...?
NO SIR— !

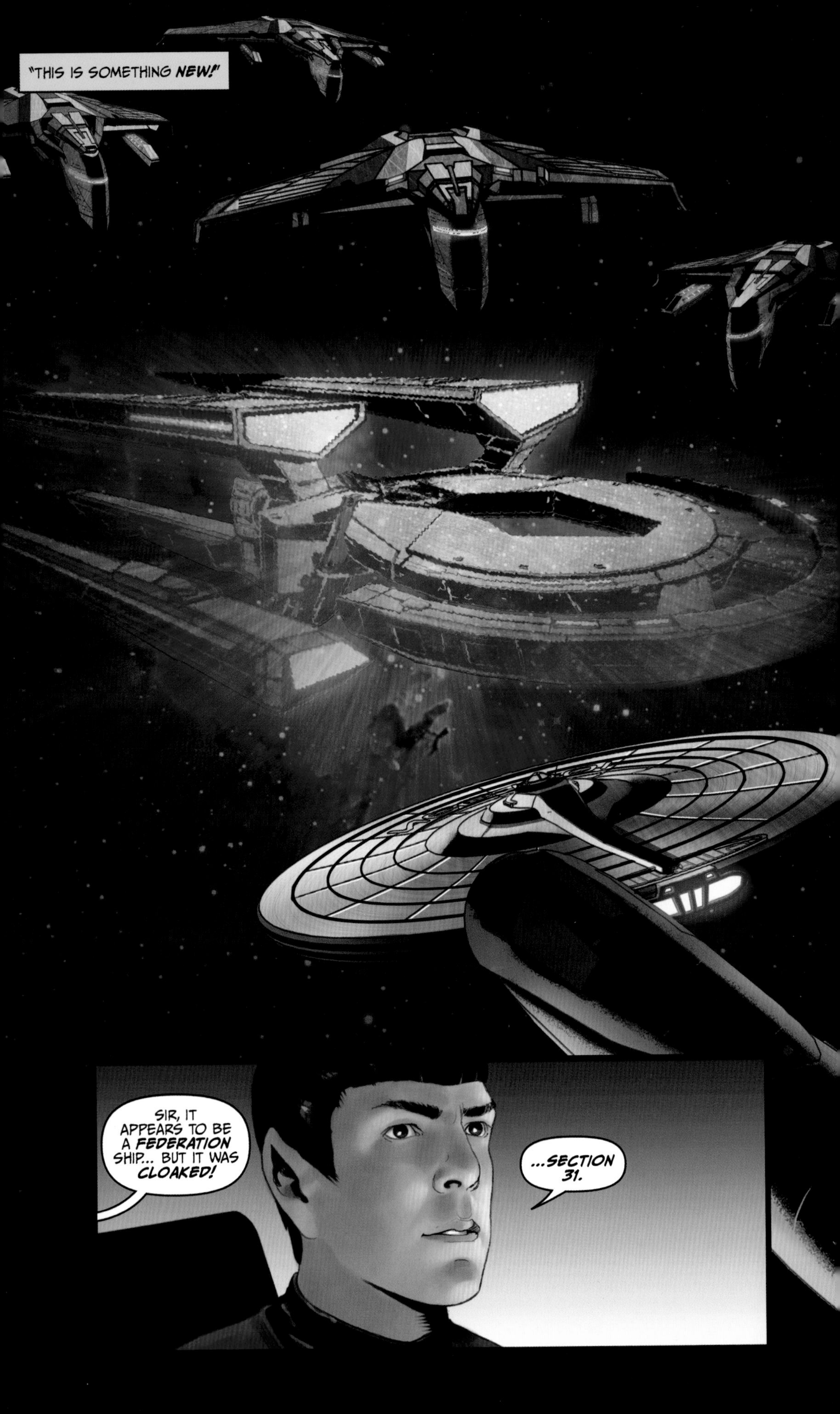
"THIS IS SOMETHING NEW!"
SIR, IT APPEARS TO BE A FEDERATION SHIP... BUT IT WAS CLOAKED!
...SECTION 31.

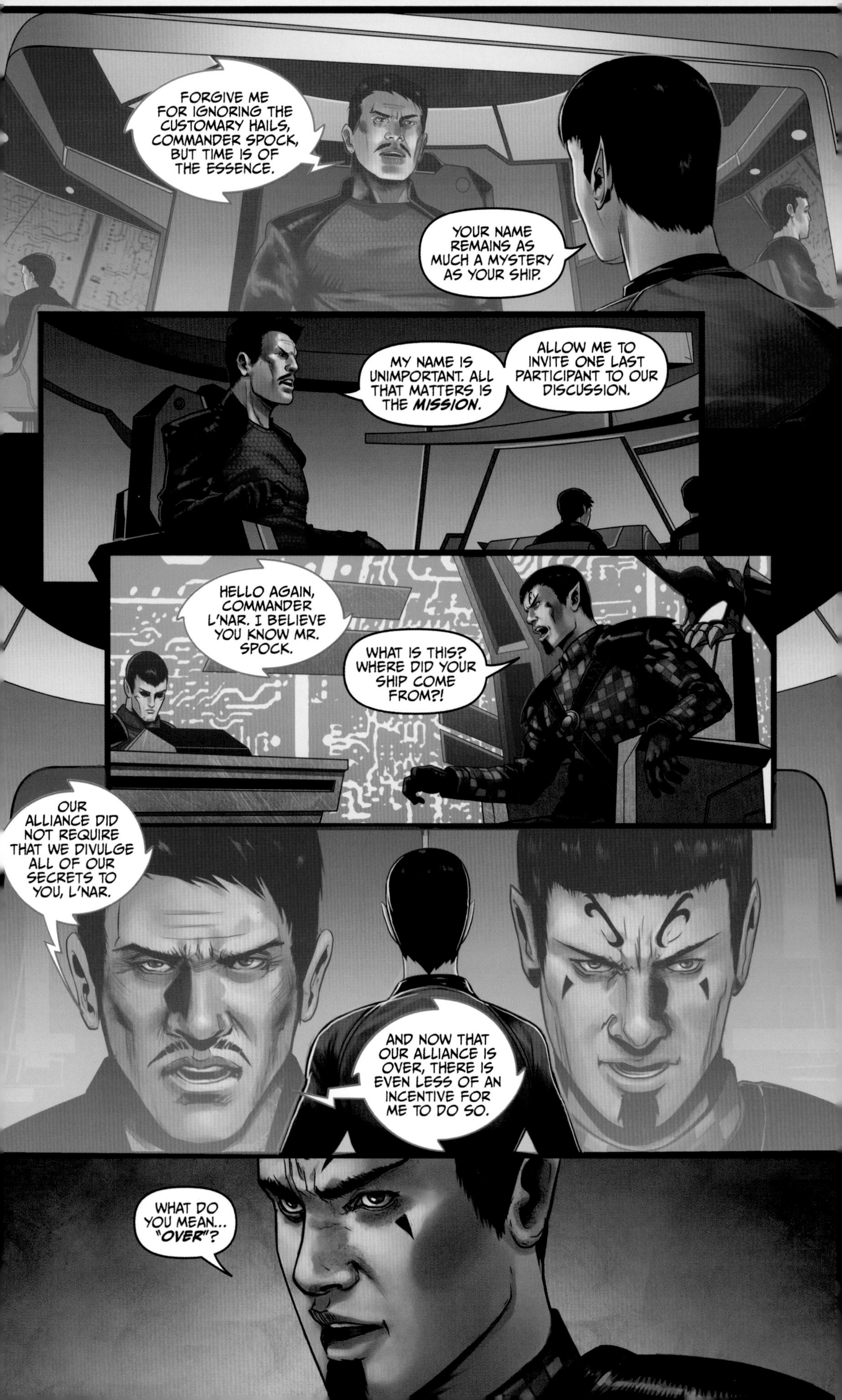
FORGIVE ME FOR IGNORING THE CUSTOMARY HAILS, COMMANDER SPOCK, BUT TIME IS OF THE ESSENCE.
YOUR NAME REMAINS AS MUCH A MYSTERY AS YOUR SHIP.
MY NAME IS UNIMPORTANT. ALL THAT MATTERS IS THE *MISSION*.
ALLOW ME TO INVITE ONE LAST PARTICIPANT TO OUR DISCUSSION.
HELLO AGAIN, COMMANDER L'NAR. I BELIEVE YOU KNOW MR. SPOCK.
WHAT IS THIS? WHERE DID YOUR SHIP COME FROM?!
OUR ALLIANCE DID NOT REQUIRE THAT WE DIVULGE ALL OF OUR SECRETS TO YOU, L'NAR.
AND NOW THAT OUR ALLIANCE IS OVER, THERE IS EVEN LESS OF AN INCENTIVE FOR ME TO DO SO.
WHAT DO YOU MEAN... "*OVER*"?

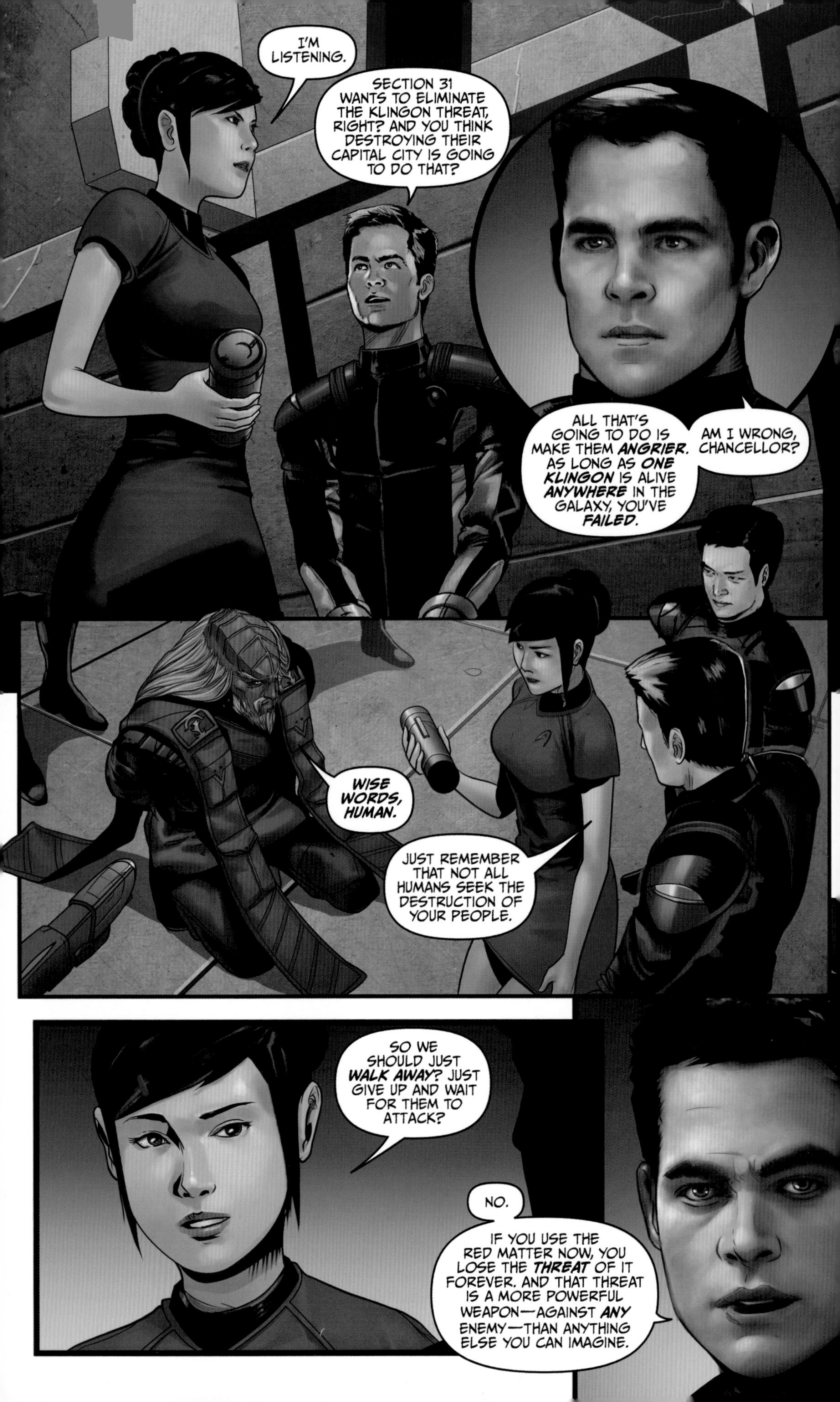
I'M LISTENING.
SECTION 31 WANTS TO ELIMINATE THE KLINGON THREAT, RIGHT? AND YOU THINK DESTROYING THEIR CAPITAL CITY IS GOING TO DO THAT?
ALL THAT'S GOING TO DO IS MAKE THEM ***ANGRIER***. AS LONG AS ***ONE KLINGON*** IS ALIVE ***ANYWHERE*** IN THE GALAXY, YOU'VE ***FAILED***.
AM I WRONG, CHANCELLOR?
WISE WORDS, HUMAN.
JUST REMEMBER THAT NOT ALL HUMANS SEEK THE DESTRUCTION OF YOUR PEOPLE.
SO WE SHOULD JUST ***WALK AWAY***? JUST GIVE UP AND WAIT FOR THEM TO ATTACK?
NO.
IF YOU USE THE RED MATTER NOW, YOU LOSE THE ***THREAT*** OF IT FOREVER. AND THAT THREAT IS A MORE POWERFUL WEAPON—AGAINST ***ANY*** ENEMY—THAN ANYTHING ELSE YOU CAN IMAGINE.

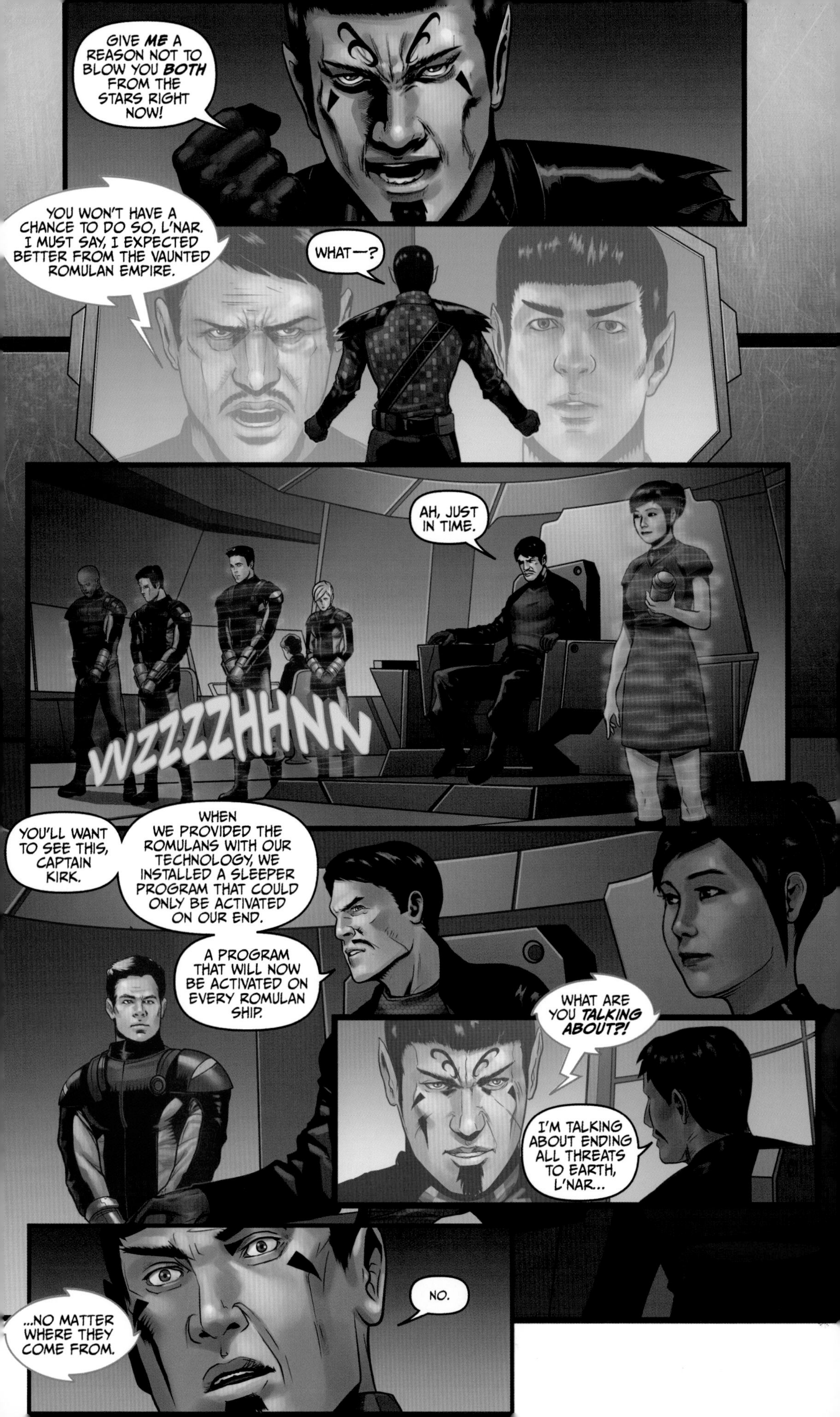
GIVE ME A REASON NOT TO BLOW YOU BOTH FROM THE STARS RIGHT NOW!
YOU WON'T HAVE A CHANCE TO DO SO, L'NAR. I MUST SAY, I EXPECTED BETTER FROM THE VAUNTED ROMULAN EMPIRE.
WHAT—?
AH, JUST IN TIME.
VVZZZZHHNN
YOU'LL WANT TO SEE THIS, CAPTAIN KIRK.
WHEN WE PROVIDED THE ROMULANS WITH OUR TECHNOLOGY, WE INSTALLED A SLEEPER PROGRAM THAT COULD ONLY BE ACTIVATED ON OUR END.
A PROGRAM THAT WILL NOW BE ACTIVATED ON EVERY ROMULAN SHIP.
WHAT ARE YOU TALKING ABOUT?!
I'M TALKING ABOUT ENDING ALL THREATS TO EARTH, L'NAR...
...NO MATTER WHERE THEY COME FROM.
NO.

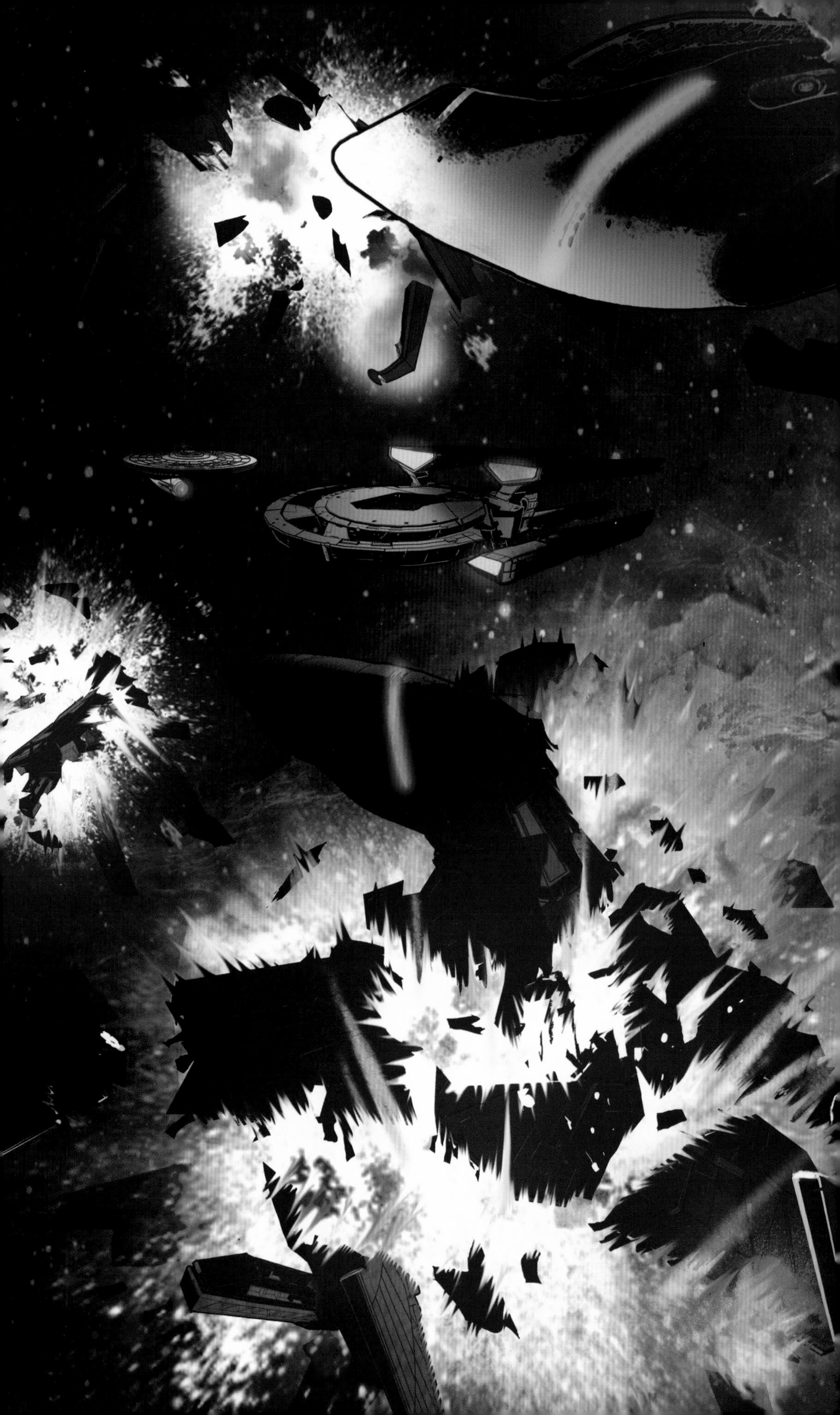

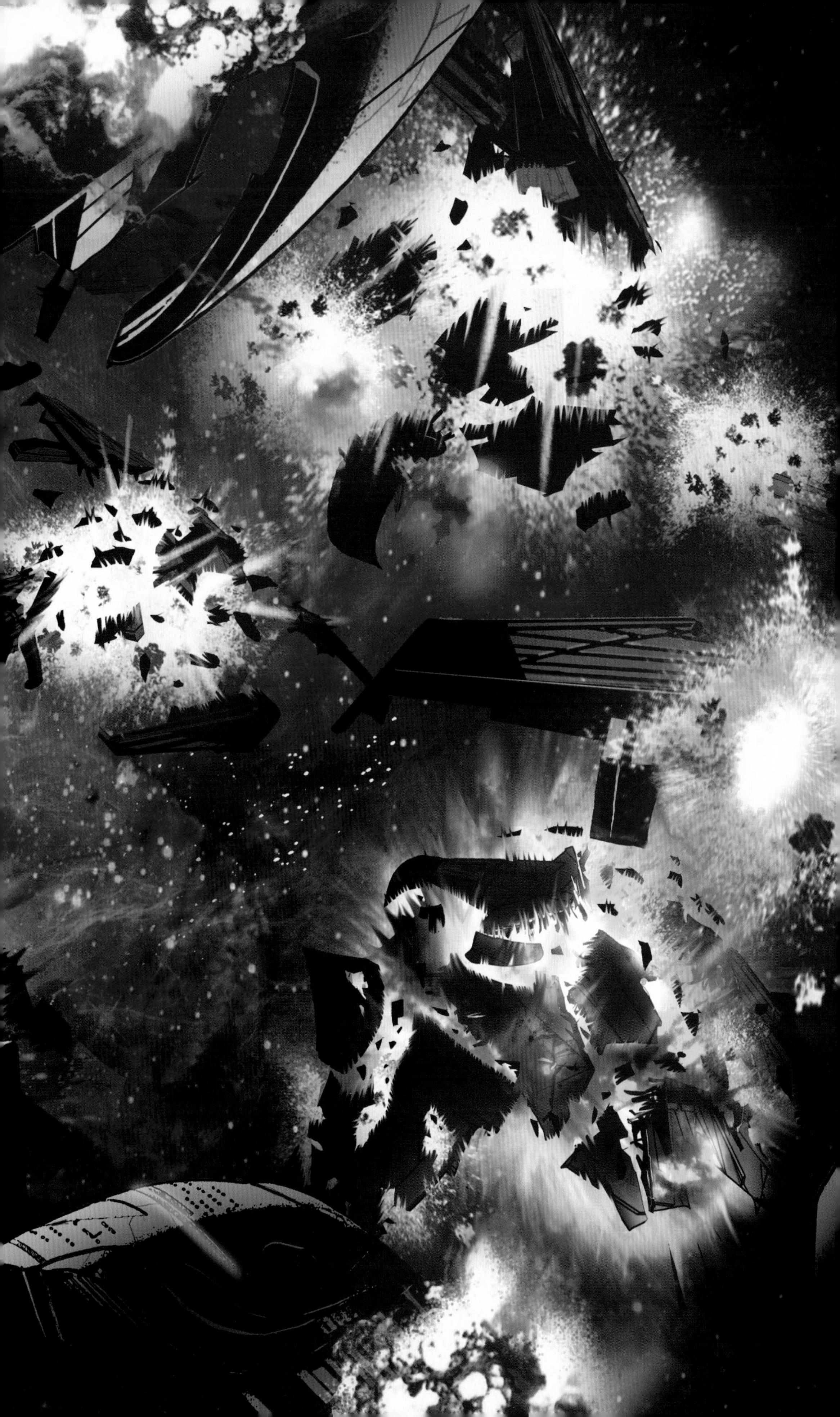

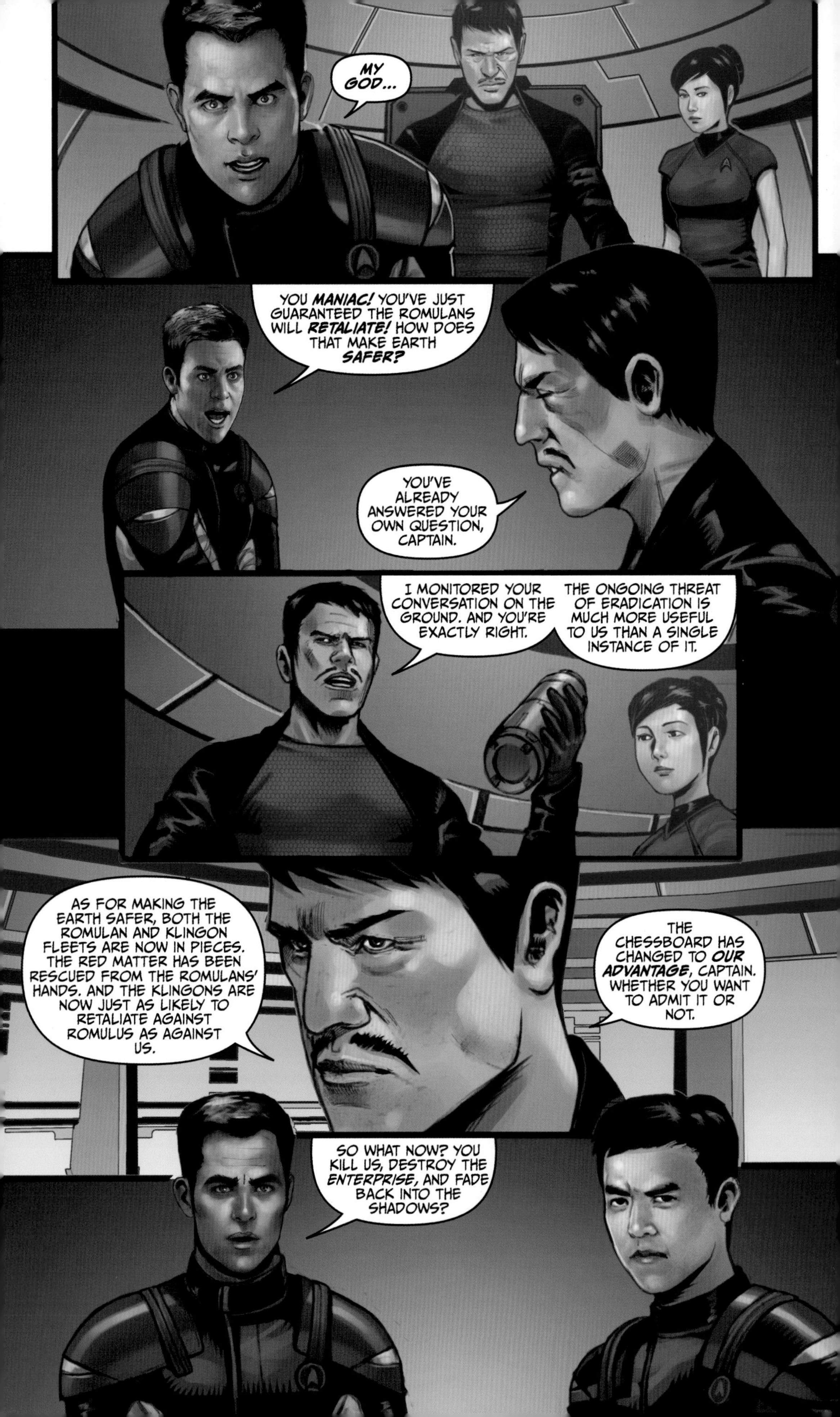
MY GOD...
YOU MANIAC! YOU'VE JUST GUARANTEED THE ROMULANS WILL RETALIATE! HOW DOES THAT MAKE EARTH SAFER?
YOU'VE ALREADY ANSWERED YOUR OWN QUESTION, CAPTAIN.
I MONITORED YOUR CONVERSATION ON THE GROUND. AND YOU'RE EXACTLY RIGHT.
THE ONGOING THREAT OF ERADICATION IS MUCH MORE USEFUL TO US THAN A SINGLE INSTANCE OF IT.
AS FOR MAKING THE EARTH SAFER, BOTH THE ROMULAN AND KLINGON FLEETS ARE NOW IN PIECES. THE RED MATTER HAS BEEN RESCUED FROM THE ROMULANS' HANDS. AND THE KLINGONS ARE NOW JUST AS LIKELY TO RETALIATE AGAINST ROMULUS AS AGAINST US.
THE CHESSBOARD HAS CHANGED TO OUR ADVANTAGE, CAPTAIN. WHETHER YOU WANT TO ADMIT IT OR NOT.
SO WHAT NOW? YOU KILL US, DESTROY THE ENTERPRISE, AND FADE BACK INTO THE SHADOWS?

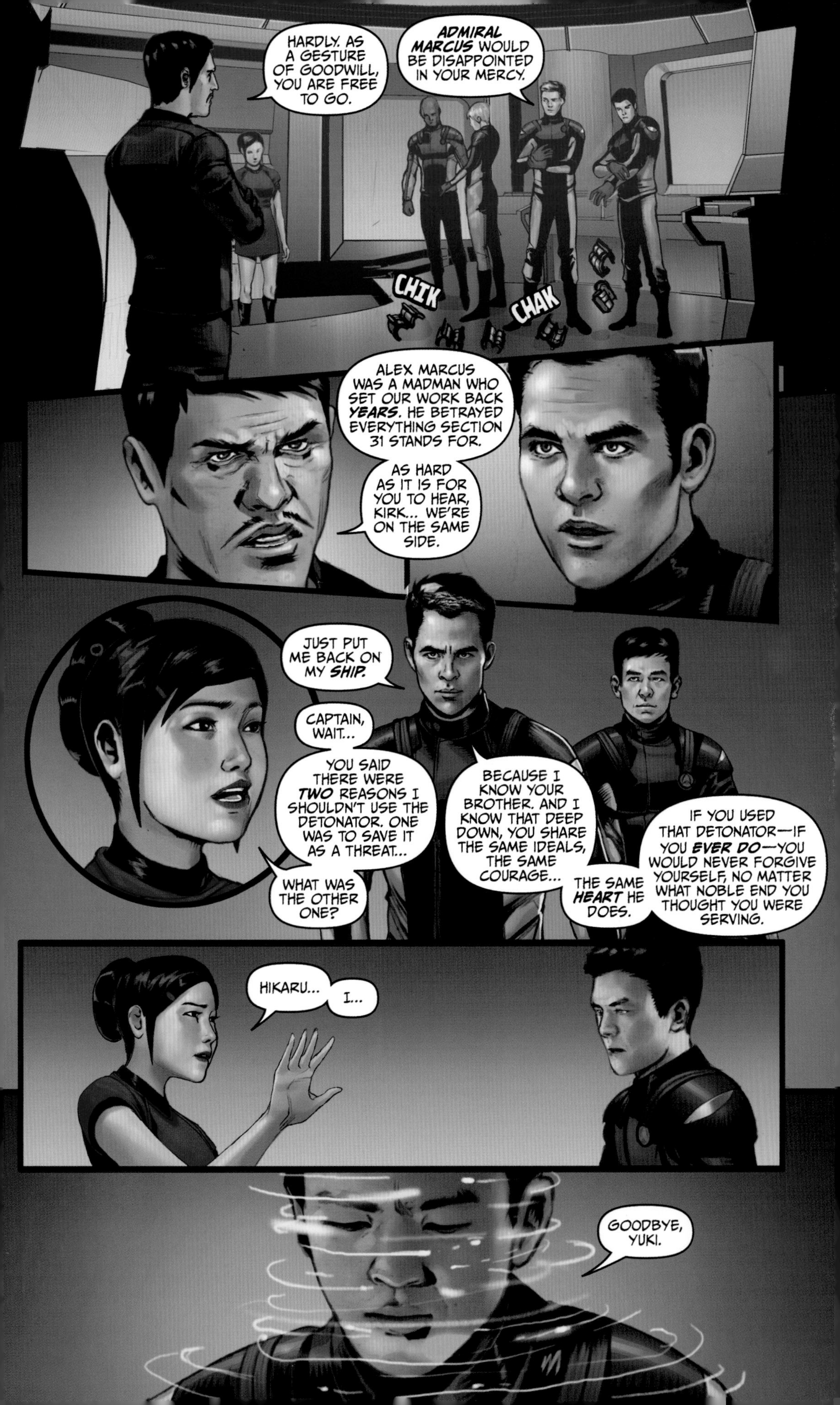
HARDLY. AS A GESTURE OF GOODWILL, YOU ARE FREE TO GO.
ADMIRAL MARCUS WOULD BE DISAPPOINTED IN YOUR MERCY.
CHIK
CHAK
ALEX MARCUS WAS A MADMAN WHO SET OUR WORK BACK YEARS. HE BETRAYED EVERYTHING SECTION 31 STANDS FOR.
AS HARD AS IT IS FOR YOU TO HEAR, KIRK... WE'RE ON THE SAME SIDE.
JUST PUT ME BACK ON MY SHIP.
CAPTAIN, WAIT...
YOU SAID THERE WERE TWO REASONS I SHOULDN'T USE THE DETONATOR. ONE WAS TO SAVE IT AS A THREAT...
WHAT WAS THE OTHER ONE?
BECAUSE I KNOW YOUR BROTHER. AND I KNOW THAT DEEP DOWN, YOU SHARE THE SAME IDEALS, THE SAME COURAGE...
THE SAME HEART HE DOES.
IF YOU USED THAT DETONATOR—IF YOU EVER DO—YOU WOULD NEVER FORGIVE YOURSELF, NO MATTER WHAT NOBLE END YOU THOUGHT YOU WERE SERVING.
HIKARU...
I...
GOODBYE, YUKI.

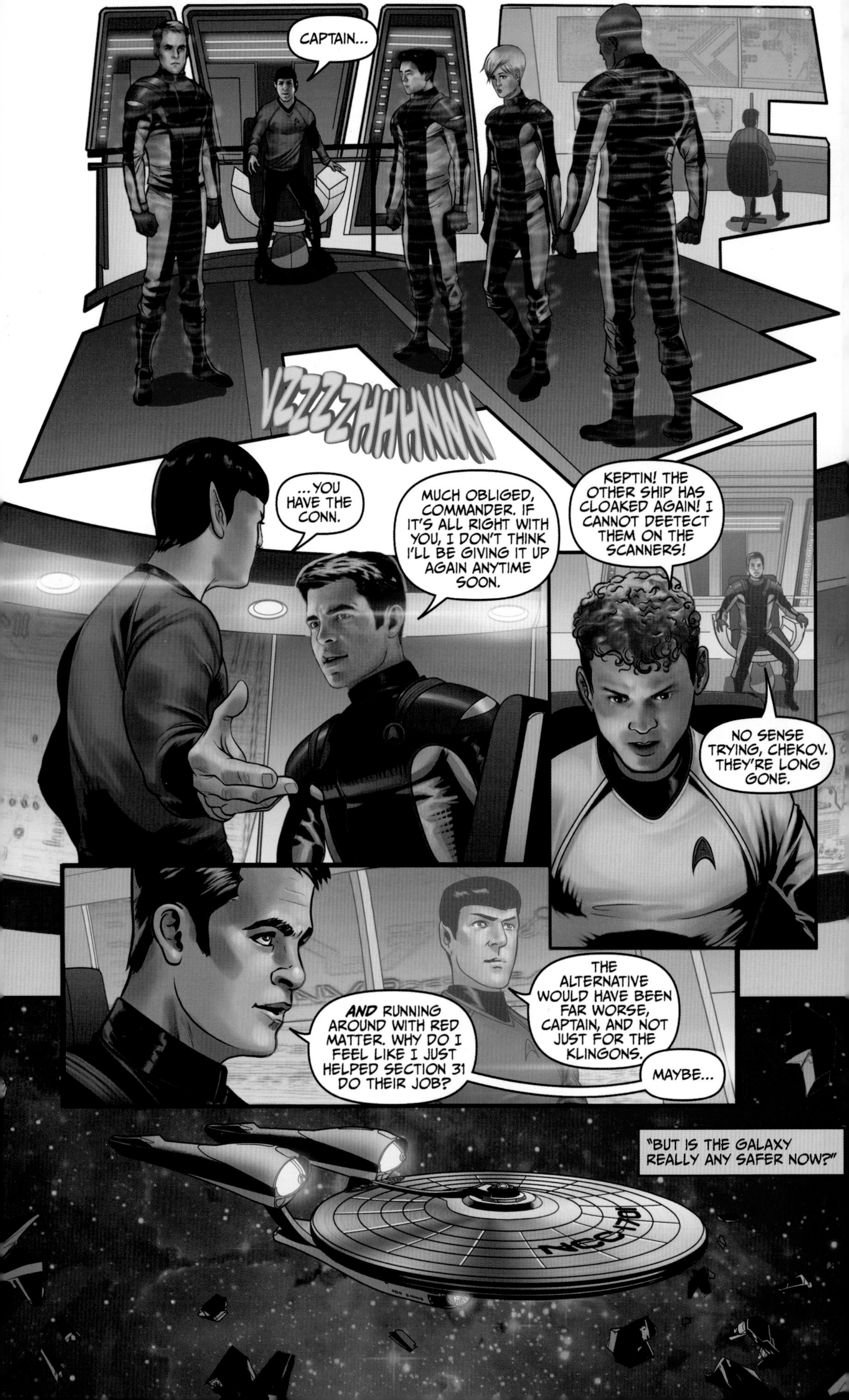
CAPTAIN...
VZZZZHHHNNN
...YOU HAVE THE CONN.
MUCH OBLIGED, COMMANDER. IF IT'S ALL RIGHT WITH YOU, I DON'T THINK I'LL BE GIVING IT UP AGAIN ANYTIME SOON.
KEPTIN! THE OTHER SHIP HAS CLOAKED AGAIN! I CANNOT DEETECT THEM ON THE SCANNERS!
NO SENSE TRYING, CHEKOV. THEY'RE LONG GONE.
THE ALTERNATIVE WOULD HAVE BEEN FAR WORSE, CAPTAIN, AND NOT JUST FOR THE KLINGONS.
AND RUNNING AROUND WITH RED MATTER. WHY DO I FEEL LIKE I JUST HELPED SECTION 31 DO THEIR JOB?
MAYBE...
"BUT IS THE GALAXY REALLY ANY SAFER NOW?"

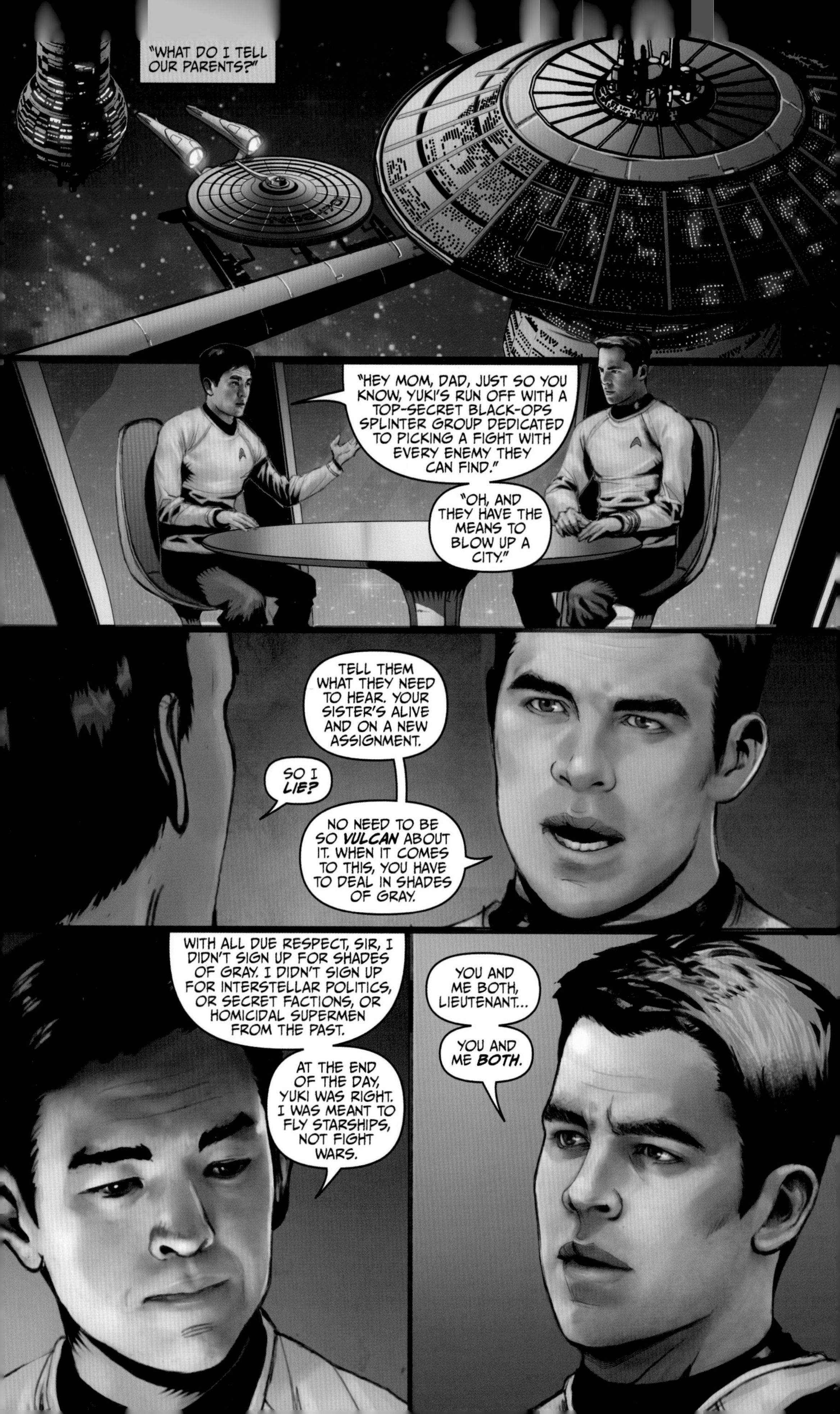
"WHAT DO I TELL OUR PARENTS?"
"HEY MOM, DAD, JUST SO YOU KNOW, YUKI'S RUN OFF WITH A TOP-SECRET BLACK-OPS SPLINTER GROUP DEDICATED TO PICKING A FIGHT WITH EVERY ENEMY THEY CAN FIND."
"OH, AND THEY HAVE THE MEANS TO BLOW UP A CITY."
TELL THEM WHAT THEY NEED TO HEAR. YOUR SISTER'S ALIVE AND ON A NEW ASSIGNMENT.
SO I *LIE?*
NO NEED TO BE SO *VULCAN* ABOUT IT. WHEN IT COMES TO THIS, YOU HAVE TO DEAL IN SHADES OF GRAY.
WITH ALL DUE RESPECT, SIR, I DIDN'T SIGN UP FOR SHADES OF GRAY. I DIDN'T SIGN UP FOR INTERSTELLAR POLITICS, OR SECRET FACTIONS, OR HOMICIDAL SUPERMEN FROM THE PAST.
AT THE END OF THE DAY, YUKI WAS RIGHT. I WAS MEANT TO FLY STARSHIPS, NOT FIGHT WARS.
YOU AND ME BOTH, LIEUTENANT...
YOU AND ME *BOTH*.

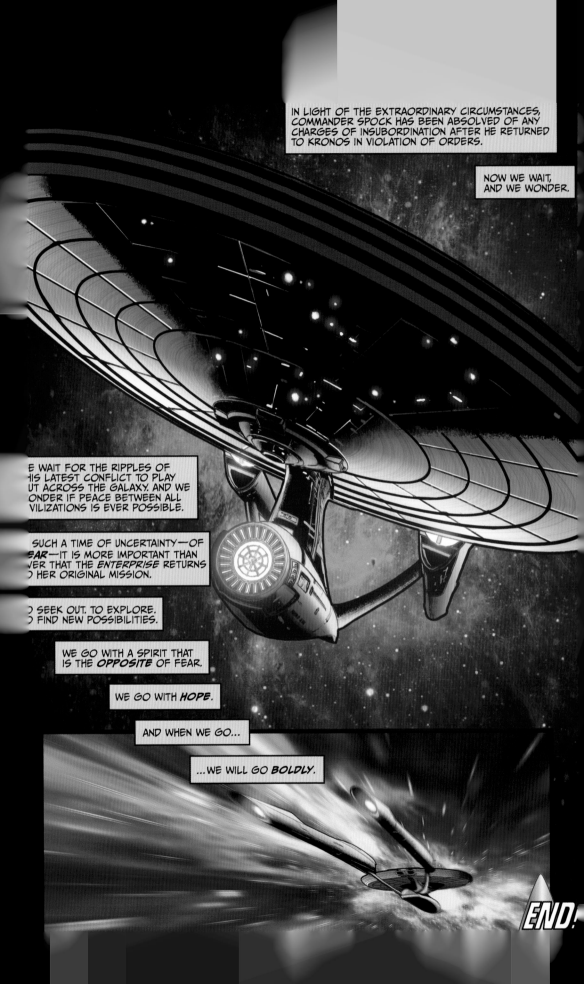

IN LIGHT OF THE EXTRAORDINARY CIRCUMSTANCES, COMMANDER SPOCK HAS BEEN ABSOLVED OF ANY CHARGES OF INSUBORDINATION AFTER HE RETURNED TO KRONOS IN VIOLATION OF ORDERS.

NOW WE WAIT, AND WE WONDER.

E WAIT FOR THE RIPPLES OF HIS LATEST CONFLICT TO PLAY UT ACROSS THE GALAXY. AND WE ONDER IF PEACE BETWEEN ALL VILIZATIONS IS EVER POSSIBLE.

SUCH A TIME OF UNCERTAINTY—OF EAR—IT IS MORE IMPORTANT THAN VER THAT THE *ENTERPRISE* RETURNS O HER ORIGINAL MISSION.

O SEEK OUT. TO EXPLORE. O FIND NEW POSSIBILITIES.

WE GO WITH A SPIRIT THAT IS THE *OPPOSITE* OF FEAR.

WE GO WITH *HOPE*.

AND WHEN WE GO...

...WE WILL GO *BOLDLY*.

END!

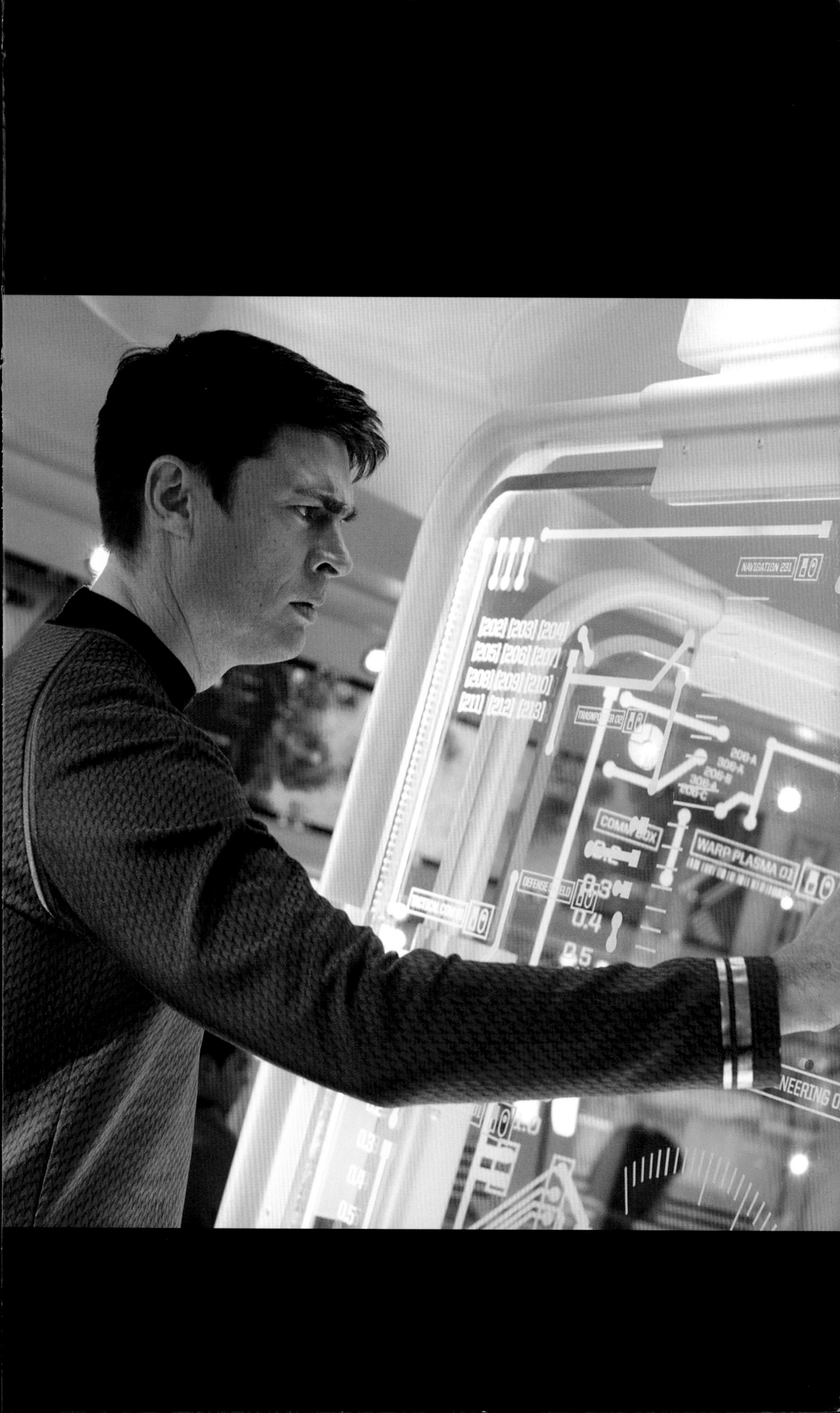
NAVIGATION 231
[202] [203] [204]
[205] [206] [207]
[208] [209] [210]
[211] [212] [213]
WARP PLASMA 01

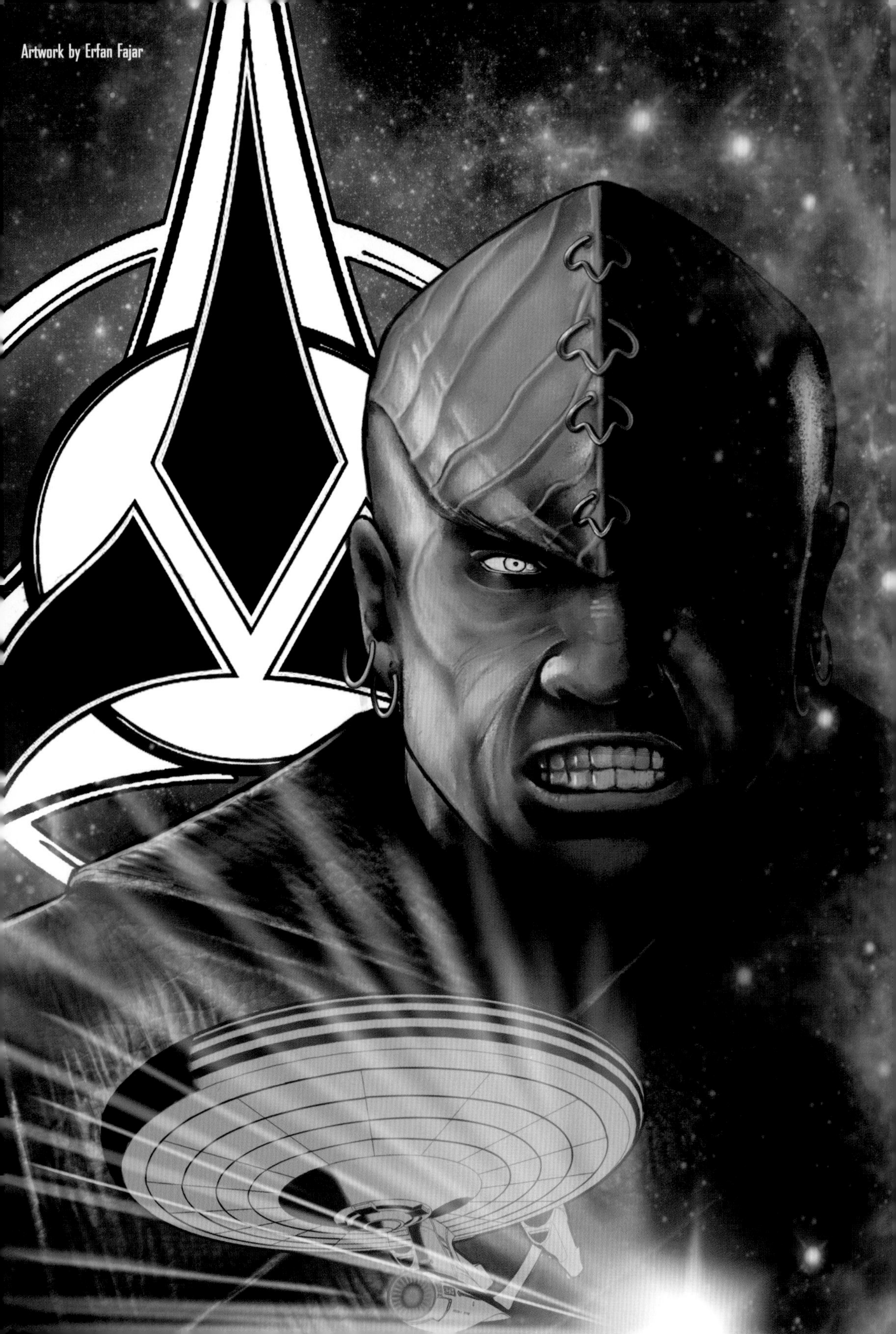

Artwork by Erfan Fajar

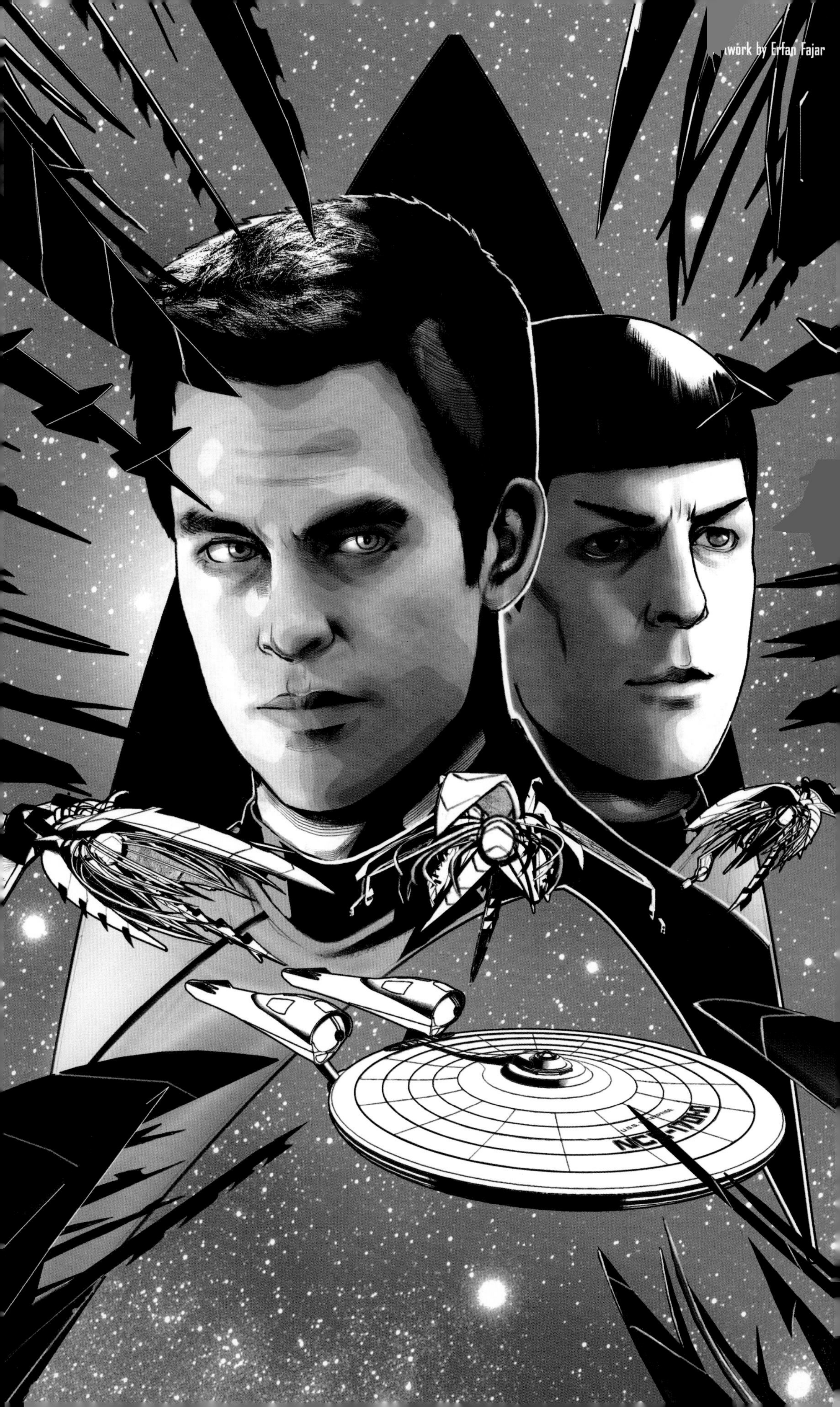
work by Erfan Fajar

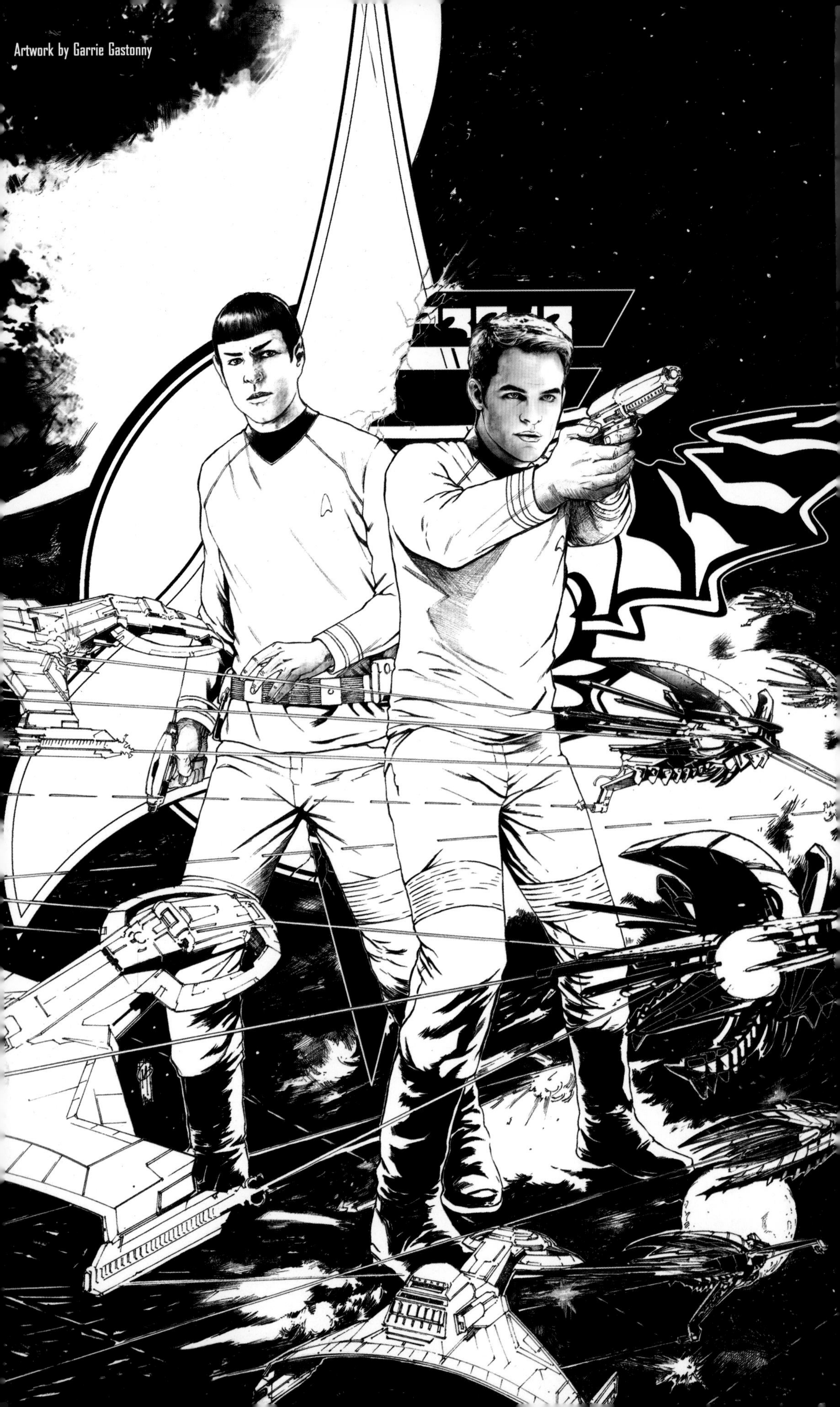

Artwork by Garrie Gastonny

Artwork by Erfan Fajar

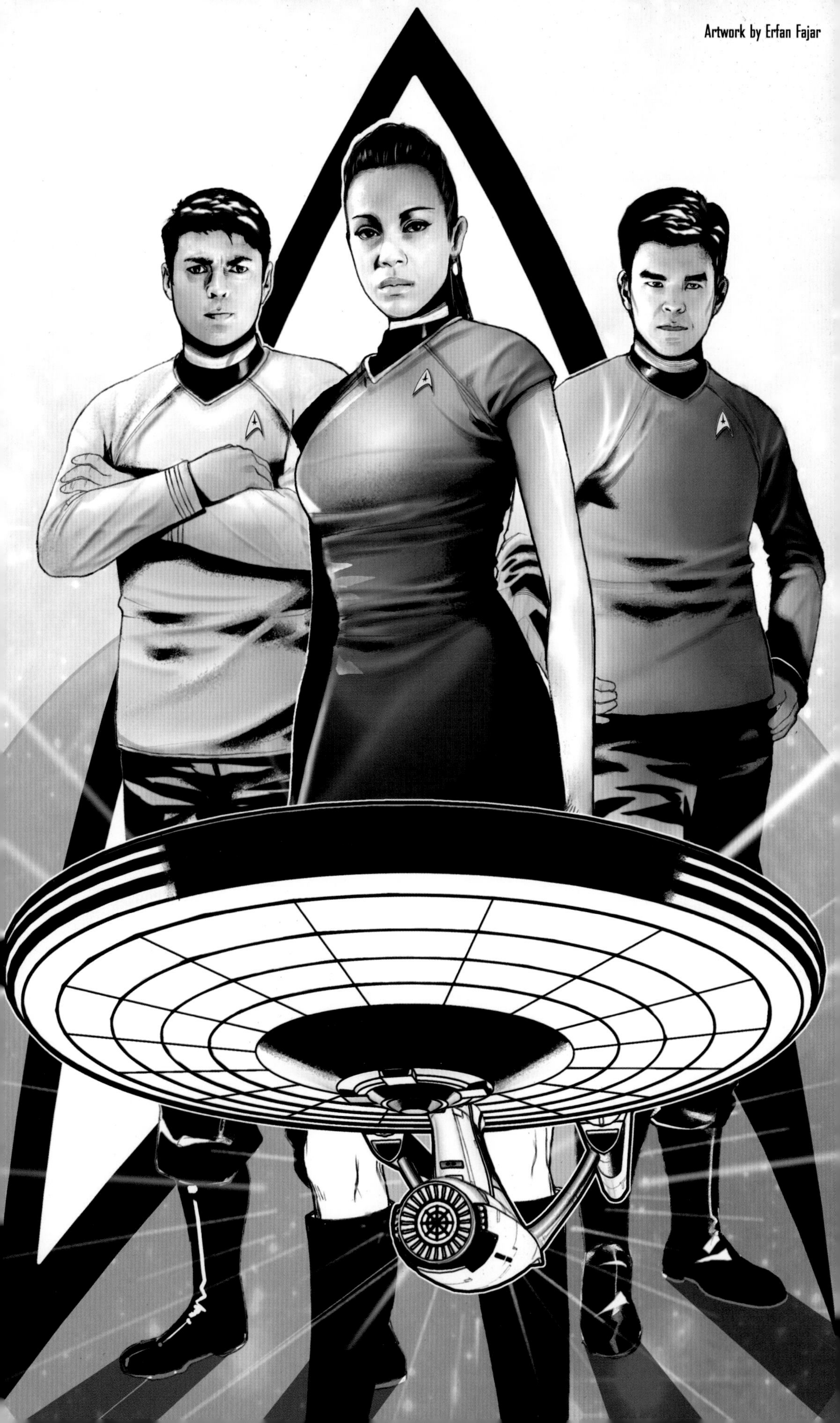

STAR TREK®

VOLUME 7

THE KHITOMER CONFLICT